SOME
LIKE IT
PLAID

SOME LIKE IT PLAID

ANGELA QUARLES

Entangled Publishing, LLC
2614 South Timberline Road
Suite 105, PMB 159
Fort Collins, CO 80525
rights@entangledpublishing.com

Amara is an imprint of Entangled Publishing, LLC.

Edited by Liz Pelletier and Lydia Sharp
Cover design by Bree Archer
Cover photography by loco75 and Anastasiia Vasylyk/Getty Images
zayatsandzayats/Deposit Photos
Period Images

Manufactured in the United States of America

First Edition November 2019

To Joshua Abraham Norton (1818 – 1880), the real Emperor Norton

Chapter One

"We need wives if we're to survive as a tribe." Connall son of Eacharn's aggravation powered his words, but they blended in with the other shouts and exclamations in the keep's great hall. Frustration making his movements jerky, he stood, the sound of chair legs scraping against stone adding to the mayhem.

"Hold your tongues, the lot of you." This time, his voice rang out in the close confines. The council members, who'd been bickering for too long, hushed one by one, and all gazes turned to him. And one by one, each intent stare added to the burden of responsibility weighing on his heart. Even his father, the chief, raised a brow and leaned forward in his seat.

As the leader's oldest surviving son, Connall's word carried authority despite his mere twenty-one winters. He rounded on their spellcaster, Mungan, who was barely visible in the murky corner, and strode toward him. "This cannot continue. Find a solution. I need a wife. As do my brothers and the other men."

"Well, I want my own back, damn you," shouted a warrior,

whose face had the stiff mien of barely restrained sorrow.

"I sympathize with your grief, my friend, but we are at an impasse."

Mungan's lanky frame unfolded from the darkened corner. He strode into the sun's rays streaming from one of the keep's windows, the light highlighting the gold-tooled patterns on his leather jerkin, crackling energy surrounding him. Even the dust motes seemed to dance in a pattern around his youthful face.

"Aye, there is a way." Mungan's rich tenor filled the room with portent.

Cries of relief sounded, and Connall stepped forward. "Then—"

"But there is a cost." Mungan gripped his yew staff and tamped it once on the stone floor. Unlike the other men in the tribe, he kept his dark brown hair cut close to his head. "Magic, especially magic of this potency"—his gaze swung to Connall's and held—"always has a cost."

Chills raced along his skin, but he crossed his arms, pushing aside any unease the spellcaster's words caused. Mungan was the most powerful druid to emerge in their tribe in several generations. Connall trusted him with his life. "I'll pay it."

He'd pay anything. Their current situation was untenable. His responsibility to his people lay heavy on his heart, leaving him antsy, frustrated.

Mungan nodded once, his eyes never leaving Connall's. "Then we must depart for Achnabreck at once to take advantage of the sun's last emanations. The winter solstice conveys the strongest magic. Make haste and pack for an extended journey." With that, he pivoted and marched from the keep, his wool mantle swirling behind him.

An indescribable pull tugged, as if he'd handed over his fate to the powerful, enigmatic man.

Connall dragged in a deep breath to center himself. No turning back now.

The early setting sun stretched fingers of light over the nearby mountain peaks, a clear reminder of their need for haste. Connall relished the lash of the wind through his hair and the steady movement of his horse beneath him as he galloped along the wooden road to Achnabreck, one of their most sacred sites. His brothers, his father, Mungan, and several warriors rode with him. As they neared their destination, they slowed their pace to allow their horses to cool down.

Connall stared into the distance, that pull of fate stronger the closer they came to Achnabreck and the druid's energy merged with its stronger one. Slate-gray clouds, tinged deep pink, streaked the horizon, foretelling of rain.

Mungan drew alongside, matching his mount's trot to that of Connall's. Yew staff secured to his back, Mungan leaned forward in his saddle to direct a concerned look his way, the mantle of responsibility he always wore still evident but overshadowed with the warmth of familiarity and friendship they'd shared since they were lads. "Remember, hearth brother. I cannot guarantee where you'll end up."

He squared his shoulders. "As long as there are women to wed, I'll be fine."

"Well, you'll be equipped with the tools you require. The magic will see to that. Only…"

Mungan never hesitated to speak his mind before. As their leading druid, his opinion held equal weight to that of the chief.

"Tell me," Connall urged. He'd been given a lesson on what to expect and how the magic would work. Most of it didn't make sense, though he pretended to grasp it.

A rare smile stretched across Mungan's face. "You love adventure. Well, an adventure is what you'll get. No need to be afraid." He slapped Connall on the back then trotted to the path leading up to the site's edge. Connall would swear the spellcaster tossed a final word over his shoulder. "Much."

Arse.

His own horse stepped off the wooden road and threaded up the clearing of the squat hillside. What had he agreed to?

When the others dismounted at the expanse of flat rock stretching over the ground, he swept his gaze over the incised circles and indentations only those of Mungan's order comprehended. The wind blew stronger on this knoll, bringing with it the aroma of alder, peat, and the warm, sharp scent of deep, deep magic. A smell which triggered memories, ones he hadn't allowed himself to dwell on since he was a lad. His older brother and his playmates used to sport here, and he always tagged along, his heart full of yearning to join them.

Guilt knifed him now, nearly bowing him forward in the saddle.

He gritted his teeth. On the barrows of his ancestors' graves, he'd do what was right for the tribe's welfare. He'd failed them before, depriving them of his older brother. He wouldn't do so again.

Mungan murmured into his horse's ear and stepped away. Its head bobbed once, as if in acknowledgement, sending a crawling sensation down Connall's spine. The spellcaster removed his saddle bag and stepped onto the incised rock, setting his burden down near the edge.

Connall shivered in the pre-dusk winter air. The young druid poured liquid into some of the "cups" carved in the stone. In others, he pinched precise measurements of various herbs and plants, mixing them within. In another, he struck a flint and burned a bundle of twigs. A pungent, earthy smell wafted to the side of the clearing, making his nose twitch. With each inhale of its rich, heady scent, the magic strengthened and swelled.

In other cups, Mungan placed yew staffs which, when complete, formed a circle. No one knew who'd carved into these rocks, but the druids claimed to know the intended purpose and how to harness its magic. He'd heard tales of "journeying" through the rock's magic, but it was a rare occurrence, one neither he nor his father's peers had ever witnessed.

"Stand here." Mungan indicated a staff in direct line with the setting rays of the sun.

Heart pounding so hard it reverberated up his throat, Connall dismounted, grabbed his leather satchel, and did as instructed. His father, his brothers, and the rest of the attending warriors gathered around the edge and watched in silence, their faces ranging from grim to desolate. He would *not* let them down.

He stood with the staff circles at his back, as straight as he was able, and lowered his chin, ready for whatever magic the druid planned. If it found Connall a wife, he'd pay the price. The weak winter sun bathed his skin, mixing with the power in the air.

Mungan stepped back and held his yew staff to the side, his gaze checking Connall's position and stance and then roving once over the magical setup.

The spellcaster nodded decisively. "Walk sunwise around the circle of staffs. And whatever you do"—he pointed his finger at him—"do not stop until the magic is complete. You have the charmed stone that will return you, aye?"

Connall fingered the small incised object in the pouch belted to his side, the smooth surface cooling the pads of his fingers. Even this wee object seemed to pulse with magic. "I do."

Mungan pointed to Connall's left. "Then walk."

He paced across the slanted expanse of magic stone, and Mungan chanted words that were mostly lost in the wind, but snatches caught his ear, ringing eerily clear. "...two souls lost...separated in the breadth of eternity...united by..."

Heavier and heavier his steps became as the spellcaster's words slipped through the thickening air to reach his ears. Panic clutched his heart, but he gritted his teeth and sought his battle-ready calm—of a certainty, this venture would be as fraught with danger as one with swords and blood and might. As he made the next pass around the circle, the solstice sun's rays brightened to a painful degree, and he squinted. His body...by all the gods and goddesses...it was as if his bones had turned to stone.

He dragged a leg forward, and it landed with a *thud*. Next leg forward. *Thud*. He concentrated on moving each muscle in his body, the druid's words admonishing him to not stop still animating him forward despite the struggle. *Thud. Thud.* Sound grew muffled and distorted till it all but disappeared. And his heart punched against his ribs with each weighted step.

Ach, he could neither see nor hear. But then the druid's voice pierced through the thickening, blinding veil shrouding him: "Remember, you hail from a land called Scotland."

Scotland? 'Twas a strange word. And a strange name it was for their land, but he'd not question it—the druid might be young, but he was wise. Connall stumbled forward and *boom*, a pressure smacked his torso and legs, and sound rushed into his ears. The blinding light morphed to black as night, and true fear grabbed his soul as he opened his eyes wide. Light and sound swirled and resolved, and his knees buckled under him, making him stumble down...an unfamiliar green knoll.

Where—?

Using the downward momentum, Connall regained his footing by running. At the bottom of the steep hill, he sat, his breath sawing in and out as if he'd fought an army of warriors single-handedly. The dread he'd experienced earlier at the druid's evasiveness now settled into his belly like a weighted stone, for the sight before him was...was... He pulled in a shaky breath, his pulse beating a frantic rhythm. Well, it was unlike anything he'd ever seen.

The stench...oily and smoky.

The noise...discordant and piercing.

And the sight?

Mother of all his ancestors, alien it was. More people than he'd ever witnessed at even the largest tribal gathering pushed past one another on a smooth road of rock. Chariots, colorful and shiny, zoomed nearby, faster than any horse, and pulled along as if by magic.

And the people. Och, they were dressed even more strangely—colorful fabric cut in unusual patterns and sewn with great skill, their skin and hair colored vibrantly. In the distance stretched a dull red line, arcing through the air and flanked by two ladder-like structures. He frowned—the scale was odd. What was it?

Then he gasped—it was a *bridge* unlike any stone causeway or ford he'd trodden, stretching across a vast loch. How skilled were these people?

Connall dug his fingers into the grassy soil and swallowed, throat dry, then jumped to his feet, slapping his hand at his side. Instead of meeting the hilt of his greatsword, he encountered cloth.

He stared down at his person, and goose bumps broke out along his skin. Gone were his great kilt and sandals, and in their place was a tartan wrapped around his hips and the heaviest shoes upon his feet, crisscrossed with string. He held out his arms and smoothed a palm down his forearm, marveling at the soft cloth covering his upper body. A leather satchel hung at his side, held by a strap from his opposite shoulder.

What have ye done, Mungan?

A couple strolled by in their peculiar attire, chattering away in a strange language, for the cadence was unfamiliar. But as they drew near, despite not knowing the shape of the words, he understood their meaning perfectly and marveled at the strength of the young druid's magic.

Connall turned in a circle, taking in the cacophony of sight and sound and the multitude of people.

"You were right to send me here, Mungan," he whispered into the still, winter air, his breath clouding it white. For women were *everywhere.*

And then his heart chilled to match the frigid air, because the words which had emerged from his mouth were not their customary shape.

Mo Chreach. The sooner he found his wife, the sooner he could leave this strange and smelly place with its peculiar word-shapes. Besides, the druid warned him he had to accomplish his task before two full moons passed, or the tether would weaken and he'd no longer remember home. All stated with a matter-of-factness that had further unnerved him.

Connall strode to the edge of the tightly shorn, uniform grass where it bordered the arrow-straight stone path across which everyone strode. A nice-enough looking lass strolled by, staring at an object in her hand.

"Will ye be my wife? I'll treat ye well, never fear," he said in the strange words.

He thought it best to reassure them on that fact. And then he stared—she'd passed him without ever looking up from her hand. Was his voice not working in the druid's magic? It was disconcerting to think word-shapes in one way, and have them come out differently, and still understand them. Despite their unfamiliarity.

He placed his hands on his hips and used the voice that made his warriors stand straighter. "Harken on to me!"

Startled faces glanced his way. Aye, his voice was in fine working order. But instead of stopping and paying heed as they should, each and every one continued past and either looked at their hands, as they all seemed inclined to do, or talked to themselves, a hand at their ear.

He tried again, infusing his voice with more authority. "I'm searching for a wife for my hearth."

Most continued on as before, as if he were invisible, but one man slowed, his brow furrowed in concern. "You're looking for your wife?"

Connall approached, his steps eager. "Aye."

"Where'd you last see her? Is she not answering your call?"

"I haven't yet met her, and I'm calling for one now, aren't I?" Connall waved his hand toward the seething mass of humanity.

The man stepped back, eyes round, and scuttled past, shaking his head.

What was so difficult to understand? He'd been assured by the lasses in his life that he was pleasant-enough looking, and he was surely strong enough to take care of one, unlike most of these sticks scurrying past.

With that thought to hand, he approached the next lass who appeared to be of child-bearing age, though 'twas hard to look at her for her lips, cheeks, and eyes had a sharpness of color he'd never seen before. As if she had the hues of a butterfly's wing on her face. "Will ye consent to be my wife and return with me to my land?" Remembering the druid's words, he added, "It's called Scotland."

The woman only stared and said, "Freak."

Each time he approached a likely lass, he was met with the same, or with laughter or weird looks. Truly, it was enough to wound his pride.

A man approached him, all in black with tools strapped around his waist. "I'm going to need to ask you to leave the park, mister. I'm getting complaints of harassment." He carried himself with the authority of a chief, though he was a bit soft around the waist to be a warrior for these people.

"Harassment?"

"You can't stand here asking random women to marry you." He crossed his arms and glanced around. "Is this for some reality show or a YouTube stunt? You need a permit for this kind of thing."

Connall shook his head, unsure of the man's meaning, his druid's magic failing him for the first time.

"Well, knock it off, all right?" The man stepped away, muttering under his breath, only the words "cold" and "brings out the weirdos" reaching Connall.

As he departed, a young lad approached at an alarming speed on a flat, wheeled board. Connall grabbed his upper arm before he could dash past.

"Hey, watch it," the lad barked, his eyes flashing in annoyance. But as he took in Connall towering above him, his eyes widened, and he yanked two white things from his ears. "Keep your hands to yourself."

"Where can I procure a wife?" Pride be gone—surely a man his age would know.

The lad stepped on the edge of the board, snapping it up into his palm. "I don't know, dude, try Craigslist." He shook his head, hopped back onto the wheeled board, and rolled away, dodging between the strolling people.

Connall didn't know who or where Craig was, but if he had a list of available wives, he would find him. He gazed around at the bizarre people and behavior.

Aye, the sooner the better.

*

Chapter Two

As night descended, Connall worked his way back to the only haven he'd seen since appearing in this land—the stretch of shorn grass and hill he'd tumbled down. He'd not dared stray too far in his search for a wife.

His inquiries as to where he could procure this Craig's list of wives had proven baffling, the words peppering the answers not finding a meaning in his head.

He'd try again in the morn. Meanwhile, he needed a place to lay his head. Knee-high platforms dotted the area, and on them stretched various sleeping forms. While these were indeed an improvement upon his own pallet, he had to question the wisdom of sleeping with no shelter overhead. Did it not rain in this land?

Or perhaps these were set out for travelers, so they wouldn't have to sleep on the ground. With that thought easing him, he approached one of the few empty beds and put his hand to his kilt.

He grunted. This was not enough to wrap around himself. Hand still poised at the leather binding it to his waist, he studied the other sleepers. All kept themselves clothed.

He curled his lip. So be it.

He tucked an arm under his head and settled in. The constant noise, however, kept him from closing his eyes. How could these people sleep with this continuous din?

A tinkling sound grew louder, separating itself from the rest, and he angled his chin to see what new strangeness approached. A man aged at least one-hundred winters hobbled toward him, two animals trotting beside him. Though of a different form, not only to each other, but to any that he'd ever seen, the general lines told him these were some manner of dog.

"It's not safe to sleep here, young man." The older man motioned to the left. "Come, come, follow me. There's an extra bed at my shelter."

Connall studied the newcomer, struck by a sense of familiarity, despite his age.

"Mungan?"

Even as he said the name, he knew it wasn't their spellcaster. The nose, while similar, was longer. The jaw less square.

The man placed his hand to his heart and tipped forward slightly. "Norton, Emperor of the United States and Protector of Mexico."

Emperor? He knew leaders of some distant lands held such a title, and he was humbled to have come across this land's ruler so soon. Mungan's magic had come through for him.

The magic will provide equivalents for you.

And while relief flooded him, it was laced with a feeling of averting a danger he hadn't fully realized he'd faced—for Mungan to provide such magic meant he'd have been out of his depth otherwise.

What did this cost you, hearth brother?

• • •

One week later

"Come on, just a little farther," Ashley Miller murmured as the F-line streetcar slowed its approach to the stop at 5th and Powell.

Close enough. But before she took the leap, she surveyed the faces waiting at the stop or strolling by. None were the two hired goons searching for her. Goons—*such* an outdated and melodramatic term, but that was her life right now, wasn't it? When she first learned last month that in addition to being saddled with her ex-husband's debts, a bookie was also tracking her down to make her pay another one, she wanted to divorce his ass all over again and then drop-kick him from the Golden Gate Bridge.

It was why she preferred taking the streetcar with the tourists instead of BART, despite the higher price tag—it gave her the freedom to get off quicker than a bus, and no one would expect a resident to use one daily.

When would one of her shit ton of job applications come through? But wouldn't they just trace her to wherever she landed?

She shouldered her messenger bag and hopped off the side just as her phone *ding*ed with a text. She pulled it up.

Sweet. An Etsy sale. She shoved her way through the just-got-off-work crowd, angling toward the three-story former warehouse turned hipster mish-mash of upscale condos, shared office space, and the section within she was temporarily calling home—a podshare.

"Jesus, I hope not for much longer," she muttered.

With rent so high in San Francisco, this was all she could afford, but it was clean and safe, so she put up with it. God, she just wanted to lie down and sleep for like…five days? Was that too much to ask?

This morning her software engineering team had grated and frayed her last nerve, second-guessing everything and acting as if this wasn't their zillionth test run on the code. "One more week. And then I can sleep."

Aaaand, she was talking to herself. Yep. She needed some friggin' rest.

She pushed against the glass door and stepped into the warm tones of the podshare, an artsy combo of paint, exposed wood and brick, and slate chalkboards adorned with colorful, inspirational quotes.

"Cards Against Humanity Game Night Tonight. Sign up here," declared one. "Why do you love podshare living?" asked another, with scribbles below in various handwriting. And because the place was run like a well-oiled machine, the Christmas decorations had been taken down while she'd been at work and replaced with a space to write New Year's resolutions.

Writing *Get out of this podshare and dodge the bookies* probably wouldn't go over well.

She walked past them, pulled open her locker, and shoved her messenger bag onto the top shelf. She removed her fishing tackle box full of beads and other crafting supplies—she'd better fill the order now while she was still mostly awake rather than wait until she got off her bistro shift later. Because when that shift ended? Her *only* plan was to crawl into bed to grab the five hours of sleep she'd have before heading into work in the morning.

She lugged the box to her designated section of the podshare, climbed the wooden steps between two sets of bunk beds, and then crawled into hers on the right. She'd tried to make it homey, with butterfly LED lights strung across the peach-colored wall and clippings from travel magazines of places she longed to someday visit, but it was still a bed in a room full of beds. Really, it was nothing more than an upscale youth hostel, but everyone else here thought it was the dawn of a new era of living, some even choosing to telecommute from the open, shared offices in the back.

Nothing like the Victorian-era home she'd lived in less than six months ago. But she wouldn't dwell on what used to be. This was her reality now. Her nightmare. She needed to keep her head down, work hard, and just get through it. And avoid those bookies like her life depended on it—because it did.

She checked the time on her phone and retrieved the Etsy order. *One custom dragonfly necklace, coming right up.* She fished out the ordered item, enclosed it into a box, and addressed it. Since she had a few more minutes before she needed to change for the bistro, she tabbed over to Craigslist. Perhaps her notice of handcrafted items from a local artisan had caught someone's attention.

"Coming to game night tonight?" a voice called from below. Ashley peered over her railing at the perky brunette, the social coordinator for the podshare.

"Sorry." *Not sorry.* "Gotta work tonight." *Like I do every night.*

She glanced back at her Craigslist post. Nothing. She sighed, about to scroll away, but a new local ad's headline made her stop.

Scottish Lass Wanted.

Scottish Lass? Who *talked* like that anymore? And what did he *want* her for? Various plots from all the Scottish historical romances she'd inhaled in her minimal free time spun together, creating intriguing possibilities. Intriguing, *fictional* possibilities.

But she clicked.

The ancient land of Scotland beckons for the brave lass

who answers this advertisement. Scotland—where the men are real men, able to swing an axe one-handed and would never be caught wearing tight breeches. Where the men are tall and broad of shoulder and know how to please a woman. Enjoy the most enchanting, majestic spot in all of Scotland in exchange for washing and cooking duties as well as willingness and ability to increase my herd. Interested parties reply for further information.

Oh man. Scotland. The rolling green hills and craggy mountains and misty lochs she'd drooled over in travel magazines filled her mind.

But...*dishes.*

Her gaze went straight to the striking photo on the wall of a slate-gray loch in Scotland, green mountains rising on either side, their tips kissed by misty clouds. And not a soul in sight.

God, she was exhausted from not only paying off debts that weren't even friggin' hers to begin with, but also tired of always looking over her shoulder this past month. Tired of wriggling and jostling against all the people in her city.

She really, *really* wanted to answer this ad. But she wasn't a Scottish lass.

Though...didn't her mom say that great-granddad was from the Highlands? Did that count?

But...*dishes.* And her bills. Ugh. Her asshole of an ex-husband's bills. But worse than that, she could picture how her parents would react if she gave up, crawled back home, and asked for help. They'd pat her on the head, go, "my dear, you couldn't expect to handle that on your own." She would *always* be the spoiled baby of the family, no matter what she did.

That settled it. If this position in Scotland came with a nice salary, then she was all over it—any opportunity to pay off her inherited debt and avoid living down to her parents' expectations would be worth the trouble. And really, how bad could it be?

Because yes, dishes. But also...*Scotland.*

God, this line was scary long. Ashley leaned to the side and stretched up onto her toes—wow, there had to be at least twenty-five women in front of her. She glanced over her shoulder at the exit just as the door opened and three more women stepped through to file into line, their hair perfectly curled and lip gloss expertly applied.

Ashley rubbed her dry, bare, *unglossy* lips together and straightened her shoulders. What the hell was she doing here?

But all through her shift at the bistro last night she couldn't stop thinking about that ad. Her aching feet as she trod the same path between tables to bring yet another couple their dinner only emphasized that washing dishes in Scotland had to be better than this.

It would also get her far away from the men looking for money she didn't owe and didn't have. This job would be the *last* place the bookies would expect her, a tech nerd, to go— it was probably at some remote castle with no Starbucks in sight.

And if it didn't pay, maybe she would go anyway. Screw him. She refused to feel guilty. She'd married that jerk right out of college, partly because she wanted to prove to her family that she was mature.

Mature...right. That blew up in my face.

Ashley pulled out her phone and used the time in line to fill out targets in the work app for her team, hoping that would give her a head start on the afternoon in case this ran much longer and turned out to be nothing.

Sooner than she expected, a man with a Scottish brogue called out, "Next. Lass, ye ready? Are ye done staring at your wee palm?" Deep, rich tones rumbled in the air, buffeting against her as if corporeal and sending a wash of awareness across her skin.

Startled, she glanced up. And nearly dropped her phone. Because, good Lord, this should be illegal. A whole snack of Scottish virility sat in an office chair, staring at her expectantly. Even though he was sitting, she could tell he was tall, his shoulders filling out the black Henley to perfection. Most guys with long hair couldn't really pull off the right look, but the full-bodied waves would make Instagram star Brock O'Hurn weep. Black, with a small braid down each side. Blue ink peeked from his neckline in a swirling Celtic pattern.

He uncrossed his arms and sat forward, eyebrow cocked on his angular face, highlighting his deep green eyes shot through with gray smoke.

Wow, she hadn't yet said a *word*. "Um, hi. I'm Ashley. Nice to...uh, meet you." She stepped closer and stuck out her hand, shaking a little from nerves. Why? He was just a *guy*. A hot one, yeah, but still just a guy.

"Aye, the customary handshake. I'm Connall from the land of Scotland," he pronounced with care.

She glanced at his green-and-blue kilt. Maybe it was that swath of fabric revving her up. Strong calves lined with muscle ended in wool socks and black combat boots. When his warm, rough palm slid against hers, her breath caught. His gaze darted to hers, his eyes filled with curiosity as well as surprise. She yanked her hand away.

What the hell? She was *not* here to get involved with some guy, no matter how hot. Or how Scottishly hot. Or hotly Scottish. Oh damn it all. She didn't have much time to consider this so-very-out-there idea to get away, but it seemed to be the answer to her problems. And for once she was going to succumb to something she longed to do even if it wasn't the smartest move.

"I'm here about the job? In Scotland?" She opened the flap in her messenger bag for the item she'd tucked in at the last minute, in case he was wearing a kilt. "And I brought you this. I made it for my Etsy shop, but I thought…" She pulled in a breath, the enticing scent of an unsullied outdoors and freedom making her words stumble, "I thought you'd like it."

He gave a low chuckle. "I suppose it is a job at that."

His smoky-green gaze locked with hers. God, if all men in Scotland were like this, sign her the eff up. "Um, yeah, so anyway, I made this and I thought you might be able to use it to, er, secure your kilt. A kilt pin. That I made." *Jesus, just shut up.*

But there was depth to those eyes that drew her in and made her feel as if she were free-wheeling downhill, giddy and on the knife-edge of losing control. A depth that said he'd witnessed more of life than usual for his age. A prickle of awareness raced along her skin. *What does he like to do in his spare time? What are his pet peeves?* And riding this urge to know more about him was a need to *shelter* him.

She reached out to the flap of his kilt resting against his solid thigh and lifted the fabric, only a little, to slip the pin through. Her knuckles brushed soft hair and warm skin. A sharp breath sounded by her ear, and his whole body stiffened.

Abort. Abort! What are you doing?

"Well now, that's a lovely gift, it is," his voice rumbled low. "From a lovely lass."

A warmth fizzed low in her belly, and her body flushed hot. *What is wrong with you, Ash? You're not usually so forward.*

And then horror hit her—this was for a friggin' job. And

she went and *touched* her potential boss's thigh?

Holy hell.

She jerked back, drawing in a quick breath, and ran through possible face-saving apologies.

I was...er...

I did that because...er...

Nothing sounded right.

His head cocked to the side, his black hair falling with it. "If you're interested, I think we should meet again to discuss the matter."

"I'm interested." In the job. The *job*. Not him.

Heat flared in his eyes. "Very well. Tomorrow, at the same portion of the day, at the coffee establishment on the corner?"

Ashley nodded, and before she could embarrass herself further, she stood and turned away. But not before she saw him twirl around in his office chair. She could also swear he said, "I do love how these spin."

• • •

The squeak of Connall's chair cut through the chatter of waiting women. Hopefully, it masked the pounding in his chest.

As his chair finished its delightful spin, Connall motioned to the next woman in line, though his whole being seemed to be centered on Ashley's retreating form.

Yes. She's the one.

When their gazes had locked, intelligence had shone in her eyes, coupled with a hint of humor. And she possessed birthing hips, couldn't forget that. He gently touched the silver pin she'd given him. Clever lass, for sure, fashioning such a jewel for his kilt. Cleverness was a trait his village needed in a chief's wife, for chief he'd most likely be.

These last two days, interviewing so many women, had been exhausting. Who knew so many were looking for husbands? He was fortunate and overwhelmed by the attention. But until Ashley appeared, none had sparked his interest. Truth be told, the reason he'd taken another spin in the wondrous chair was to break from her pull on him. To test it. That and he felt...delighted, for which only a spin in the chair would suffice to express himself. A lightness suffused him, the likes of which he'd not felt in a long, long time.

Even now, though she'd departed, the full impact of her gaze on him—those dancing brown eyes—sent his senses reeling. That saddle-brown hair appeared as soft as silk, framing an open and honest face.

She's most certainly the one.

And glad he was of it, too. Mungan had warned him that he needed to be quick. His first full moon had passed mere days after his arrival. He had twenty-eight nights left to accomplish his task, or he risked forgetting his home and family—everyone he knew and loved.

Later that day, he shifted metal hooks to the side, searching for his size in this trading center he'd learned was called a men's clothing store. In the week since he'd arrived in this metropolis called San Francisco, he'd been dizzy from everything he faced. And had to learn. At least the weather had turned warmer after that first day—almost as warm as summer.

His personal trade assistant, a very cheerful man, pulled out a pair of dull blue trousers called jeans. "These will look perfect on you, trust me."

Connall nodded. "I trust you. My thanks."

"I'll add these to your stack, then." He marched away to the small room where they expected people to try their clothes on before purchasing. If Connall concentrated hard enough, the magic let him know what was expected. But it was hard concentrating today when all he could fix on was the lovely lass he'd met with earlier.

Ashley.

Tomorrow, they'd meet again, he assured himself.

He tested the fit of the jeans in the tiny room and looked in the marvel of a mirror. Why men wanted to cram their pride into these tight monstrosities he'd never know, but he was tired of all the staring as he walked around this forsaken land in his kilt. He was the only man wearing one; it emphasized that he didn't belong here. With his new garments selected, he turned to the wooden door and gripped the handle, concentrating. *Pay with the black card at the long table.*

Before Connall had left, Mungan explained the spell would match his wealth, belongings, and knowledge with the land's equivalent. If it wasn't for that and his new friend Emperor Norton, he'd have been lost.

Connall nabbed the clothes he wished to take from the store and strode to the table. His trade assistant beamed. "Did you decide on anything?"

"Aye." He slung the jeans and several shirts onto the table and pulled out his black American Express card. His ten cows back home allowed him much here in this land, it seemed. Now, he'd have a fresh change of clothes to meet Ashley.

Anticipation and a sense of rightness suffused him as he stuck the card in the slot of the tiny device on the long table. Soon he'd be meeting his future wife, and all would be well— the hard part was over. No more clomping around this sharp, smelly place.

• • •

Ashley paused at the street corner and squinted into the gray clouds covering her city. Was she really about to do this? Step inside that coffee shop?

She rubbed her palms down her thighs and pulled in a deep breath. The truth was, she couldn't stop thinking about him.

No. It wasn't *him*. It was the *job*. One in *Scotland,* and the escape it represented that had her hot and bothered—not the sexy Scotsman.

Butterflies dancing in her stomach, she marched up to the mom-and-pop coffee shop and pushed open the door. A chime sounded overhead, and she immediately found him sitting at the old-fashioned counter. When the butterflies collapsed in a dead faint, she snorted.

Yeah, right. She wasn't fooling anyone. It was *him* she was anxious about seeing again.

He'd been peering around the quaint coffee shop, and when his gaze caught hers, he did a double take and immediately stood.

"You came." The words were low, but his voice carried to her easily, its effect on her instantaneous—everything inside her perked up, including the butterflies.

Damn, he wasn't wearing his kilt today, but those jeans molded to his powerful thighs. With him standing there in the tiny shop, it was even more obvious how tall and just...huge he was. An air of authority radiated from him that she rarely encountered. Authority that sat naturally on his shoulders instead of forced there to puff up the owner, like she came across in so many of her past bosses. She could easily see him as a warrior of old, fending off the English in the Highland mountain passes with just his sword.

I need a vacation.

"Of course I came." Thankfully, her voice didn't expose her internal chaos.

She slid onto the red vinyl cushion of the soda-fountain style seat, acutely aware of how close he was to her as he settled beside her. And that yummy, masculine scent was *not* him. It was *not*. And she'd keep spraying herself with eau de Denial as long as she could, thank you very much.

A puzzled look scrunched his forehead. "I've seen others in your land wear such, dangling from their ears." His large fingers touched the end of her silver earring. "The design reminds me of home. It's beautiful."

Wistfulness tinged his voice on the word *home*, and her body heated with desire and embarrassment—desire because the gesture felt intimate, and embarrassment because she'd worn these particular earrings to get his attention. They were a Celtic design.

"Thank you. I made them."

His gaze popped to hers. "You are a gifted metal worker. I shall treasure the piece you crafted for me." He tapped his chest. There, pinned over his heart, was her Celtic sword pin she'd given him yesterday, the tip pointing down. With the flaring, angled points of the hilt, it almost looked like a *Star Trek* communicator. And with him tapping against it?

"Ha ha, good one." She tapped her chest. "Beam me up, Scotty."

Instead of playing along, he frowned at her. Ooookay, not a *Star Trek* fan.

The waitress rescued Ashley from having to save face. Though her heart beat as fast as a caffeine-fueled coder typed, she said calmly, "I'll have a coffee with cream and sugar, and that chocolate-chip muffin you displayed right in front of me."

"Ha. They do look good, don't they?" The waitress lifted the glass dome and retrieved a muffin with a pair of tongs. She placed it on a white plate and poured a cup of coffee.

"I'll be having the same," Connall stated next to her.

Was that relief she detected in his voice?

He slid a black Amex card onto the counter. "Do you

take this as your form of barter in this place?" The waitress nodded and stepped away to run his card.

What the hell line of business was this guy in? A *black* Amex? And did all Scottish people have a strange way of talking?

She blew on her coffee. "So... Scotland, huh? And thank you for the treat." She lifted her chin and met his gaze, challenging herself not to look away.

He gave a slow nod, and his eyes darted to her mouth and back. He angled his head slightly, his black hair shifting and one braid swinging forward. He could be an Instagram influencer with just his luscious hair.

Keep talking. You are not *ogling your potential boss.* "How long have you been in San Francisco?"

He blew on his coffee, too, before answering. "Eight nights."

"That's all? How are you liking it?"

He looked into his coffee. "Arriving was lonely and strange. I knew no one until I met Mr. Norton and his two dogs." He said the name with a hint of gratitude, and a cord of sympathy stretched from her to him.

"I don't have close friends myself," she whispered. She'd discovered that fact after the scandal of her divorce.

"He stinks, and others seem to shun him, though I know not why." His nose and forehead wrinkled. "But he was a friend to me when I needed one most."

Her heart squeezed, and she had the inexplicable urge to put her arm around this stranger who'd found comfort from a homeless man—everyone who lived or worked in this part of the city knew "Emporer" Norton—and seemed perplexed that others shunned such a kind soul.

She swallowed the hot ball of emotion gathering in her throat and sat up straighter, determined to shift the conversation to the reason they met in the coffee shop. "So, about this job..."

"Not sure why ye insist on calling it a job."

"It entails washing and cooking, your ad said. In exchange for my trip there?" How hard could washing and cooking duties be? Especially if it was just half a day and she could explore the rest of the day.

Explore *Scotland*.

Working herself to the bone to pay off her bastard of an ex-husband's debts, well, she needed a breather. A break. A ray of sunshine to peek through the gray clouds choking her present circumstances. So she'd know all this hard work was *worth it*.

He was answering her question, but the enormous bicep parked *right next to her* pulled her focus from his words. How was a girl supposed to think? Well, about anything other than—would it be rude to put her thigh alongside and see which was bigger? Because, honestly, she wasn't sure if hers *was*. She nodded along and managed to ask the one thing she wanted to be clear on. "This is just for part of the day, right? Four hours a day?"

She picked up the muffin, but nervousness had taken up all the room in her stomach, so she set it back down.

"Well, that's much less than the other women in my village, but aye, I might have an idea of other ways you can spend your time." He gave her a charming wink.

He spun around on the stool and faced her, placing his hands on his knees, his fingers long and strong. It put him more in her personal space, and it was all she could do not to match his movements and face him. He leaned forward, his two braids swinging toward her. "So we're in agreement?"

She pulled all the giddy parts of her into a tight ball so this feeling wouldn't control her, and took a deep breath. She could do this. She *deserved* this. "Yes."

"Then let us depart."

"What, now?" She scrambled up, hitching her purse onto her shoulder.

He drew a squiggle on the charge receipt and grabbed his card. "Aye, I'd rather be getting started."

This was happening so fast. "Okay, but let me pack my things first. I don't have much." A part of her wanted to do the responsible thing and ask for time off from the places she worked, but excitement and a daring, brave feeling infused her, which was so rare she wanted to seize it, let it fill her. Let it *be* her.

And what better way to throw off the bookies than to completely disappear?

. . .

Connall gripped the sides of the large chariot which ran on tracks without any visible steed to pull it, the wind pushing against his hair, the noxious smell of this metropolis even more odious as it whipped against his skin and into his nose.

Steed or no, this chariot ran as fast as the fleetest horse, and he hung off the side like Ashley and so many others, her long brown hair riding the air, her bearing as strong as any warrior. It took his full concentration to hang on as he watched the stone street *whoosh* past.

Finally, Ashley said, "This is our stop."

He concentrated, and the meaning became clear. He readied himself. When the contraption slowed, she hopped off, and he did the same, gratified he landed squarely on his feet. He grinned and looked back as the beast moved on.

"I'm right over here," she called.

He spun around and glanced up at where she pointed— one of the massive buildings he'd seen but not dared enter.

Ashley pushed hard on a clear door, and he reached over her shoulder to swing it forward for her. A rush of lust tightened his loins as he inhaled her sweet scent.

She seemed unfazed by his closeness, though, and ushered him inside.

"I don't have a lot. Had to sell most of my belongings after my divorce." She waved a hand into a large room beyond the smaller one they stood in, filled with jarring colors, beds, and people.

He tensed. *Divorce. A way of legally separating from a spouse.*

"It grieves me to hear of your marriage dissolution."

"Well, it doesn't grieve *me*." She stepped over to a bright, shiny wall and pulled open a clever door, a rattling sound emitting from it. He followed, placing his hand on the surface. Coolness met his palm. 'Twas similar to a sword's material, but thinner.

"Is this where you and your family live?" He took in the clumps of people, aged the same number of winters—most sitting at tables, or on their beds.

"No," she scoffed, her voice low, her words only meant for him. "I don't really know any of them. This is just temporary. Till I can get back on my feet."

"Are ye not standing on those appendages as we speak?"

She cocked her head. "You have an odd sense of humor."

He frowned but ignored her puzzling assessment because a more pressing issue confronted him. "You live in such close quarters with strangers?" The unnaturalness of it tightened his skin, but then so much of this land and its ways were strange.

She shrugged and pulled a flat, metallic object from a shelf then slid it into her shoulder satchel. Then she pulled a square object made of cloth out from under a bed and began tossing clothes inside.

This was how people lived in this land? Even in his village there was more privacy and space than this. And they all knew and cared for each other. Toiled and celebrated together.

He took in a shuddering breath. *And cried together.*

The thread of guilt for taking her from her home dissipated. True, she'd agreed to come, but he sensed she wasn't quite understanding her new role. She kept insisting on calling it a job, as if being married to him would be a chore.

Surely, she would prefer his home. The air was cleaner. His people friendlier. The food better.

She straightened from a crouch and closed the distance between them, and a part of him relaxed as she drew nearer, the larger satchel pulled on ingenious wheels. She smiled up at him, her eyes bright with excitement and a hint of daring, which poked at something deep inside himself. Aye, this was the right thing to do.

"Ready," she said. "When does our flight leave?"

He returned her smile. "Now." He grasped her wee hand, and a surge of protectiveness swelled in his chest—she was his responsibility now. His to cherish and protect. For while his home *was* more pleasant, he was well aware it posed certain dangers.

She startled at his touch but didn't pull away, and a slight flush pinkened her cheeks. Then he fingered the incised stone in his pocket and uttered the words Mungan had made him memorize. Sealing their fates. Sealing their bond as man and wife.

• • •

Ashley gripped Connall's hand hard. Hard enough to cause pain, she was sure, but she couldn't help it. She was in the middle of some kind of fit, and he was her only lifeline—as if she'd fainted but was still awake, or something, because the room spun, all had gone dark, but she was still awake. What the hell?

Her knees buckled, and sound became hushed, as if her ears were stopped up. But by her temple, Connall's deep, panty-melting voice murmured, "I have ye."

"What's happening?" she whispered.

Then gray seeped into the darkness, and sound rushed back in. She stumbled forward and gasped—and immediately sank to the floor.

No, not floor. *Ground*. Dirt and grass met her palms.

Where the eff am I?

Chapter Three

Chills slalom-raced down Ashley's skin, her heart thumping so hard it was an insistent drumbeat in her ears. Gone were the cheerfully painted walls and the strangers she shared the space with. She was outdoors, the sky the muted gray of twilight, the landscape dotted with dead-looking clumps of vegetation and rocks, and in the distance loomed snow-topped mountains.

And no sound.

She put a hand to her forehead. *What the—?*

She tugged her earlobes and moved her jaw to try to clear her ears.

"What happened? Where am I?" Her voice shook, and even its tentative, thready tones pierced the quiet air. Though, hallelujah, the sound meant she hadn't lost her hearing. It was just so...*quiet*. No hum of electricity. No honking of cars. No shouts or laughter. It was almost as if she'd dipped into a pool of water, but even that had its own noises.

Something rustled beside her, and she latched onto the proof of existence like a lifeline. The hot Scotsman strode into view, his large body blocking the mountains and rugged landscape. He waved a hand behind him. "We're in Scotland."

He said this as if it should be completely obvious, but there was the matter of how the hell they'd gotten here. Had she blacked out during her fit? Had he *drugged* her?

"I...I don't remember traveling. And why are we in the middle of nowhere?" Her heartbeat pulsed in her veins like a living thing, beating out its scared rhythm. What the hell was going on?

Why can't I remember anything since he held my hand back at the podshare?

He squatted in front of her, concern etching his face. Her skin broke out in goose bumps, because he was wearing a different kind of kilt—not the modern kind, but the big, drapey kind that wrapped around his waist and up over a shoulder—with her pin still on him, holding up the portion over his shoulder. And he was also wearing...oh man, was that a friggin' sword strapped at his hip?

Er, God, yes. His hand clasped it to keep it angled off the ground, as if it was something he did every day. A thick silver choker, with a gap in the front, circled his neck.

She pulled in a shaky breath.

It's a dream. I must have passed out.

And he wasn't the only one who had changed. She wore some kind of tunic dress and a fur-lined mantle. The suitcase was gone, and her laptop bag was now a leather satchel. She put a hand to her head; her hair was in one long braid.

Yeah, her brain decided to go all out. But it was more detailed than any dream she'd had, because despite the fur-lined mantle—nice touch—she was *freezing*.

He leaned into her space, and she caught a whiff of his maddening, masculine scent. He reached toward her, then dropped his hand to his knee and balled it into a tight fist. "'Twas magic which brought us here. Druid's magic." His voice was gentle, soothing. "It's too late to journey back to the keep, so we'll make camp here and head there on the morrow."

OkayOkayOkay. She'd just make nice with the hallucination of the hot Scot from earlier because she'd wake up soon. "Sure. Fine." She shivered in the darkening twilight.

Connall searched her face again, and the weight of his concern sent her pulse fluttering for another reason. He nodded once then vaulted to his feet, and she immediately missed his nearness.

He gathered twigs and small branches and then arranged them into a neat pyramid off the side of the large expanse of rock she was perched on. He produced flint from the pouch at his waist and struck it, his cheeks hollowing as he breathed into the smoke and coaxed a flame to life, the sizzle and crackle of fresh tinder catching fire filling the evening air.

Impressive. But then again, this was her dream casting him as a warrior of old who'd know how to make fire from nothing but a piece of flint.

Even though it was a dream, she still hated being cold, so she stepped off the rock and inched closer to the now-blazing glow.

He removed her pin from his kilt, looking at it with a frown and then a small smile. He tucked it into his pouch and tugged his great kilt off, leaving him in some kind of shirt that covered him to mid-thigh, which should have looked silly but didn't. He spread the voluminous fabric near the fire and lay down, bringing half of it over him. He looked up at her and held up a corner, his eyes unreadable in the growing darkness. "Lay here. You'll be warmer, for it will only be growing cooler tonight."

It was a dream, right? She'd at least snuggle up to this muscular Highlander with black to-die-for hair and penetrating green eyes. *Thank you, dream mind!*

She knelt beside the fabric, barely discernible in the dying light.

"I'll not touch ye, if that's your concern."

Not really. It was a fantasy, so she might as well get some action. She crawled inside the warm cocoon he'd made and snuggled her back to his muscled side. He covered her with the remaining fabric, tucking her close. Soon her chills faded, because the man was a friggin' furnace.

As her lids grew heavy, she assured herself she'd be waking up soon. But couldn't her brain at least have given her a nice make-out session?

. . .

Ach, the nicely rounded rump of a fetching lass was pushed up against his hip. He flexed his fingers to prevent them from taking on a mind of their own and circle around her wee waist and pull her tighter against him. And possibly more.

But when they'd traveled through the druid's disorienting magic from her land to his, she'd been as skittish as a colt, and who could blame her? Even his own innards had squirmed, and that had been his second trip. Thank the gods he didn't have to go through that torture again.

His misfortune that they'd arrived too late for him to take her home. *Mo Chreach! My wife should be in a proper shelter.*

Perhaps this was the gods' way of punishing him for his earlier cowardice, by forcing him to sleep where he'd lost his older brother to a slave raid.

Fractured images crowded his mind, fuzzy from the passage of time but sharp enough to wound just the same—of him insisting to play with the older lads in their war games, of the shouts of the raiders, and, worst of all, the dank hole in which he'd cowered.

Aye, his brother had told him to run, but he shouldn't

have listened. Connall shivered now as if he were still hiding in that hole until he'd heard no more sound. Hiding until it was dark. Only then did he crawl out like the worm he'd been, shaking and stinking of fear, to discover he was the only one left.

He'd failed them. He'd failed his oldest brother as well as his childhood playmate. But he would not fail his tribe again.

As always, the reminder of his shortcomings left him antsy. Unable to walk it out as usual, he touched his nose to Ashley's soft hair, seeking solace. Her sweet scent stole over him and some of his tension eased. And instead of the nightmares he'd expected for having dredged up the past, he fell into a deep, restful sleep.

. . .

Ashley slowly rose to consciousness. Her side ached, and her neck had a crick. Ugh, she must have fallen asleep while watching TV on the sofa. She blinked heavy lids and stretched.

What time was it? What day of the week? The heavy, slept-too-long achiness infused her limbs.

Oh shit. Work! She jackknifed up and then swayed, slapping a steadying hand down onto the ground. The *cold* ground.

What the eff?

She rubbed her eyes—yep, she was on a kilt stretched across a slope facing downhill to one of the most stunning, snow-capped landscapes she'd ever seen. The ground dropped off, and beyond the winter-wilted but leafy shrubs—rhododendron?—a valley lay far below, the sparkling whites and dark browns fading gradually into the slate-blue haze of distant mountains and water.

It was as if she sat in some giant's amphitheater, staged to watch the antics of mortals in the valley below.

Where the friggin' hell *was* she?

Her mind raced, piecing memories together. At the podshare with Connall—him taking her hand—appearing here as the sun set.

But that had been a dream. Right?

Maybe it still is. She squeezed her eyes shut. *Wake up, wake up, wake UP.* Nothing happened.

To her right was a flat rock incised with geometric swirls and circles.

She rubbed her arms and hunched forward, unease slithering across her skin. *Am I alone?*

A twig snapped, and Connall appeared from behind, leading two horses. Her jaw dropped as relief swished through her veins so fast she swayed.

It's him.

But why relief? Okay—she wasn't alone up here. That was why. But shouldn't she be pissed at him? Heat climbed up her neck at the memory of her snuggled against him last night and her hopes for a dream-tryst.

It can still be a dream.

"You're awake. 'Tis best we head out." He marched over to the remains of a fire and kicked dirt into it, scattering the ashes. He handed her a dark piece of bread. "And if you're wishing to take care of personal needs, you best be doing so now."

"Head out? Where are we?" That trickle of unease bloomed in her heart, her breath catching. Because his words were different. Somehow, he was speaking in a lilting but foreign language, and she'd not only understood every single word, but had answered in the same language.

To distract herself and, well, because her stomach chose that moment to growl, as if it knew she'd just been handed food and was all, *Gimme, woman,* she took a bite of bread.

The yeasty flavor burst on her tongue, along with the taste and crunch of oodles of grains. No dream she'd ever had was this vivid. The details were sharp, down to her being cold. And to the odd taste and texture of the bread. And her hunger.

The taste, though—a fuzzy memory poked. She took another bite, trying to chase it. Whatever it was, it had been buried so far in her past she couldn't form it. Except for a fleeting, wonderful feeling of being cherished.

"Aye, we need to break camp and head to my tribe's stronghold. And we're in a land called Scotland."

That last word was *not* in the same language—instead it was in her own—and he said it as if it were a strange word to him.

"What happened? How did we get here?" She'd asked this last night, but maybe he'd change his answer.

He strode toward her and knelt. She appreciated he would no doubt repeat himself but took the time to listen to her and patiently explain. "Mungan, our spellcaster, weaved strong magic. Brought me to your land, and then brought us both back here." He held up a round stone incised with two parallel deep grooves around its center. As if that explained everything.

The hell it does. Some dude, even in a dream, was just whisking her about?

He waved to the two horses. "They left us mounts to ease our journey."

She swallowed, trying to work moisture into her parched throat. "How long will it take to get to your...stronghold?"

"Only part of the morning."

"How many hours?"

"Hours?"

"Yeah, how long? How many hours?" Was her *Star Trek* Universal Translator on the fritz already? The word "hours" had come out in English.

He shook his head and frowned. Then he pointed to the sun just barely visible as a pale glow behind morning clouds. "As long as it takes the sun to travel from there"—he slid his finger just a few inches away—"to there."

She pulled in a deep breath. Oookay.

He marched over to a shaggy brown horse, grabbed the saddle, and swung himself up into it with one swift motion, like she'd seen in old cowboy movies.

Wow, that was hot.

She'd ridden her share of horses growing up in Nebraska but had never perfected that technique. She stepped up to her horse and stroked its mane, pulling in the musky scent of the beast, letting him smell her, adjust to her. The animal's fur was thick and curly, its coarse hairs springing through her stroking fingers.

Is this real?

She stared at the imposing but gentle Highlander, and then at the horse she was supposed to ride. If she did as he asked, she'd no longer be "playing along" with her dream. She'd have to face what she hadn't wanted to admit yet— hopping onto this horse would be accepting this wasn't a dream. This step, this moment, felt real. Tangible.

As her queasy belly rearranged her breakfast by grain size, she stretched a hand toward the reins, then stopped and made a fist.

Magic brought her here? Or did she have a psychotic break, the workload and stress of paying off her ex's debts finally becoming too much for her?

Then she put her hand on the saddle and...stared. No stirrups! While the saddle was about shoulder-height, it would still be a pain to mount. There had to be a rock somewhere to step—

Hands gripped her arms and scenery *shooshed* by.

Holy hell, the Highlander had just picked her up by her arms!

She frantically scrambled onto the horse's back and settled in, the folds of her skirt bunching up around her legs.

"Um, thanks," she said, out of breath. Jeez, the strength that took. And he acted as if he'd just picked up a twig instead of a full-grown and *rounded* woman.

He nodded ahead and tapped the sides of his mount. She followed close behind, the horse adjusting to her seat, though it was odd not having any place to stick her feet.

He led the way down a switchback until they reached level ground and then...stepped onto a *wooden* road. What? Her horse followed, as if completely at ease, and she swayed with the movement, her leather saddle creaking softly.

The road wound through the scrub and marshy area, like a long boardwalk through sandy beach dunes. Though wide enough for two horses to walk side by side, she opted to stay behind Connall.

It was like the yellow brick road in Oz, winding away to the horizon, but wooden. Connall *had* mentioned magic. Did the wizard await her at the end? That thought made her snort, followed by a hiccup as she tried to swallow a burst of laughter. After all this, nothing would surprise her now.

With no phone, Ashley had no idea how long they'd been traveling. She guessed maybe a half hour when the road petered out, morphing into a dock. Beyond stretched a lake, its waters slate gray like the sky and as smooth as a mirror. Connall dismounted and looped his horse's reins around a skinny stone about waist-high. As she drew near, she could make out rune-like carvings running up the side.

Words formed in her mind, *Friends, a hundred thousand*

welcomes to Dunadd.

Her heart gave one slow thump. *Holy shit. I can read that.*

Dazed, she slid off her horse, her thighs turning to jelly. He stepped into her space, his gaze intent on hers, and lightly clasped her fingers, pulling the reins away. And damn, just that small touch—paired with his scrutiny—sent a tingle all over her skin. He looped the leather around the stone, his movements quick and efficient.

Storm clouds gathered to her left, a dark smudge bleeding into the lighter gray cloud cover overhead. As if punctuating her observation, moisture-laden wind swirled over her, loosening hairs from her braid. A herringbone pattern of ripples pocked the lake's otherwise-smooth surface. Halfway across, a jutting bluff rose from the water, its dark slope taking up most of the horizon. This was so friggin' surreal.

"Come." Connall held his arm toward the boat, silently asking her to step down that dock and go toward the only obvious destination—the stronghold perched ahead.

She took a step forward. And another. Whatever this place was, it was still away from San Francisco and her troubles.

I'll figure it out later. At least I'm safe.

Five more steps—the leather soles of her shoes barely making a sound—and her toes skirted the edge of the wooden dock, the small wooden...vessel slightly below. To call it a boat seemed ambitious. Vaguely oblong in shape, it was more a cowhide-covered wicker *bowl* with two wooden benches cutting across the middle.

Connall stepped past her and hopped in.

He held out his hand, but she hesitated.

No turning back after this. Well, not easily by the looks of it.

Over her shoulder loomed snow-tipped mountains and darkening clouds. She bit her lip. As far as she could tell, they were the only two people in this barren but ruggedly gorgeous landscape.

The only other option was to be alone out here. She slid her hand into his.

Again, warmth from the contact suffused her. Warmth from his rough skin but also warmth that was part of him—part of his personality.

She stepped into the boat, carefully keeping her feet on the thick wicker crosspieces, unsure the hide would take her weight. She braced her feet as the *bowl* swayed and switched her focus to the Highlander standing in its center, still holding her hand and seeming completely confident of its seaworthiness. She pulled her fingers from his and carefully settled onto a bench.

Connall took the bench opposite, closed his large hands around the oars, and shoved the boat away with the tip of an oar against the dock's sides. He dipped them in and pulled back, water sloshing against the sides, the workings of his strong muscles visible under his shirt as he set a steady rhythm.

She brought her knees up against her chest and clutched them. The boat rocked slightly with her movement. "I…have some questions." The chances of this being a dream were pretty much zero now. Time didn't pass like this in a dream, and it was all too real. Whatever was happening, though, she needed some answers.

His eyes held hers, and she shivered at the raw power and sensuality emanating from their depths. Directed at her. "I figured ye might." His voice was gentle, patient.

She jacked a thumb over her shoulder. "That stone post back there. I could read the runes."

He nodded, and a corner of his mouth tipped up. "That's lovely." Was she mistaken or was that…pride…in those same eyes? He dipped the oars in again for another powerful stroke.

"You don't understand. I shouldn't be able to. I don't even know what language that is." Her voice pitched higher as she neared the end.

"Well, it's the druid's magic, isn't it? That's Ogham. Could ye read back in your land?"

"Yes."

He arched a brow and brought the oars forward. "Well, there ye have it."

She growled in frustration. "But I couldn't read *that*."

"It's as I said, 'tis the druid's magic at work. Anything you had—knowledge, possessions, abilities—is transferred into a similar equivalent here in this land."

He said it so matter-of-factly, as if magic was just a given. And could do that kind of stuff. As he sat there and rowed a weird wicker boat across a lake as if this were all quite normal.

This was too freaky.

That's it. If this is real life, then I'm having a psychotic break.

At least my wild imagination gave me a hot Scotsman to hang with.

His brawny arms shot them across the shallow lake to the rocky slope looming over them like some kind of brooding lair of a fantasy-movie wizard.

The boat scraped up onto a pebbled shore, bypassing a nearby dock lined with larger wicker boats. He leaped up and jerked their boat farther up the shore, and she gripped the sides to keep balanced, still too flummoxed to do anything productive.

Connall grasped her hand, the roughness of his skin oddly gentle across her palm. He tugged, and she clambered out onto the pebbled shore, slippery from the nearby water. Reeds fringed the shoreline, gently dipping in the soft but growing breeze, shadowed by the twisty branches of a stunted rowan tree. Up ahead, a steep incline cut into a terraced hillside.

She followed him up the slope, and her thigh muscles and calves quivered with the strain.

Damn. Had I known I'd be traipsing through Scotland like this, I would have worked out. Ha, *when* exactly?

She breathed through her nose to not give away how out of shape she was. Up ahead lay level ground. *God, just make it to there, okay?*

At the level area, though, Connall continued to eat up the ground with his powerful strides. About a dozen thatched-roof, round, stone houses filled the clearing, though some were missing their roofs. How remote was she in Scotland?

He kept going. Up *another* slope of the big-ass rock of a hill.

They kept going. And going. And she fell behind. Finally, he stopped, seemingly realizing that she was no longer near. "Are ye all right? Need me to carry ye?"

She scowled at him and tugged off her fur-lined mantle, the march uphill having warmed her up a good bit. "No. Just not used to this much exercise."

He frowned but waited until she drew close, and then resumed his relentless pace up the hill, his leg muscles having no trouble climbing up this slope. *God damn.* He certainly was in shape.

Finally, they reached a larger terrace filled with stone huts, and at these she found other people. A blacksmith banged around in a forge, or whatever they were called, and everyone was dressed like Connall, toiling out in the open spaces. Hair stiffened on the back of her neck. Every single one greeted her guide as if he'd been absent for a while, and he returned their greetings cheerfully. Smiles broke out when they spotted her trailing behind. They dropped their tools and began lining the path. Needing to escape their scrutiny, she turned away and placed her hands on her knees.

And gasped. She was higher up than she'd figured. And the view. God. The lake they'd left behind appeared small, though it stretched around and out to sea. From here, the looming mountains weren't as imposing.

"Ashley." Connall's voice startled her. He waved toward yet another, steeper slope. Unlike the unadorned, gentle slope uphill they'd just walked, this was a sharp staircase of stone, the steps unevenly laid into a natural ravine between two hills. Carefully, her thighs going *Seriously, Ashley?* she picked her way upward until they reached a small courtyard lined with stone, dead grass, and moss. On the far side, a dozen people, mostly men, busted out from the entrance of another thatched-roof, stone building, this one two stories high. Immediately they were surrounded. Like before, the language sounded unfamiliar, but she could understand every word.

An older man, with a trim brown beard flecked with gray, embraced Connall in a stiff hug. "We were worried about you, laddie. Gone more than a full moon's span, you were."

"Greetings, Father. More than a full span, you say?" Connall stepped back, shock clear on his features. "Where I was, only eight nights had elapsed, I'm sure of it."

"Mungan said time might move slower where you were."

A younger man took his turn at a hug, the strong angle of his cheekbones and proud slope of his nose very similar to Connall's, despite his dark red hair. "Or *when* ye were, if I understood him correctly."

"When?" she asked at the same time as Connall.

"Aye," said his father. "Apparently, the bastard sent you not only to another land to find a wife, but to a time in the distant future."

Wife? Distant future?

His father ran his gaze up and down her figure, but not

in a creepy way, more like a general assessment. "And I see ye brought back a lovely wife at that. Well done, son. Well done."

The strange people, the rocky courtyard, the darkening sky—all of it eroded into a fuzzy, muted wash of color. She swayed as everyone surrounded her, chattering their greetings, some punctuating their welcome with gentle pats on her shoulder. Her smile was stuck on for politeness' sake—inside, her body roiled, and the sting of bile rose in her throat.

What the hell was this wife business? Because she'd *for sure* remember marrying this dude—she'd vowed to never marry again.

Deep breath.

The weight of an arm draped across her shoulder, and Connall's voice rumbled by her ear as he tucked her against his side in a protective gesture. "You all right?"

The dizziness faded, and the crowd surged around her, leading her inside the stone structure. It was like she was on some track, these events and people pulling her along to yet another destination.

Would she ever feel in control of her life?

Chapter Four

"And they have these massive structures crafted of a clear but hard material." Connall sat back in his seat, enjoying a winter sun unfettered by clouds. They'd convened in the great hall, but since the day was without rain, they'd thrown open the doors and set their chairs just inside to take advantage of the light and warmth.

His father and brothers settled across from him, leaning toward him with interest. He'd left his wife with some of the older women to get her acclimated to her new home.

"And the sheer number of people," he said. "More than any I've seen."

While part of him had been fascinated by all he'd witnessed, and the tools wielded by Ashley's people, he was glad to be home. Home, where it smelled better, and the loudest noise intruding on his senses was the *tang-ta-tang* of the blacksmith's hammer down the slope.

But would Ashley miss it? Would she demand to return? For the first time, unease at the prospect settled in his gut. She'd been a bit anxious on her arrival.

His father and brothers were intrigued, but not enough to shuck their lives here for those wonders. Except for his youngest brother Giric, who'd been peppering him with questions, his eyes round and eager. He probably didn't realize that he'd even moved his chair closer to Connall's.

Connall set down his mug of heather ale and propped his feet onto a low stool. "Glad I am to hear the people in her land are unable to reach us. Though I espied no weaponry, their tools were such that I imagine their weapons are superior. Better even than the Roman interlopers along the wall."

Ten winters prior, the Romans had pushed farther north and built a second wall across the land to the east of Dunadd. Few of his own people had ever seen a Roman, but Connall felt confident he could discern one on sight. Surely a people arrogant enough as to build such a barrier would be arrogant in appearance as well.

His father scratched his gray-speckled beard. "I remember hearing from my own grandfather that when they first arrived, *we* had the better weaponry. They imitated *our* methods. And instead of wooden roads, they built them of stone." He leaned forward. "And speaking of Romans, while you were away, some made the trek over the high mountain passes and through the waterways to our bit of land and proposed an alliance. How they managed to find us, I know not. The council met, however, and agreed that in light of our weakened position, we would be wise to accept."

Then more than a few had seen a Roman now. Connall pushed down the curiosity and missed opportunity of seeing one for himself. He nodded and took a sip of ale.

His father lifted his own mug and extended it toward him. "And I'd like you to venture to the Roman outpost along their wall. We wish for you to—"

A commotion at the door interrupted them. Eithne, one of their elderly women, rushed in. "You have to see this. You do! Connall's new wife—she's a Diviner."

Connall's feet thumped onto the ground from their perch on the stool. "She's what?"

"A Diviner, thank the ancestors."

. . .

Ashley sat back on her heels and shoved her shaking hands between her clasped knees, unwilling to let those gathered see how unnerved she was. All around, the villagers chattered, their voices pitched high in excitement. She, however, was *so* not excited. After Connall had left her with some elderly women so he could consult with his father, she'd been trying to not draw attention to herself. She figured that was the best strategy. Until she got a better handle on what the eff was going on. But when she'd walked by a worker on the second terrace casting dirt across a stretched piece of leather and idly wondered what dangers existed here, words had popped into her head as if in answer.

And she'd said them out loud.

That had been freaky enough.

But the words... The words themselves made her hands shake. Still.

Romans shall bring strength but also danger. Ware the Painted People at the cragged rock.

Romans? Why had she said Romans? And why had she blurted the whole thing out anyway? It was as if the words just appeared in her brain right when the tossed dirt formed into a pattern. Her knees had buckled, and, yeah, now she was sitting on the rocky ground, staring at the leather, going *ohmygod.*

She rocked forward and back.

Oh, she'd lost her mind. Yep. Only explanation.

Connall and his father pushed through the small crowd.

"What happened?" Connall crouched in front of her, his green eyes alight with concern and excitement. Was it horrible that she latched on to that concern from the only pair of eyes she knew here?

"She can divine events," an older man said, his thin arm pointing to the stretch of leather. "She did a foretelling."

Connall's gaze now filled with a look of pride.

Shaking, her legs so much like jelly she was afraid she couldn't stand without support, she put a hand to the ground and pushed herself upward. She stepped to Connall's side, trying to ignore how close everyone was as well as their chatter. Chatter about *her*.

"Can I speak to you alone?" she asked in a low voice. Since Connall was the only familiar person here, she wanted some damn answers from him.

He nodded and ushered her to a waist-high stone wall that lined the courtyard. She placed her hands on the cool, rough stone and gripped it. Hard. No way they'd shake now.

God, her family would be *laughing* that *she* was in this situation. The helpless member of the family who had relied on them, and then her husband, for everything. No matter that she'd changed.

She would *not* be that helpless and weak person she used to be. Nor allow anyone here to form that opinion of her.

Needing a moment to ensure her voice came out strong, and to gather her thoughts, she peered over the wall's edge from her dizzying height to the vast expanse of barren land. Ruggedly beautiful even in winter, but still barren. Wind whipped up the hill and pushed against her face and upper body, chilling her, but she refused to curl into herself. She tucked the loose strands from her braid behind her ear.

Clearly, the impossible had happened, and she had traveled backward in time. With some freakish new skills.

Connall settled against the wall beside her, his presence

somehow reassuring and lending her strength. He remained quiet, seemingly content with giving her the time she needed.

She rounded on him. First things first. "Exactly *when* and *how* did we marry?"

"We were pledged to each other when you took my hand and we traveled here."

"Wait. What? That's it?"

"Cleaving two persons to a life together by clasping hands is a common practice. I would have preferred a druid as witness, but in—"

"Hold up—don't you require my agreement?"

"Of course."

Relief slumped her shoulders. "Then we're not married. I didn't agree."

He straightened. "What trickery is this? You *did* agree, but you mean to deny this? I would not take an unwilling woman to wife."

"When?"

"At the coffee shop."

Huh? Honestly, that had been a blur of biceps. But before she could ask him to explain, he continued, "And the druid's magic sealed our agreement when you put your hand in mine."

Magicmagicmagic. OMG.

This was an even more fucked-up thing to process. She took a deep breath. Oh God, was she really about to ask him this?

"Tell me about this magic that brought me here?"

"To explain the magic is impossible."

"But how am I able to understand you?"

"Transference, I'm told. The same happened for me when I visited your time and place. I could speak your tongue, and my wealth was reduced to that black flat thing. I'll not question it, because it bought me what I required, but your currency is a strange thing."

Transference? She flicked her hand to the crowd of people still gathered around the leather, pointing and talking. "Could it explain what happened there?"

He straightened and stepped closer, so close she'd swear his heat buffeted her. "Were you not a Diviner in your land?"

She shook her head, determined to stand her ground. His black hair streamed to the side as the wind whipped over the wall. He tossed his head to make some of the strands leave his face.

He frowned. "You don't have a skill or ability with its equivalent?"

"Not that I can think of," she whispered. God, this was all so unreal. She really, really wanted to move into his arms and let his large body shelter her.

How messed up is that?

To stop herself from touching him, she gripped the wall even tighter. She relished the realness of the stone biting into her skin. "Can I speak to the druid?" She'd just ask him to undo the spell and send her back.

"Which one?"

She dropped her hands. "You have more than one?"

"Druids are our intellectuals, our healers, judges, and priests. Of course, we do." Pride infused his voice.

He knew *exactly* which one she wanted and was being cagey on purpose. "The one who cast the spell." Well, if he thought she'd just accept her fate, he was abso-friggin-lutely wrong.

'Cuz which girl was fucking tired of men directing her, defining her, carving the shape her life was to take? This one!

The muscles in his jaw worked. "He's not here. After I left he had to take a healing journey, needing solitude." He waved a hand out over the barren stretch of land. "He'll not be back until the full moon." His gaze flicked to her body, and he stepped between her and the wall, blocking the wind. Was it her imagination, or did those smoky-green eyes soften?

It was unfair of him to have that combo of eyes, black hair, and sharp cheekbones. And damn, that jaw, too. And the ability to anticipate her needs.

So unfair.

But her body relaxed a fraction, no longer being blasted by the chill whipping through her strange clothes. "And when is the full moon?" she asked, desperate to stay on track.

"Twenty nights from now."

Her chest squeezed tight. *Twenty nights?*

Dammit. Well, as soon as this druid deigned to make an appearance, she was going to be all up in his business until he sent her back to her own dang time, cuz there was no way she was staying in the past.

Wait. I'm talking about druids. This is all kinds of whack.

But twenty nights?

The vastness of the land around her and the collection of stone huts desperately gripping this promontory became like a weight pressing into her.

Could she survive here that long?

• • •

As a new night began, Connall ushered his wife down the slope to the next-highest terrace. Cormac's domicile was his to claim, his father had told him, one of several now lying empty. He'd inspected it earlier and had found it clean and free of personal belongings, ready for him to make a new hearth with his wife. A wife as skittish as a colt ever since he'd brought her to his land. Seeing her at the wall—cold but too proud to admit any weakness—he'd longed to take her in his arms and warm her. He'd shoved the other ways to provide warmth aside—against a wall was *not* how he'd like to bed his wife for the first time.

Her prediction about the Romans worried him. Who were the "painted people" they needed to be wary of?

The terrace opened before them, and he steered Ashley with a hand lightly placed on the back of her arm. Even now, wariness stiffened her stride, but he took heart that she didn't shy from his touch.

As his hand gripped the hearth latch, doubt lashed him—'twas a simple door, but... It represented crossing into their new life together.

His jaw clenched—no good came of doubting himself.

Swinging the door wide, he ushered his wife within. Someone had started a fire for them, and several torches flickered and sputtered along the wall. Ever since the talk by the wall and her request to speak to Mungan, Ashley had been quiet.

"What are you doing?" she said.

He whipped around, her words both a shock and relief. "Only closing the door. You can't be telling me people in your land slept with them open for I witnessed none such behavior."

She stood in the center of the room, the light bathing her features. Her back was as straight as a yew arrow. Her eyes narrowed. "I mean, why are you inside this hut with me?"

Hut? She made it sound demeaning. Like all the hearths on this terrace, it was one large room with a bed along one wall, spacious enough for a small family. The stone was cut smooth as a babe's behind and tightly fit together, preventing any drafts. It was a fine home, and would be even finer with a woman's touch. "Where else would I be?"

She flicked a hand toward the door. "In your own room, or hut. Definitely not in mine."

He crossed his arms. "As your husband, this is my place as much as yours."

She took a step forward, shaking her head. "Oh no, buster, we're not really married. And I'm not sleeping with you, so if you have ideas in your head about that, you can just get rid of them."

Now she'd put that image right back to the forefront of his mind, hadn't she? Growling in frustration, he strode over to the fire and poked it into a roaring blaze with a length of iron. "The magic—"

"I don't care what the magic did, we're not married. I thought I was answering an ad for a part-time job in Scotland. Not an ad for a wife."

He swung around. "I'm sorry you misunderstood, but it was not my intention."

She marched over and settled cross-legged on top of the bed, as far away as she could get. This night was not going as he'd expected. Not at all. While, aye, she was on the bed as he'd imagined, it wasn't an invitation. More of a *watch your loins if ye value them*.

And he did.

While it went against his purposes, he admired her strength. Her willingness to speak her mind to someone much stronger. And since it was in private, there was no harm in enjoying her spark.

Sparks made hearty blazes.

She'd learn, in time, who was in command.

She closed her eyes, and her chest rose and fell on a deep breath. He tried hard not to notice how it stretched the fabric across her full bosom.

When she reopened her eyes, calmness seemed to settle over her features. "Why didn't you just get a local woman to marry you?" She assessed him from toe to nose. "You're not bad-looking. Surely one of the women here would jump at the chance."

He barely suppressed a smile. More than once a faint

blush had tinted her cheeks after a surreptitious inspection. His upper arms seemed to draw her particular notice. He deliberately widened his stance and clasped his hands behind him, allowing the muscles along his arms to flex.

Aye, she darted a gaze there, and her tongue quickly licked her lips. She fooled no one.

"Yes. I could have convinced one of the women to be saddled with the likes of me." But then his good humor left him on his next words. "But all marriageable ones are gone."

"Gone?" Her forehead wrinkled. *"All?"*

"Aye." The fight went out of him. He rounded the table and collapsed onto the bench facing her, his elbows on his knees. The weight of all that he was responsible for, all that his tribe had suffered, pushed down on his shoulders. By the ancestors, he was tired. "About a lunar month ago, we were attacked while most of the warriors were away, including myself. The raiders carried off most of the women and many of the children. To sell them, no doubt."

A gasp cut through the room. She'd pulled her knees up to her chest, one arm wound tight around them and her other hand clasped to her mouth.

Her hand lowered, though her eyes were still wide. "That's horrible. Slavery exists here? In this time?"

An old pain pinched his chest, and his voice choked out, "Aye."

"Can you get them back?"

"We would if we knew who took them. Some of the men lost wives and children and wish for nothing more but to march on their stronghold to reclaim them." They'd been returning from a successful hunt, joking and telling tales of their plans for when they reached home. They'd been absent five nights, leaving behind a small guard of younger men. As Connall and his companions crested the top of the last hill, though, all chatter died as angry smears of smoke spiraled upward from their stronghold. They'd kicked the sides of their mounts and raced to Dunadd, only to find most of their women and children stolen in a rare raid on their coast.

Anger filled him anew. If his mother had been alive still, she'd have been gone as well. Unable to take the shock and empathy she directed at him, he focused on the door. "We've sent runners to neighboring tribes, but none are close. On one side is the sea, and on the other are lochs and nearly impenetrable mountain passes, especially in winter."

"What about survivors? Didn't they see the raiders?"

"Aye, but in all the chaos, all they could tell was that they were not from nearby—their clothes and language were not ours."

"Oh God." Her choked words brought his attention back to her. She favored one god more than others? A nameless one, at that?

She was still curled against herself, her face paling. "I…I can't believe… I must have gone pretty far back for Scotland to still have slavery." Her eyes found his. "What year is it?" she whispered.

"Year?" The word sounded like one from her own tongue, not his, and he was unfamiliar with the meaning. Her tone indicated it was an important one, and he wished on all the gods that he could answer.

"Yes. I come from 2019, so this is…"

He frowned, still unsure of what she was asking.

"A.D. Anno Domini?"

"You speak the tongue of the Romans?" The rhythm sounded like the snatches he'd heard from local tribes who'd traded with them.

She put her hands to her face and then dragged them down. "So the Romans are still running around here? That should be a big, fat clue as to *when*. God, why didn't I pay attention in history classes?" She unfolded her legs and gripped her knees, staring at him. "Look, I'm sorry about what happened to your women, but I can't be your wife. I have a life I need to get back to. As soon as that spellcaster returns, I'm having him send me home."

He nodded. "Well enough, but know that by then, you probably won't wish to return."

Some of the spark returned to her face, her eyes. "Think that much of yourself, huh?"

He shook his head. "The tether will weaken for you the longer you remain. If you truly accept where you are, you will eventually forget your other life and be happy." While he'd not felt much weakening—for there was no chance he'd accept life there—just the small amount had spurred him to finish his mission, enlisting Norton to aid him in placing the notice on the list of Craig's.

She surged to her feet. "Wait. What? This magic will make me forget my former life by the next full moon?"

"After two full moons pass, aye. And it won't *make* you. It's only if you truly belong here and accept this as your home."

"When is the second full moon?"

"Forty-nine nights from now."

She paced to the far wall then back again, her gait jerky and stiff with tension. "Well, then, even more reason for me to not get all comfortable with you." She gave a choked laugh, though it was still tinged with the heat of her anger. "This is not the job I signed up for."

"It's not a *job*. I'm not sure why you keep insisting this. Regardless, I told you what you could expect before you left."

"When?"

"At the coffee shop, just before you agreed to return here with me."

Her gaze went unfocused and then pink tinged her cheeks. "I, um...I didn't quite hear all that."

"I said them plainly in your tongue."

She flapped her hands. "I was under the spell of your biceps, okay?"

"Biceps? That sounds like a word in your tongue not mine."

She marched back to him. And pointed. At his upper arm muscles. "Those. Happy now?"

A surprising burst of pleasure filled his chest, but he kept very, very still.

Then she folded her arms and lifted her chin. "Anyway, I can't stay here. This is *not* where I belong."

He held his tongue. She was wrong. He was sure of it. She only needed time to adjust. She'd come around.

But having confirmation of her attraction gave him a new idea. He'd been mulling over the druid's explanation of the magic. If he teased her, drew this attraction out longer, she'd eventually give in to her desire and join with him.

The way he saw it, if she initiated, she was telling the magic she belonged here.

He would simply have to exercise restraint. Somehow.

"I'm assuming we're too far back for a shower?" she said.

"Shower?" This word was also in her tongue, as if the magic didn't have an equivalent.

"A bath? Where's the bathroom?"

He frowned, which made her eyes get rounder.

"Oh shit. Don't tell me." She flapped her hands around. "Where am I supposed to *pee*?"

That he understood. He pointed to a bucket in the corner.

She turned slowly back to him. "You have *got* to be kidding."

"Why would I jest about such matters?" At the horror dawning across her features, another stab of uncertainty hit him as to whether his land was a better alternative. Of a certainty, they had a more efficient method for such matters.

"Why, indeed," she whispered. She turned pleading eyes to him. "I can't pee in a bucket. Not with you watching. What am I supposed to do with it after?"

"Throw it over into the south ravine like everyone else."

She pointed to herself, then waved a hand around. "Me. Not where I belong."

He sighed, stepped into the crisp night air, and closed the door behind him, giving her the privacy she required. Her adjustment might be harder than he figured.

Chapter Five

The elderly woman, Eithne, pushed open a quaint wooden door at the end of a stone-lined tunnel, her wiry body hiding her strength. She reminded Ashley of one of those older women who looked all innocent—fluffy white hair, pillow-soft cheeks, wide blue eyes—but could throw down if you crossed her in a bridge tournament. It was Ashley's first full day at Dunadd, and Connall had left her with Eithne—she had her new duties as washer woman and kitchen aid to learn. When Connall had woken her up that morning, she'd asked for coffee, but right when the word came out in English instead of his language she knew her answer.

Morning with no coffee?

Yesterday had been so overwhelming, there'd been no time to ask. Now she was struggling to be something other than a useless, coffee-less slug. It had been bad enough to pee into a bucket last night, but to also do it with morning brain fog? And then lug it outside again?

Ah, fun times.

The Bridge Battle Axe stuck a torch into the room

beyond, the light flickering against stacks of barrels and leather sacks. "And here's the storage room," Eithne said. "It's full now, aye, as we laid in a fine stock of supplies to carry us through the winter. Even more so now that..." Her voice trailed off with resignation and sadness.

She seemed to shake herself and then winked at Ashley, fine lines radiating across her face with the movement. "It's nice to have some younger people to help me again. My joints are stiff." She ducked into the storage room, and Ashley followed. This room must be *under* the main floor of the keep, accessible from a tunnel that led from the detached kitchen.

"It grieves me to ask you to do such manual labor as the wife of the chief's son," Eithne continued, "but you have to understand, the raid left us shorthanded."

Most of the people around were men and elderly women. Very few children, and only a few women her age. Her throat clogged—what they must be *going* through. How awful. And that people throughout history had dealt with similar heartache—having their loved ones stolen. There one day, gone the next.

She leaned against the door opening and peered inside. No bigger than a streetcar, the room looked as if it were straight out of some fairy-tale dungeon with its low ceiling, tight confines, and a tiny slit up high letting in just a squeak of light.

She stepped inside and pulled her mantle tighter around her neck, shivering from the room's cooler air. The smell of dank earth and stone was richer in here, along with the deep tones of aged wooden barrels and supple leather. Soft clouds of her breath floated into the space.

"First, can ye fill that leather sack with grain from this barrel?" Eithne shuffled to one along the left wall and pointed. "We'll be needing it for today's baking."

Easy enough. Ashley rubbed her cold nose with the cuff

of her mantle, a low-grade headache scouring her skull. She set the sack on the floor and tugged the barrel lid off as the other woman held the torch high for her to see. Inside lay a wooden scoop, its edges lighter from repeated use. Digging it in deep, she used it to transfer the contents to the sack, which Eithne now held open for her.

God, she ached from having barely slept last night, and most of it spent with her body drawn up tight and tense. Oddly, it wasn't Connall's presence, asleep on a makeshift pallet on the other side of their hut, which had her mind spinning out of control, unable to relax into sleep. She felt safe around him. Safe enough to let her mind latch onto all her other worries and how she was going to handle it. In the early hours before finally slipping into sleep, she'd realized— it would have been New Year's Eve back in her time.

Happy New Years to me.

At least everyone's been nice so far.

Last night, she decided that, to stay sane, she had to accept Connall's explanation for how she found herself back in time, even though she'd never believed in magic.

When Ashley poured the last scoop into the sack, the woman tied the top off with twine. They headed back to the kitchen. The magic "translated" her knowledge and possessions, he'd said. If true, most of her odd abilities could be explained, like being able to speak their language and read the runes.

But what could have allowed her to do that foretelling yesterday?

Because if she'd had that skill back home she'd have for damn sure asked it things, like was her ex-husband a slime-ball-douche-canoe before she'd married him? Though Google might have done the trick. The right search term... Then she snorted. Ha. As if. She'd have never found out that way because it would never *occur* to her not to trust him.

So, so naïve.

Then she stumbled. Good Lord. Google? Could that be it? She'd had her laptop with her when she whirled through time, and it was no longer in her "translated" messenger bag.

She drew in a shaky breath and continued following behind Eithne, who now opened the kitchen door.

"Affraic, have ye met Connall's clever new wife?" Eithne stepped up to another older woman, this one as thin as a pogo stick and crumbling herbs into an iron pot hanging by a hook before a hearth fire.

She smiled, her eyes warm and welcoming. "And glad we are to have ye." A bit of tension eased around Ashley's chest, though her headache grew. The woman nodded to a knife-scarred table nearby, one end filled with wooden vessels and leather bags of various sizes, and the other side bare. "You can set your burden there, I thank ye."

Ashley carried it to the indicated spot and gently set it down, her muscles giving an oh-thank-the-Lord sigh. The kitchen was blessedly warm, almost to the point of stifling, but she relished the feeling, for a chill had settled into her bones. And a heavenly smell permeated the air—cooking meat sizzled on a spit as plops of fat dripped onto the hearth stone, the scent overlaid with fragrant herbs and yeast baking and blooming.

That same memory tugged—the one when she'd eaten the grain-heavy bread—but with her brain fog and mounting headache it quickly sank.

Eithne smiled at her. "You look worn out. Why don't we walk about, and I'll give ye a tour of the buildings until we're needed back here?"

Ashley nodded, relieved, because yay, no more carrying today, but jeez, more walking?

Before they went outside, though, she placed a halting hand on Eithne's bony shoulder. "Can we visit the person who was dressing the leather?"

Eithne's white brows rose. "You want to do another foretelling?"

"I...just want to see if it was a fluke." She swallowed, her heart kicking up a bit. She needed to test her theory.

"Aye, we can't be calling you a Diviner if that was the only one in your hand, now can we?" She winked and led the way down to the second terrace.

Ugh. I'll have to come back up *this dang slope when we're done.*

"Eithne, can I ask you a personal question?"

"Aye."

"Where do you bathe?"

"Why, at the river. Didn't your husband show you?"

She pursed her lips. "No. Can you show me after?"

"Of a certainty, I can."

Soon they were at the hut from yesterday, where a man was stretching and dressing hides. Like most she'd seen who weren't warriors, he was elderly—thin but fit. Eithne explained her request, and Ashley scooped up a fistful of dirt then squatted in front of a stretched hide, the cool earth in her palm growing warmer as she stared at the leather.

Holy shit. Am I really about to do this?

First question—where the hell was she? Dunadd, Scotland didn't exactly narrow it down. She flung the dirt toward the browned leather, the wind whisking some of the tiny kernels downslope. Most *swooshed* across the hide, though, and settled into a pattern. Ashley went still. Again, the answer formed in her mind. *Dunadd, on an Argyll peninsula between the Sound of Jura and Loch Fyne.*

Damn—it *was* her very own Google.

Heart pounding, the beats echoing now with the aching throb spreading in her head, she cast another scoop and learned that the Argyll region was on the western side of

Scotland and part of an ancient kingdom called Dal Riata, the origin of the Scottish-Gaelic language. Later a stronghold of the Campbell clan.

A shadow cast over the leather and she glanced up. An elderly man with a lantern jaw and sharp green eyes had joined them to watch. "What is it telling ye?"

"Where we are."

He frowned at her. "We already know that."

"But I didn't."

She brought the fist holding her dirt to her lips and kissed it. Okay, let's do this. *What year is it?*

She tossed the handful of dirt, and a pattern took shape. *156 AD.*

She fell back onto her butt. *Holy shitballs.*

Fuckity-fuck-fuck-fuck. 156 friggin' A.D.? For real?

Her whole body flushed cold and then hot, goose bumps breaking out on her skin, followed by a cold, cloying sweat. Oh God, she needed to lie down. This couldn't be... Oh, Jesus. She knew she was back in time, but *that* far back? Unbelievable.

Despite her already-sore muscles and now shakiness, she pushed herself to a stand. Her knees buckled, but she caught herself against the smooth stone of the leather-worker's hut. Fuzzy white spots filled her vision. The three Scots watched her with curious expressions. Their rough clothing dyed in simple colors... The primitive stone huts... The mention of Romans from her earlier telling when she'd wondered about dangers...

Every single friggin' tiny-ass hair on her body popped up stiff, and the contents of her stomach acted like they were on a damn trampoline.

Oh God.

She stumbled over to the terrace wall and draped her arms over it. Vast, empty land stretched toward the horizon.

Wind whipped across her sweaty skin, chilling her.

And then she puked over the side.

• • •

Connall stepped away from the warriors. "And make sure ye have enough dried meat this time, will ye?" Their journey over the lochs to the Roman outpost would be a long one.

To the north, clouds, bruised purple and heavy with moisture, crowded the horizon, foretelling an evening rain. He sent a quick prayer to Add, their local god, that on their journey's start, the weather would be clear. He'd find time today, though, to venture to the river they'd be traveling and make an offering to Danu, the goddess residing in, and presiding over, its depths. Perhaps he could bring his new wife along and show her their ways.

He rubbed a hand across the back of his neck and strode through the courtyard to the keep. Ever since his father had explained the mission this morning, an idea had formed in his mind and kept prodding.

He found his father by the keep's central fire, conferring with several of the older men.

"How are the preparations?" his father asked.

Connall settled on an adjacent bench and nodded to all assembled. "Well enough. We should be able to leave in two or three days' time. However, I wished to broach an idea with you. My wife's skills could prove useful."

"Other than in general?"

"Aye, I'd like her to accompany us on this journey."

"Of course ye do," one of the older men interjected, winking at Connall.

Connall ignored him and concentrated on his father. The truth was, while he'd been impressed by his wife's skill, he had to be honest with himself—this request was purely an excuse. A restlessness he hadn't previously realized resided within him eased whenever she was near.

His father sat back and narrowed his eyes, taking him in. "I need her skills here. She could warn us of coming attacks."

"What if she did a foretelling before we departed? We've never journeyed to the Roman outpost or dealt with them directly. Much could go awry."

He kept his features neutral, awaiting his father's reply. Finally, his father nodded. "This sounds acceptable." But before his father dismissed him, his gaze drifted to Connall's leg and then back up to him with an eyebrow lifted.

He'd kept his face neutral, but he'd forgotten about the rest of his body, for his leg had been bouncing. He immediately stilled it and drew himself straighter.

"Bed her before ye leave, son. It'll go better for ye."

By the ancestors, his father could always read his moods. And, by the ancestors, how did he know he *hadn't* already?

"I'm giving her time."

All three men looked upon him as if he were a stranger.

"Whatever for?" asked his father. "You need to be producing sons and daughters for the tribe. If all goes well, Domnall will use the same magic to find his own wife at the Summer Equinox."

He crossed his arms. "Trust me. I know how to handle her." She was in a new, strange land. She couldn't be expected to accept her situation so readily, but his father would find that reasoning weak.

Unbidden, thoughts of the time he'd pleaded as a child to allow his childhood playmate—a girl—to play and train with him and his older brothers crowded his thoughts. And of how disastrous that had ended.

Never mind that he had a new plan to implement—entice her until *she* made a move. And this trip would help.

"You're being too soft on her. You haven't much time.

You know what Mungan said. She needs to be settled before two full moons pass."

"I'm not being soft." Connall clenched his jaw and stood. He'd not show *any* weakness to his father or the other men. Sooner than he'd wish, he'd most likely be elected chief. And he needed to be worthy. If they viewed him as weak, he couldn't lead properly. And a failure to lead properly could prove fatal to one or many.

But a leaden feeling settled in his gut at the idea of manipulating Ashley. And instinct told him that bedding her by seduction was the wrong strategy if he wanted her to stay.

Aye, I want her to stay.

She needed to come to *him*.

. . .

Yesterday, it was a massive caffeine-withdrawal headache. Today, the shits.

Literally.

Holy-mother-effing-dang gazillion grain bread and wholesome-effing food.

Ashley's legs shook as she held her squat by the river. Cuz, yeah, her muscles were also sore and aching from all the climbing.

Fuck my life.

At least back home she'd be miserable on a toilet, not squatting behind some bush at a river in second-century Scotland.

When she'd thrown up yesterday, she'd at first thought the nausea and ice-pick-through-the-head pain was from the shock, but as it persisted she'd realized—it was a friggin' caffeine withdrawal.

She brushed the tears off her cheeks and hugged her knees. *This place is trying to kill me.*

Two days later, Ashley knelt outside the hut she shared with Connall. Her mornings were still rough, but each day the headaches were less intense and her digestive tract no longer mutinied.

She tied off her braid, her hair still wet from her quick bath in the river. She might have only been able to afford cheap shampoo at Target, but that shit was better than the hunk of "soap" she'd been given. Her hair was starting to feel coarse.

Lately, a new energy had suffused the courtyard, though her "husband" wouldn't tell her what was happening. Well, she'd just find out on her own. A piece of leather stretched across the ground. Since her surroundings were rocky, a sackful of dirt sat alongside, ready for any divinings.

She cast some dirt onto the leather. *What do they have planned?*

Nothing. As in no answer—not that they weren't planning anything. She sat back on her heels.

She cast dirt again, asking the same question. Still no answer.

After the fifth time, she sat and stared down the incline. A dog ran up in a rolling gait, a bone clutched in its jaws, tail wagging.

It kind of made sense—Google didn't know what everyone was doing everywhere all the time. It might be able to tell her the bigger events in this time, because either it was historical record, or it would be like Google traffic or Wayz that would give her a sense of some movements. It was the only explanation that made sense with the transference aspect of the druid's magic.

She folded her legs up to her chest and wrapped her arms tight around her shins. She propped her chin on one knee and looked at her hut's door. The door that led to the room she shared with Connall at night.

She'd expected pushback on their agreement, but—thank God—every night he slept on his straw pallet while she took the bed along the opposite wall.

But getting *to* those separate beds each night was another freaking matter—torture, pure torture. An awkward dance of *let's pretend we're not completely conscious of the other's every movement* as they readied for bed. The stillness of the night punctuated by the trickle of water in the bucket as he cleaned himself with a cloth. The sound of clothes being discarded. The rush of vulnerability as she stepped behind the curtain she'd erected in the corner to hide their "bathroom." Each time he brushed by her, a weird…tug would make her want to turn and lift a hand and say, *wait, I…*

But what? What could she say? I want you?

How could she even *feel* that way about him? With that sneaky hand of his, he'd pulled her from her own time to have her as his *wife*, for Pete's sake. And she'd had enough of controlling men.

Thank you for that lesson, you douche of an ex-husband. He better be miserable, wherever he'd scurried off to hide from those bookies.

She snorted. Nothing would shock her less than to learn that he was living in the cottage on her parents' ranch in Nebraska. Charles was probably sipping a beer with her dad, while they shook their heads over her. *Her.*

Because, yep, that douche had not only ruined their marriage and her finances but also used his infinite charm to gaslight her parents into believing it was somehow her fault. And since that played into how they viewed her—immature baby of the family—they believed him. Believed him over their own flesh and blood.

Oh, she'd tried to tell her side, but pushing against the

quintessential Midwestern attitude of her traditional parents was already an uphill battle. *Stick by your man, and all.*

In a way, it *was* her fault. Too eager to get out from under their controlling behavior, she'd hopped onto the first good thing to breeze into her life—Charles. And because she *was* unprepared for life on her own, she'd let him control everything about their marriage.

And so much was out of her control right now, too.

Since her relations with Connall were something she *could* control, then dammit, she would. She'd also resist the urge she'd been feeling to learn more about him—what made him tick, what made him hurt. Oh boy, did she resist. Because the words he'd said—about her accepting her life here, and him—making her forget her old life? Yeah, not happening.

Though, when she saw Eithne with her husband earlier, still affectionate and caring after all their years together, she did wonder what it would be like to find a relationship like that.

Someone who looked out for you, instead of taking advantage. Someone with integrity. Someone who saw her as special, worthy of being treated as an equal.

As if conjured by her thoughts, Connall's tall form came into view from up slope, his strides long and sure. And angled right for her.

She stood and brushed the dust off her butt. Then caught herself. The hell? *I am* not *primping.*

She crossed her arms in front of her then let them fall to her sides. Then she put them behind her, grasping a wrist with the opposite hand, but that only made it look as if she were trying to show off her boobs, so she dropped them to her sides again.

God, she was being ridiculous. She met him halfway, enduring his scrutiny.

He rested a forearm on the top of his sword hanging by

his side. That people just carried swords around like it was no biggie was one of the harder mental adjustments. "We're departing for a long journey, and you will be accompanying us. We leave at first light on the morrow."

She stepped back. "Wait—what? Why?"

"Other than I'd like you to accompany me?" He took a step, closing the distance between them again and touched the tip of her braid.

Resist. He just ordered you around again.

She flicked her head, swinging her braid away from his touch. She crossed her arms again, which she realized—too late—still emphasized her boobs as his gaze darted there and back. "Yes. Other than that," she said crisply.

His body straightened. "We will need your skills along our journey to ensure not only our safety but also our success."

A thrill shot through her. Well, when he put it like that... Life might suck major hairballs here, but at least she could be *useful*. And she had a unique skill this tribe apparently valued.

She soaked that feeling up like a dried-out sponge. "How long will we be gone?" Because despite the thrill of being useful, she was not going to miss the spellcaster's return.

His full lips pressed into a thin line. "We'll be back well before the full moon arrives," he replied, correctly guessing her main concern.

Her chest eased a little at that. Seventeen days left before the full moon and that sneaky druid was still nowhere to be seen. She'd been hoping he'd return before then, despite what he'd told the others, so she could jet on back home. Hot shower... Shampoo *and* conditioner.

"Where are we going?"

"To the closest Roman outpost on the wall."

"Hadrian's Wall? *That* wall?"

He shook his head. "That would be an even longer

sojourn. This new one is being called Antonine's Wall. After their current emperor."

Huh. She hadn't heard of that one. "Has Mungan returned early?"

"He has not, but I did question my father as to his whereabouts and learned he plans to stop by that outpost as well in his wanderings. Something about needing to trade for rare metals and rocks for his healing magic."

Well then. Best-case scenario, they caught up to him and she got to return home early, before this mind-wiping business happened. Worst case? Well, nothing different than what her situation was when she woke up this morning, counting down the days until he got back.

Connall put a hand on her shoulder. "Before we leave, my father wishes for you to perform a divining."

Oh jeez, while she liked the idea of being useful, a bout of performance anxiety smacked her. "But it doesn't always work."

He squinted at the keep. "He'll just have to accept that outcome."

With a resigned sigh, she allowed him to lead, his hand now at the small of her back, its heat and subtle pressure both thrilling and annoying—another sign of not being in control of her life right now. Hey, at least she wasn't getting as winded as before. A new feeling of ease and strength powered her thighs and calves.

When they reached the keep, he held the door open. "Allow me to do most of the talking."

Not knowing much about his father, she decided to let him do just that.

This was only the second time she'd been inside, and that was when she'd been freaking-the-eff out. Now she was able to take in the stone floor strewn with dried herbs and straw. Unlike their hut, a thin layer of plaster covered the walls, stretches of which were painted with colorful Celtic designs, while other parts had smoke-blackened smudges from the torches lighting the space.

Their footsteps crunched across the floor, and all eyes were trained on their approach. His father gestured to the other men arrayed on either side. "Leave us."

Ashley tried to keep her steps steady, but man, it was difficult knowing that this was a guy who had full power to do anything he wanted to the people he ruled over. Though he had to be in his mid-to-late fifties, his body was still that of a warrior—powerful arms attached to an equally powerful chest from the looks of it. No Dad-bod for him. Traces of Connall's strong jaw and brow were visible. A gold brooch on his shoulder held up the folds of his kilt. And instead of a silver torque on his neck like Connall's, his was gold.

She swallowed—he also had the same penetrating stare, as if he were assessing her.

The departing men brushed past, all nodding to Connall, with a few also acknowledging her presence.

The chief gestured to a bench before him. "Sit, please."

As she took her seat, Connall settling beside her, she caught sight of the stretched leather on a cleared surface of the floor, a wooden bucket of dirt beside it. Performance nerves kicked up a notch in her belly.

"Has Connall told you of your journey?" He said the words with a brisk tone, all business.

"Yes." She cleared her throat. "Yes, he did."

"Well, before we let you leave, we'd like to ensure all is safe here." He motioned to the stretched leather. "Can you divine that for me, lass?"

"Father, she—"

He held up a hand. "Allow her to speak for herself, if ye please."

Beside her, Connall stiffened but didn't argue. Ashley

took that as a sign to answer him. "Sir, I'd be happy to, but I can't guarantee that it will work."

He frowned, leaning forward and placing an elbow on the arm of the chair. "What do you mean?"

She looked off to the side. How to explain? "The, er, knowledge I had access to was limited. It doesn't know all that happens. In fact, it can't predict much, except the weather and other natural phenomenon."

He pursed his lips and studied her. She tried not to squirm under his penetrating stare. "Then how were you able to do a foretelling?"

She straightened and gripped her knees. "I wondered that, too. I think it's because it was also a record of earth's past."

"Earth's past?"

"Yes, of history. The big events. And since a lot of that hasn't actually happened yet in *this* time, it's as if I can divine the future. But you need to know—the time you're living in now is remote to us. I doubt we knew every battle." She looked at Connall then back at the chief. "Or every raid."

The chief's attention flicked from Connall to her. "So you guessed what has me worried."

"Yes."

He rubbed his chin. Then nodded. "Fair enough. Can you try, though?"

She relaxed. "I can try."

She settled before the leather and scooped up a handful of the cool dirt and cast it, asking about potential raids. She spoke the answer as the words came into her mind, a jolt of surprise hitting her that something *was* coming through.

"The one who will be known as Saint Patrick will be taken in a raid by the Irish and made a slave."

Huh. Wow. Okay.

"Saint Patrick?" Connall asked. "Never heard of either

name. And certainly none named such here."

Either name? "You don't know what a saint is?"

"Is it not a name?"

Whoa. Okay, so in 156, Christianity hadn't yet made it here. "In a way."

"More importantly," the chief said, "it sounds to me as if it's not a raid we need to worry on if none have this name here."

She'd always associated Saint Patrick *with* Ireland, so this slave raiding *by* the Irish was news to her. She also had no clue where he'd been taken *from*, so she threw the dirt several times until she gained a clearer picture. "No, you don't need to worry about that particular raid." While one of the probable birthplaces on the western coast of Britain *was* nearby, it was still several hundred years from now.

She tried again, narrowing it to the second century on the Argyll peninsula, but nothing specific emerged. Her shoulders slumped. "No. Sorry. I think it's because Saint Patrick is pretty famous, so we know about that one."

And like with Google, she needed to properly phrase the question to get the desired answer. Google-fu still mattered.

The chief sat back, but if he was disappointed, he hid it well. "I thank ye for trying. I won't keep you any longer from your preparations."

Dawn seeped over the mountains to the east, casting pink shadows across the loch spread out before Ashley. White birds circled the water in the distance, their calls barely audible with the wind coming down from the north.

She shivered and wrapped her mantle tighter around her as, once again, Connall held his hand out to help her step into a larger version of the kind of boat that brought them here.

This time, they were leaving the stronghold, and this craft was one of a dozen or more bumping up against the dock. Warriors shouted and leaped onto two of them.

Connall flexed his fingers.

Ugh. Clasping that damn hand back at the podshare had landed her here. While a part of her loved the idea of touching him, another part worried—could every touch and interaction tie her closer to this time?

No, she was being silly. She placed her palm in his and the roughness of his warrior's skin sent a bolt of heat from her chest. She looked up into his face, and his eyes darkened. He wrapped his strong fingers around her smaller hand, and she stepped into the boat. As soon as she was onboard, she snatched her hand away, but the sudden movement rocked the boat.

"Whoa," she whispered, and stuck her arms out for balance.

Steps *thunked* behind her, and Connall's strong hands gripped her waist, steadying her body but unsettling her insides.

He was so close. So close, his heat buffeted her. So close, his enticing scent sparkled through her senses. So close, the moment his breathing hitched—slight, soft—twanged the air between them.

To distract herself from the rush of unwelcome awareness of *him*, she asked, "Will we—" She cleared her throat. "Will we be traveling by boat the whole way?"

"Most of it, aye." So close, his breath tickled her ear. She shivered.

He came around and blocked the wind, and she chastised herself for the irrational need to stomp her foot in frustration for him moving *away* from her.

"In my great-grandfather's day, I'm told we were perched between two great waters, but every year the water recedes, little by little. Now all that remains is this shallow loch, and we'll need to thread through a river before it spills out into Loch Gilp and Loch Fyne." He smiled. "I imagine by your time, this loch will be gone."

He was probably right, but it was hard to picture—to her, this *was* how Dunadd looked. How it *should* look. A dark, terraced butte rising out of crystalline waters.

"Will we be going out into the open sea?" She eyed the still-too-tiny craft, and a flutter of unease grew in her stomach.

He shook his head. "We'll be staying close to land."

Okay, she could do this. She gripped her leather satchel tight to her side and settled on a bench. This boat was much larger, the sides stretching up higher, leaving a deep space inside. Seven rows of benches lined either side of the main mast, though the sail was wrapped up tight. Around her, warriors boarded, taking positions along the sides to man the oars. Connall, thank God, sat beside her to row.

The men shouted directions to each other, and soon the boat slipped away, cutting into the still waters of the loch. And then a chant began in time with the rhythm of their oars. Before long, they were flying across the water, the wind whipping against her skin.

Connall's biceps bunched and flexed, his motions matching the other men as he sang the chanting song, his voice a clear bass. Even though it was one of several deep tones, his would have been easy to pick out even if he hadn't been beside her—strength, competence, and pride laced the rolling words, weaving their spell deeper into her, causing her breath to quicken and her stomach to do a slow, but inevitable, *flip*.

The other boat slipped away from the dock and followed in their wake. Fourteen men manned that boat as well as this one. "Will there be enough men to guard Dunadd?"

He stopped singing at her question, though he didn't lose

the rhythm. "There are. We'd grown lax in the peace we'd known for the past decade, and most of the men were with the hunting party when the raid occurred. We have twice this number of able-bodied warriors, as well as some crotchety old-timers to guard while we're away."

As Connall resumed his chant, she stared toward the distant horizon. What awaited her there?

Chapter Six

Later that day, Ashley was about to jump up and down just to do *something*. This was the longest she'd ever gone without having an activity to occupy her—reading, watching TV, playing a game, running errands. She'd even wash dishes, for Pete's sake, just to alleviate her boredom.

Connall was busy either rowing or sailing their ship. At least back at the keep, the overburdened women kept her busy with chores.

The number of ribs making up the hull had been counted—eighteen—and every visible knot in the wood—forty-two. Landscape features had been named—there was now a Misty Mountain, a Mystic River, and a Walden's Pond, though lately they were getting names like Fraggle Rock and Honeycomb Hideout.

As they floated downstream, the clouds made rippling shadows along the sides of the snow-capped mountains, entrancing her. She'd spent enough time in Scotland now to know that *this* particular beauty was not a static thing. Depending on the weather, or the time of day, this same spot would cast a different spell, providing those who regularly saw it with an ever-changing parade of gorgeousness.

She'd lifted a hand, as if she could touch it. She was *in* that photo of Scotland hanging over her bed at the podshare.

Around midday, they'd emerged from the twisting river and into a loch where they'd pulled ashore, scarfed down a meal, and the warriors took up the loose boards in the middle aisle of the boat and made a deck, completely hiding all but a few benches in the middle. They ran up the sail and, once everyone was onboard, set out into the more open waters of Loch Fyne. It sure *felt* as if they were on the open sea, with the shore receding and the other only just kissing the horizon.

Lately, though, everyone was casting worried glances toward the dark clouds crowding low on the western horizon. Connall cinched a sail line tighter and secured it, his eyes constantly darting to the ominous sky. He stepped over and squatted, looking down at her. "Can ye do a foretelling? You said the magic allowed you to predict weather. I'm not liking the looks of that mass of clouds."

She'd *guessed* it would, since the weather in her own time was something she had access to via Google. Since it was something she'd normally know, she hoped the transference magic replaced weather satellites here and could tell her the weather.

She nodded and then laid her divining leather and sack of dirt on the deck. Several warriors crouched beside Connall, their faces set in worried lines. One was his brother Domnall, a quiet man who had the same good looks and a silver torque on his neck. None of the others had these torques, so it must be an indication of their rank.

She rubbed sweaty palms down her skirts and grabbed a fistful of dirt. Pulling in a deep breath, she cast it across the leather and waited.

The answer came, chilling her.

She glanced up at the men's eager eyes and sought Connall's. "It's going to be bad. Gale force winds. It'll be here within the hour." Wicked-cool—so the magic *could* mimic Google.

"An hour?"

She pointed to the sun. "The time it'd take for the sun to go from here"—she moved her finger slightly—"to here."

Connall's eyes flashed with determination, and he leaped to his feet. The others followed, and all were shouting and running around the deck as they redirected the sail and steered their boat to the distant shore. She ran to the side and scanned the coast.

"There's a large bay around the southern tip of this isle. We're heading there," Connall shouted to her.

Being on land alone wasn't going to help. They needed shelter. Plus, they were running out of time—the storm was approaching too fast.

They skimmed along the southern tip, which she'd divined earlier was the Isle of Bute.

"There!" She pointed to an inlet they'd just passed. It cut back into the land in such a way it was like a narrow hall between two cliffs, which could shelter them from the brunt of the wind.

That wind, though, was carrying them to the open waters of the Firth of Clyde.

Connall glanced over his shoulder to where she'd pointed and then shouted, "Tie up the sail. No time to uncover all the oars, so we'll need to double up on these two and work together."

The men rushed to obey, and Connall strode to the stern. He cupped his hands and shouted to the boat following just behind, "Follow us and row hard!" He rounded on her. "Stay out of the way."

Ashley didn't take offense at his brisk tone—he was in

command mode. It was going to take strength and luck to go against the wind to that inlet, but—God—watching and not being able to help? She twisted her fingers into her skirt and bit her lip as the need itched along her skin. But vital seconds could be lost if she pitched in and messed up, or they stopped to chastise her.

The darkening clouds loomed closer and the wind picked up, whipping and snapping her skirt against her calves.

C'mon. C'mon. C'mon.

She gripped the rail and concentrated on watching the cliff grow incrementally larger. The men's muscles strained as they heaved the oars as a unit, their chants now low and urgent.

"Screw it."

When their arms stretched forward again, she slipped into the space between Connall and one of the men.

"I told you to stay out of the way," he growled low so only she could hear.

"I can help," she whispered. As the oar approached her, she wrapped her fingers tight around the well-worn wood, careful not to tug or try to direct. She let her hands ride the oar and only when she felt them pull back toward them did she also pull with all of her weight, her butt scooting forward. When the others eased off, she slackened her grip and braced her feet on the bench in front. Soon she fell into their rhythm, anticipating the pulls with the timing of their singing chant, an urgent and dire-sounding one this time.

Soon the rocky cliffs of the inlet skimmed past on both sides. Connall deftly slipped under the oar and leaped onto the decking, and with shouts and hand signals, directed them to a short stretch of rocky shore. A scraping noise soon followed as the wooden bottom hit the ground. She slumped forward at the sudden loss of momentum, but then scrambled out as the men hauled it farther inland.

"Connall, the other boat!" Domnall shouted. "It's struggling to make it."

Connall looked up from where he was tying the boat to a stout, wind-distorted tree. He pointed to two men. "With me."

Before she could ask what he planned to do, all three dashed along the narrow stretch between the western cliff face and the water. And then, *whoa*, they stripped off their kilts and shirts, tossing the fabric onto the ground. Even though she was shivering from the cold and the first drops of rain, as well as worry for the men in the boat, a tiny, tiny part of her couldn't help but admire the flex of Connall's ass cheeks as he ran, his powerful legs leaving the other two men behind.

When he reached the inlet's opening, he dove into the water and swam for the struggling boat.

They churned through the water, and icy fear crawled up her spine. She was scared. Scared for *him*. It had nothing to do with the fact she might be stuck in this godforsaken place.

I need you to live.

They reached the prow and hauled themselves onto the boat, water sluicing off their muscular bodies as their powerful arms hiked them upward. Though it was hard to see through the now-blinding rain, she could make out that they were removing boards to expose another set of oars.

Her heart beat in time with the rain hitting the rocks as Connall and the others steered the boat into the inlet. "Come on. You can do it," she whispered.

When the boat was finally safe, she dashed down the rocky stretch toward their discarded kilts, ignoring the startled shouts behind her. She avoided the rocks she knew would be slippery now from the rain and kept to the gray-black sand, though occasionally she had to slap her hand to the cliffside to catch her balance.

Breath sawing in and out more than it should for the short run, she rounded up all three kilts—along with their belts and shirts—and worked her way back. Ahead, the second boat scraped up onto the black beachhead, and the men onshore crowded around its sides, hauling it in. The men in the boat were slumped over the oars, their backs heaving as they caught their breath.

While they worked to secure both boats, Ashley wrung out their clothing as best she could. Something sharp bit into her palm. Wha—?

She looked down. The metal of her kilt pin glinted in the weakening sun, still attached to one of the kilts. She put that kilt in one hand and the rest in her other.

Then Connall rose from the bench in all his naked glory, his black hair plastered to his skull, the long strands curling against his neck and shoulders. Steam rose from his heated skin as rain peppered him, leaving his muscles glistening. He was a god, newly forged and rising from the mist.

Don't look.

But she did.

Oh. My.

Heat bloomed in her chest.

Because holy fucking shit.

Clearly defined pecs with a sprinkling of black hair led down to abs any gym rat in America would give their left nut for, she was sure. The sprinkling of hair arrowed down, highlighting that perfect V that made her want to lick. Or bite.

Her core clenched. The man was *hung.* Thick and long. When his cock stirred, she wrenched her focus upward to find his eyes latched onto hers, his gaze hooded.

Oh shit.

She swallowed, her throat dry, and ran up to him. She thrust his kilt in the general direction of that chest, but he clasped her wrist instead of the cloth. Heart thunking, she glanced up.

"Thank you," he said, his voice gravelly that, frankly, was like tossing more logs onto the fire. Still looking into her eyes and holding her wrist, his strong fingers right over her pulse point, he reached out with his free hand and slowly tugged a shirt from her other hand. Every bit of cloth swished across her skin as it left her grasp.

As soon as the fabric pulled free, he released her and stepped back. He donned the shirt. Then he slowly drew the kilt from her hand, still stupidly poised in the air as if she'd been turned into a statue, and deftly wrapped it around his waist.

Then he gave her The Look as she was starting to think of it—those smoky-green eyes radiating promise and passion and a quick flare of heat—his fingers securing the folds at his shoulder with the kilt pin she'd made for him.

She cleared her throat.

Do not get caught up in his snackalicious orbit.

Connall brushed by her. The remaining naked men worked alongside the others, hauling tarps from the two boats as if being bare-assed around one another was completely normal, but their urgent movements pulled her out of her daze, and she scanned the shore, looking for shelter.

The cliff receded at this portion, creating a hook-shaped beach that ended abruptly partway around another cliff. A thick grove of trees crowded the rest of the inlet's shore, marching up a steep hill. She hiked up the slight incline and found a stretch of cliff where erosion from water had undercut the rock. Not enough to make a cave, but enough to provide some protection from the rain. She shoved the other kilts and shirts in the dry space it provided and sprinted back down to the activity. Some men were lashing the boats tighter, but she studiously ignored their naked bodies and helped them retrieve supplies.

As she passed Connall, she nodded up ahead. "There's a small shelter along the edge."

Connall followed her line of sight. The wind blew stronger, whipping his wet hair behind him. He turned to the others. "Shelter there," he shouted against the growing storm as she ran with one of her loads to the spot.

"Take shelter," he said to her when she returned. "We'll bring up the remainder."

But she gathered another load. No way would she squat under the rock while they did all the work.

Soon they had the supplies on top of one tarp under the overhang, and they draped the loose end back over the top, securing the ends into the ground.

They made two more tarp enclosures under the overhang. Connall never pushed her to take shelter again, too busy with securing their safety, though he darted disapproving glances her way.

Fourteen warriors crawled into one, their weight securing the ends that overlapped.

Connall grasped her upper arm and indicated the remaining tarp. "You crawl in first but stop halfway, aye?"

She crawled inside, shivering. Once she reached the middle, she sat cross-legged. Connall entered on his hands and knees, his broad shoulders taking up the whole width. On the other side, his brother Domnall burst in, shaking his body like a dog.

She squeaked. "Domnall!"

He threw her a sheepish grin. "Apologies."

As the rest followed and the last entered on either end, they pulled the edge down and anchored it with their butts, shutting all fourteen of them tight inside.

She snorted. It was a burrito of Highlanders.

Hot sauce, please?

She snort-laughed, as the stress and fear found an outlet. She doubled over with teary-eyed laughter.

A heavy arm curled around her shoulder, and she succumbed and leaned against Connall's side as she pulled in deep breaths, trying to calm herself.

"Are ye all right?" His low rumble sounded by her ear, sending fresh chills across her skin, but not from the cold.

She gulped in another breath and wiped her eyes. "Yes," she whispered. "I think it was all the stress."

She angled back, but he moved so she leaned against his rain-soaked but warm chest instead of the wall. But still she shivered, her shakes becoming almost violent.

"Lean forward," he whispered in her ear. "If you'd obeyed me and taken shelter, you'd not have taken a chill. In the future, you need to obey my directives as your husband."

Too tired to protest, she did as he said. His large hand cupped her head and pushed it down slightly. Then his fingers scraped her hair off her nape and brought it over her head to hang in front. His hands came around her and into view, twisting the ends between his fists until no drops emerged, his strong fingers flexing and squeezing inches from her face.

Then he carefully combed her hair back and tugged it, over and over, in a rhythmic pattern. *Oh my*, he was braiding her hair.

The sweetness and caring it showed threatened to bring her to tears again. Which was silly. She pulled in a shuddering breath. No one, not even her ex-husband, had ever shown her such care. She'd been the youngest in a family of five, and they'd been too busy to pay any real attention.

A tiny voice in her mind admonished that her resolve was weakening with him.

Fuck that voice. She was exhausted.

Then the weight of the braid landed in front of her shoulder and he pulled her back to lean against him. He brought one end of his kilt around her and wrapped them both up tight within. At first, she flinched from the wet cloth, but the wool fabric soon trapped their body heat. She did *not* allow her mind, or her hands, to wonder how much of himself he'd exposed to get that much fabric around them.

She relaxed against him, too worn out to protest.

"Better?" he whispered.

She nodded against his shoulder. He'd tied the end of her braid by making a knot of her own hair.

Though the overhang and the cliff blocked the gale, pockets of rain pelted against their tarp as curls of wind found their shelter. Darkness descended early, and the storm screeched its fury. Soon their shelter grew warm from the trapped body heat, and the air thickened with the smell of damp wool and skin.

Gradually, the chill left her bones and drowsiness weighted her head and eyelids.

Thoughts whirled through her brain as she tried to convince herself that his braiding her hair didn't mean anything. He only did it because he valued her as the tribe's diviner and his brood mare.

He's so sweet, though. And fuck-hot.

Especially that whole stripping and diving into the water thing to save his men. Perhaps it was just his nature to be protective.

She shouldn't read into it any further than that.

Then his strong fingers brushed the back of her neck, and he kneaded her muscles there. *God, that's amazing.* She almost groaned.

Screw it.

She turned more into him, but he scooped under her knees and pulled her up onto his lap. She stiffened and he stilled, his face creased with worry. Worry for her.

She relented and tucked her head against his chest,

curling into his warmth as he continued to massage her neck and shoulder muscles, his strong fingers finding every knot and easing them into delicious warmth.

She'd forgotten how much she liked being touched by a man.

This is dangerous.

• • •

As his wife finally slipped into a restless sleep, he tightened his arms around her and shifted. Her stamina earlier had been impressive. Of a certainty, she'd saved their whole party. If they'd been caught out in the loch or even sheltering along its banks when the storm hit, they'd have certainly lost men.

Still could, before the night is through.

He banished the thought—they were well protected, thanks to her. She'd not uttered one word of complaint, instead pitching in to help with her wee muscles and large strength of will.

Half his men were in love with her already, and his chest swelled with pride, though he'd been angry at her blatant disregard of his orders. He'd need to make sure she understood that as the potential new leader for the tribe, he needed his people's respect. And his wife couldn't undermine him in front of others.

But there was still time to make her understand.

Chapter Seven

"Oh, wow." Ashley gripped the railing on the boat's bow and pulled in a shaky breath.

Acres and acres of mud stretched along the shore, exposed by the river's low tide, looking like an alien landscape pockmarked by rocks, divots, and seaweed. Birds circled and swooped downward, eager for easy prey.

To her left marched a wall from the water's edge inland, curving to her right and blocking the horizon. Along the shore, wooden docks poked across the mud flats and into the water, each like a porcupine with all the ship masts crowding it. The land facing the harbor had been stripped of trees, and it teemed with activity.

The wall...whoa. Very *Game of Thrones*-y. Goose bumps popped up all over her arms, and she shivered.

Holy shit. This was no CGI recreation of a Roman port for some period movie—it was the real thing.

They'd spent an uneasy night hunched in their tarp as they rode out the storm's rage. She'd dozed in fits and starts, but one constant was Connall's warm, strong arms wrapped tight around her. In the morning, they'd crawled out and the loch shone like a blue jewel. The *tink-tink-tink* of rain drops swelling at the ends of leaves and plopping onto a landscape littered with shredded leaves and dead branches was the only evidence of the storm's passing. Thankfully, Connall and the men had secured the boats well, and after a quick breakfast of hard cheese and gazillion-grain bread, they'd loaded up and set sail.

A week ago, she'd have freaked that she couldn't brush her teeth—cheese breath was the worst—but she chewed the mint leaves Connall handed her now, taking pride in her philosophical attitude. A hot shower or even a proper bath, though? She'd still throw down for that shit.

As they meandered from one body of water to another, she'd used her divining leather, so she knew that this was the River Clyde, and the fort sprawling before her was called Old Kilpatrick in her own time. As they neared, the docked ship masts grew, and soon their smaller vessels slipped into berths nearer to the shore, their bow bumping against the wooden piling, rocking them. She gripped the wooden bench until it settled, the sluggish waters beneath her a *swish-gurgle* against the hull.

Connall levered up and picked his way through his men, who were staring at the wall, most with their mouths hanging open. At the bow, he faced them and spoke, his voice loud enough to carry to their other ship docked next to them. "Half of you, stay with the boats. Do not seek trouble." His weighty stare punctuated his message. None of the men had commented on her helping during their emergency, but she didn't think it was her imagination that today they looked at her with more respect.

They straightened from their gawking and must have silently decided who would accompany Connall, because half from each boat hopped up onto the wooden dock. Ashley remained perfectly still.

Part of her was dying to get an up-close eyeful of a real Roman fort, but a new fear washed through her. *Anything* could happen in that crowd. She couldn't just text Connall if she somehow got separated and say, *hey, I'm at that goat-thing statue by the gate*, or whatever.

A shadow blended with hers, and Connall reached out a hand. "You will accompany us."

Her earlier reluctance to touch him seemed silly now after the night they'd spent in the storm. He pulled her up, bringing her flush against his chest. Her breaths quickened at his closeness, then—his hands strong and sure around her waist—he lifted her clear of the boat.

His men formed a guard, and as a unit they marched down the wide wooden dock, the leather soles of their shoes barely making a sound across the length despite the metric-ton of brawn flanking her.

A dozen or more wooden horses dotted a cleared area, and men leaped over them, one after another. Roman soldiers trained in a muddy field beyond, their metal weapons clashing with a staccato *tchrang-tchrang-tchrang*, interspersed with the softer *whack* of wooden staffs beating against each other.

"Incredible," Domnall whispered, loud enough for those closest to hear.

Ashley peeked at him and the others, and while their posture and strides exuded warrior confidence and grace, it was clear in the shine of their eyes that it was a struggle not to appear awed.

"So is this how massive Ashley's settlement is?" Domnall asked.

Connall shook his head, and Domnall gave her a look she could only describe as sorry-this-upstages-yours. It was uncanny how much he resembled his older brother, despite his dark red hair.

"This is tiny and primitive in comparison," Connall said.

All heads whipped around toward her, their faces filled with wonder.

"This...this is..." Domnall waved at the Roman fort. "*Tiny?*"

"And primitive, aye. Her land possessed strongholds, one after another, with nary a space between, and each taller than that wall." Connall gestured with his chin and his voice held a note of pride. "Some fashioned of stone, like these, but others from the shiniest sword metal."

It was surreal seeing the Roman fort through their eyes and hearing it compared to her own city. She was feeling awe, *too*, but for very different reasons. The men in their party murmured and stole glances at her. She stiffened, worried it was suspicion and fear. But now their facial features and mood matched their confident strides—it seemed they were feeling more confident because they had someone in their party *more* sophisticated than these Romans.

They pushed through a small gathering of bickering traders and were confronted by the fort's stone wall. A wooden palisade rimmed the top with Roman soldiers standing all stoic with their crossbows at the ready, folds of red cloth whipping behind them in the wind, or walking its length, the leather flaps of their kilt-like uniforms making a soft *thrump-swhoosh* as they passed. Shallow ditches were cut into the ground, circling the fort.

The gate's guard—clearly from Africa—waved them in. These Romans sure liked their red—most wore red tunics under their armor and leather kilts, and along the wall were loads of stacked red shields. For quick defense in case of an attack?

Here and there were citizens dressed much like Connall's people, though a few wore the togas she associated with Romans. Just inside the gate, an enclosed wooden platform stood on stilts, presumably a guard tower.

They were directed to a large stone building in the center.

"Ready?" Connall asked his men. Receiving nods all around, he pushed open the door into a room brightly lit by torches set into the walls. In the center, flames danced and sparked from a fire pit built into the floor.

A half dozen armed Roman guards stood along the far wall, flanking an older man behind an ornate wooden table. The fort's commander, she presumed. And while he carried himself like a soldier—spine straight, shoulders back—his paunch said he'd spent longer behind the desk than he had in active duty. Across his forehead, his bangs were styled in perfect little hooks.

Connall placed himself between her and the commander, and his men closed around her. Connall's deep voice rang out with pride. "I represent my father, Eacharn son of Eacharn, and the people of Dunadd, the Horse People, whom you call the Epidii. We've come to secure an alliance with your people."

The Epidii? She'd have to "Google" that later.

The commander rounded the squat table, causing the papyri weighted down with smooth river rock to flutter. He stretched his arm out, and they clasped forearms and shook.

The man began speaking, though she couldn't understand a word.

Huh. So her Universal Translator didn't work for every language. Which made sense—she only spoke one language back home.

A rough-looking man sporting blue tattoos like Connall's tribe stepped forward when the commander paused.

"You and your men are welcome," he said in Connall's tongue. "And I appreciate the journey you have undertaken."

Mr. Funky Bangs spoke again, and the interpreter said, "However, you'll need to proceed to the fourth fort along the wall, for you will need to speak to Manius Tatius Tacitus who is authorized to secure this alliance on behalf of the Emperor, Imperator Titus Aelius Aurelius Ceasar Antoninus."

Lord. What a mouthful.

The interpreter told them that they were welcome to rest here for the night, either by camping on their boats or near the fort, and to have their fill of supper, courtesy of the emperor. "You will want to leave your ships here and travel onward by land along the wall. Easier that way to find the outpost without a guide, but also the river veers sharply away, so your travel time will be shortened."

They were given, as a sign of good faith, horses for them to ride.

"These needed to be delivered tomorrow, so they are expecting them, and you will save us the trouble."

Connall listened to all of this without saying a word, and her respect for him grew. Coming to this formidable outpost and not masking any sense of inferiority with swagger and bluster? He was a man who knew his strength and worth. Once the explanations and the invite were extended, he gave a quick dip of his head. "We thank you for your generosity. We shall pass the night on our ships and proceed at first dawn."

Farther into Roman territory? While seeing all this was wicked-awesome on an intellectual level, it was no virtual reality simulation she could just abort if things got dicey.

• • •

The next day, the gravity of Connall's mission weighed heavier with each step they took. He was in awe of the power and craftsmanship these Romans had at their command. It was well that his tribe sought an alliance with these people.

After several hours' journey by horse, he called a halt.

Up ahead, a cleared area filled with drilling soldiers signaled that they'd reached their destination.

Hearing about the Romans and their wall was one thing, but seeing it was another matter entirely. If he'd not traveled to Ashley's land and witnessed the wonders of her time, he'd be impressed indeed by the Romans' handiwork. Though seeing their imprint imposed on this landscape felt…wrong.

At one point they'd stopped at a colorful stone sculpture embedded in the side. Ashley used her divining leather and told them it was a milestone marker, celebrating the wall's construction, though he was not overly fond of the depiction of people much like him, kneeling and subdued by Roman forces.

"Can you do a foretelling before we proceed?" he asked.

After they dismounted, she retrieved her leather and stretched it on the smoothest part of ground. She crouched and cast her dirt several times across the leather. "Light showers in the evening with a humidity level of seventy-seven percent, but other than that, nothing. Is there anything you'd like to ask specifically?"

Humidity level? "Will we have difficulty in our mission with the Romans?"

She frowned. "I doubt it could know the answer, but I'll try." She threw the dirt and then sat back on her heels. "Sorry, it doesn't say."

"We'll be having to take our chances then, but thank you." He reached out his hand. Ever since her arrival in his time, she seemed reluctant to touch him, except during the storm when she'd been exhausted. He hated her uneasiness around him, though he'd detected only a slight hesitation yesterday when she'd taken his hand. A victory, that.

But now her wee palm slipped readily into his, her skin so soft. He closed his fingers around hers and hauled her upright.

"Thank you," she whispered.

He blinked, for a slight tinge of pink bloomed on her cheeks.

Progress? Hope worked its insidious way inside him. He pivoted away before he said or did something to spoil his headway. "Let's stretch our legs and walk the rest of the way. We'll not be wishing to give the appearance of attackers."

If he thought their mission would be accomplished without delay, he was sorely mistaken. When they arrived at the fort, the official was there, but the forecasters had declared this day was an unlucky one for business. All official matters were closed.

"You'll have to come back tomorrow," the interpreter informed him.

Connall stepped away with his brother Domnall. "Superstitious Romans," he muttered. "Whoever heard of declaring a whole *day* unlucky?"

Domnall only shrugged. Before they reached the door to the outside, though, the interpreter stopped them. "Tacitus, however, wishes to invite you to take your ease in our baths and enjoy your stay."

Having heard that the Romans held strange attitudes about their women, he turned back. "My wife is with me. May she use your baths as well?"

He frowned but nodded. "As long as the men aren't using one of the rooms at the time. You'll want to set guards, however, so none of the soldiers enter."

Of a certainty he would do so.

His news regarding the closure of business was met with the same puzzlement as his own. "The behavior 'tis strange, but we can do aught about it. They offered ease at their baths."

The way it was offered sounded as if it were more of a treat than his own typical baths with a sponge or river.

Ashley gasped and stepped forward. "Roman baths?"

She beheld the fort with eyes round with excitement and... longing? Soon, he told himself, she'd be regarding *him* that way.

He shifted in front of her, blocking her view and stealing some of that longing. "Are these worth visiting, then?"

"Oh, wow, yes." She leaned to the side and looked beyond him. "I have no idea if these will be like the ones I've heard about, but the Romans were famous for them."

He frowned. "This isn't the first time you've referred to them in the past tense. Are they no longer an empire in your time?" It was still difficult for him to wrap his mind around her being from a different time, but it was fascinating.

"No." She chewed her lip. "Their descendants still live in a country called Italy, but their great empire fell. Dramatically. I'm not that much into history, but even I know that their collapse was a big deal. A watershed moment."

He glanced back over his shoulder at the fort, narrowing his eyes. *Hmm, maybe not so powerful at that.* "Do you know when this happens?"

She pulled her leather out from where she had it stashed in her saddle gear. "No, but I guarantee you I can find out."

He gave a curt nod. "Please do."

She worked her gift. "Not for another three hundred years or so." At his frown of confusion at the unfamiliar word, she added, "Three hundred winters from now."

"Still powerful enough for our needs, then." He helped her stand, delighted she again took his hand so easily. His patience was paying off. "Let's partake of their hospitality."

As they led their horses to the barrack stables, he drank in the sight of his wife walking tall and proud at his side. While he'd of course been pleased that the magic had supplied him with such a fine-looking woman, he was surprised by the protective warmth suffusing his chest. Intelligent and composed in the face of adversity, she possessed traits that were welcome in a future chief's wife.

Traits that would mix well with his own to create fine sons to lead his people.

And while he'd been patient with her, despite his father's advice, he was getting impatient to be making those sons.

To take his mind off what he'd rather be doing with her, he focused on their destination.

What would these baths be like? Of a certainty, they'd have water. "And while we're within, do the laundry. Our clothes are begrimed from our journey."

She whipped around. And glared. "Real men ask nicely."

"Real men know how to give orders," he growled. While he admired her strength of will, would it ever be tamed?

She rolled her eyes in response.

. . .

Roman baths?

Oh heck, yeah. A warm, relaxing bath was just what she needed to forget Mr. Bossy.

Do his laundry. She'd like to do...something to him.

Ugh. She'd like to *do* him.

As they rounded a corner, they nearly ran into someone. Beside her, Connall stiffened and glanced at her.

Who is this? Before she could ask, Domnall slapped the man on the back. "Mungan. We heard you were here."

The druid?

Finally. She almost did a fist pump.

Whoa. This hot guy was a *druid?* Not as hot as Connall or his brothers, but the guy would turn heads. She'd half expected him to be wearing a blue wizard's hat with stars on it or something, along with flowing robes. He was dressed in a rich-red belted tunic and sported open-toed sandals. Blue ink, like the other men in Connall's tribe, snaked up his arms in dips and swirls.

And while the other men wore their hair long, with a single braid at each temple, Mungan had thick brown hair cut close enough for her to see a jagged scar on one side of his scalp, though he left it a little longer at the top—just enough for its natural curl to give him that smoldering, bad-boy look. Jeez, strip him of this tribal gear and put him in a tight T-shirt and he could be some UFC fighter-dude.

He shot an annoyed grimace at Domnall and stepped away. His gaze narrowed on hers, and then he raised an eyebrow at Connall. "So you were successful, hearth brother? Glad I am to hear it."

She opened her mouth to demand he send her back, but a strange tug of panic mixed with regret hit her, stilling her from the shock of it. Because...what the hell? She *definitely* wanted to go back.

Didn't she?

The muscles in Connall's jaw tightened.

Yeah. It was just the idea of missing out on the Roman baths that she would regret. Nothing more. It had *nothing* to do with leaving this man. And his laundry-washing wishes.

Roman baths, am I right? Her scalp sang.

"You're their spellcaster," she said. "You need to send me back to my time. Now." Yes. Now.

Or maybe after the baths.

His brown eyes regarded her solemnly, making her heart pound, because it felt...as if her fate were being decided. "Alas, I cannot." He bowed and stepped around them.

"But— Wait!" She grabbed the edge of his red tunic, and he glanced down at her hand and then at her. She let go.

No touching the druid, got it.

"There must be some sacred stones or a sacred spot nearby that you can use."

"There are, but that is not the issue. I lack the strength

to do it. I'm still recovering from the prior spell, and so you'll need to wait until the spring equinox thirty-eight nights from now. For then the magic will not only be naturally stronger, but I will be as well." He backed away, his gaze darting between her and Connall. His lips lifted in a tight smile. "Until then." He disappeared into the crowd.

Not until the spring equinox?. Dammit. And what bothered—and scared—her even more? Relief had surged through her when he'd denied her request and she was given *more* time with Connall.

Thirty-eight nights instead of fourteen.

"I'm sorry," Connall whispered, stepping closer and continuing in a lowered voice. "I know ye had hopes he could return you to your time sooner."

She crossed her arms. The thing was, he *did* look sincerely apologetic. But she'd been played for years by her ex and that was *not* her anymore. "Did you know?"

"Know what?"

"That he could only do it at the spring equinox?"

"On my ancestors, I swear I did not. I wasn't aware of his limitations for this magic until now."

She blew out a sharp breath. "Okay, I believe you. Man, now I *really* want to try out these baths."

Connall led the way again and stopped at a large stone building toward the back and near the wall. "Let me first ascertain what this entails." He gripped her shoulder. "The commander said you'll need to bathe separately from the men."

"I should hope so."

With that, he stepped inside, but soon returned, his eyes round. He motioned with his head to the interior, his braids swinging. "The whole *building* is dedicated to bathing. The caldarium, whatever that is, is free at the moment, which has access to a hot bath." He looked to her. "Does that interest you?"

Uh, yeah! She nodded.

He motioned to the others. "The rest of you—make use of the other rooms, and I'll guard Ashley."

He ducked inside, and she followed with the others close behind, their eagerness palpable. Sputtering torches illuminated a slate-lined floor, and a wet stone smell fogged the air. Romans—naked Romans—looked up from where they were setting their clothes on inset shelves along the walls. They nodded to their party and stepped through the door on the far side. A mural of a tropical land covered the walls, the large green fronds almost alien. Benches dotted the sides, under which leather sandals and more stacked clothes lay scattered. A changing room? Up high, near the ceiling, rectangles of light poured into the room from glass-lined windows. *Glass.*

A woman draped in white robes stepped from behind one of several wooden poles lining the room's center, her blond braids twisting around the crown of her head in an elaborate up-do. "Tacitus sent me to guide you, as I speak your tongue."

"You're Roman, though?" Ashley asked.

The woman smiled slightly. "I'm not a citizen. I'm a slave from an area southward, but I've interacted with people who speak your tongue."

Ashley stepped back. *Holy shit.* Her stomach tightened. A slave?

This time period is so fucked up. And this woman seemed to accept it as normal. Was she taken in a raid like Connall's people and sold to the Romans?

Connall's jaw was clenched.

Even though she wanted to grab her arm and march her out of there, she knew she couldn't do a damn thing about the situation.

The woman cocked her head. "This bothers you," she stated softly.

"The fact that you've been made a slave, yes, not you yourself," she quickly said, to make it clear.

The tall blonde shrugged. "I'll be given my freedom in another year."

Oh. Well that was slightly better. "What's your name?"

The slave startled, her eyes flaring in surprise. "Seberga," she whispered, her voice tentative. With that, she turned on her heel and pushed open a stout oak door. "Normally, you would disrobe here, but I'll lead you straight to the caldarium—the hot room, in your language."

Apparently, it was okay for *her* to see naked men, but not the other way around.

Fine by me.

Seberga motioned to the door on the left. "Your men may change in the room we just left and either join the other men in the sudatorium, which means Room of Dry Heat"— she motioned to the right—"or in the cold bath."

"You," she said, indicating her and Connall, "follow me." The new rooms were noticeably warmer and filled with naked men lounging, talking, or gambling. These walls boasted a fresco of a tropical, palm-tree lined island.

Holy shit. The man hours alone… If a remote outpost looked like this, what did *Rome* look like at this time?

They entered a smaller, and *hotter*, room, and Seberga motioned to the walls and floor. "Hot air and steam circulate behind these stone slabs. Have you ever used a room like this?"

She was about to say yes, but her experience in a sauna wouldn't be the same. "Um, no, I haven't."

"You can change in here. Cover your skin in oil and scrape it off with the stirgils to help remove the oil and any grime." She waved to an opening on the right. "And then you may enter the hot bath. Your husband can either accompany you or stand guard, whichever is your custom. Bathe for as long as you like, then return here. Repeat the oiling and scraping and bathing until you feel clean."

"Where does the heat come from?" Connall studied the room, eyebrows lifted.

"From a boiler on the other side of this wall. From there, it's piped into hollow chambers under these floors and behind these walls."

Impressive. Already, sweat trickled down her back from the heat.

Connall bowed. "We thank you. You've been most helpful."

Seberga nodded solemnly and left, and Ashley slumped against the wall, staring at Connall. "The Romans have slaves?" She looked to the side. "I think I knew that, but it's horrible facing it in reality."

His eyes searched hers. "I take it you don't have slaves in San Francisco?"

She rolled her lips inward. "I'd like to think we don't. It's illegal, but unfortunately there are some horrible people out there who deal in human trafficking." She clasped her hands to her stomach and sat down on the bench. "You don't have slaves, do you? I don't think I saw any, but…"

He settled beside her. "No. Our people never have, but there are tribes down the coast or across the water who will raid from time to time. We're so remote that we don't have much trouble from either quarter."

"Until this winter," she whispered.

Connall nodded and looked down at his leg, where he was gripping his knee. "And once before," he said, so low she almost didn't hear the words. Words which came out stretched with old pain.

"What happened?"

He cleared his throat and pulled in a deep breath, his nostrils flaring. "When I was young, I was playing with my brother and his friends, and with…with my childhood playmate, a girl named Muirgheal." Misery was evident in his words, along with grief.

"She should not have been among our number, but I was adamant she had a right to fight and play with the boys until I finally won her a spot. We were at the same place we traveled back and forth to your land. It's sacred, but like all young ones, we were careless and believed ourselves untouchable. Then a ship of men landed on the shore, and…"

The fingers gripping his knee tightened, the only indication—other than the brief flash of pain—that this was a difficult memory to relate. She lifted her hand and stopped, flexing her fingers.

Her heart went out to him. Screw it—she covered his broad hand with her small one. "You escaped?"

He tensed and then relaxed under her hold. "I did." His jaw worked as he focused on where their skin touched. "But not my brother and his friends. Or Muirgheal."

"Domnall was taken?"

"No. My older brother Cairbre."

Whom she hadn't met. "He's still gone, isn't he?"

He nodded, and his Adam's apple bobbed on a swallow. "I didn't see enough to aid the council in their search. We never found them nor heard from them since."

Oh *God*. She squeezed his hand. "That must be awful. I can't even imagine."

Poignancy seeped into the silence and the space between them.

A poignancy whose intimacy and attendant expectations seemed more than she could handle right now.

"So instead of raiding along your shores for a wife, you raided my land." She kept her voice light.

He jerked toward her and clasped her hand between both of his. This time his eyes held a note of pleading. "'Twas not my intention, you must believe me. Everything was strange in your land. 'Twas only the List of Craig which saved me."

She gave a soft laugh. "Craigslist."

"That one. And Norton was the one who composed it for me. I told him the duties and what I wanted."

Despite everything, a bark of laugh escaped her. "So you thought the wife-finding part was a given and didn't need to put that important fact in the ad?"

He shook his head, his braids swinging slightly. "I expressly asked for someone willing to bear my children."

She drew back. "I think I'd remember *that* part. It just said something about washing and cooking duties. And taking care of your cows, though that's never come up."

"Taking care of my cows?" He shifted so he faced her fully. "I never asked him to include such."

"Well, he did. Though it was more along the lines of being able to increase your herd—oh!" She snorted.

He frowned. "What?"

"Um, yeah. He *did* put those duties in there, but either the magic translated your request wrong, or, more likely, Norton was being *delicate*."

He gently cupped her face, and her chuckle turned into a gasp, the rough calluses on his battle-hardened fingers strangely sensual as they brushed her skin. "It was not my intention to deceive. Regardless, the druid..." He searched her eyes and then glanced away, though his palm remained on her face.

"The druid what?" she prompted. He touched her gently, as though she were precious to him. Even though she should, God, she couldn't pull away.

His eyes flared with heat. "Before I left, he assured me that the magic would help me find the one meant for me."

His thumb brushed her cheekbone. Back and forth. Her heart picked up its pace. "And you think the magic worked? That I'm meant for you?" she whispered.

"Yes, ever since you stepped from that line of women."
His eyes searched hers. If she leaned forward, or licked
her lips, or even glanced at his mouth like she really, really
wanted to, he'd kiss her.

And then she'd know how he tasted. How he kissed. How
he possessed.

She pulled back, and his hand fell from her face.
Disappointment flickered in his eyes, quickly masked.

She slid her hand from his, the rough pads of his fingers
skimming against her skin. She clenched her hand against her
stomach, repressing a shudder of desire. "I might believe you.
I just…I need time to absorb this. You say the magic made
sure I'm meant for you, but…" She contemplated the door
where the slave woman had exited. Her first instinct was to
hide any weakness, but he'd been honest with her and she
owed him this much. "I'm not sure I'm meant for this time.
For this way of life."

She stood up. Breaking away from that potential kiss,
breaking away from his pull, it was one of the hardest things
she'd ever done. If he was right, and she was meant to be here,
then any interaction she had with him just tied her tighter to
this time period.

Would make her forget her old life.

"I'm going to take that hot bath now," she said over her
shoulder.

"As you wish."

The door shut. Leaving her alone.

How much longer could she resist him?

She eyed the door.

Not much longer.

She better find out if there were herbs or something she
could purchase here to help prevent pregnancy.

Yes, she'd fish out her divination leather ASAP.

Just in case.

Chapter Eight

"We are in agreement, then?" Connall asked Tacitus, the fort's commander, via the interpreter the following day.

The man sat at a richly carved desk, his back straight, as if he were a statue made of flesh.

His light-brown hair was cropped close to his head, streaks of gray at the temples. He formed a triangle with his hands and tapped it against his chin, watching Connall closely. Domnall shifted on his feet, his movements visible from the corner of Connall's eye.

His brother needed to learn to quell his agitation for it gave too much away.

Tacitus lowered his hands. "Yes, but we require a show of good faith."

His gut tightened. Of course it couldn't be this simple. "What do you require?" His mind raced with possible requests and responses.

Tacitus stood, placing his hands on the desk. "We are having trouble with the people north of the wall. The Caledonians. At a time of our choosing, you shall send twenty of your best warriors to fight with us and quell their antics."

Connall considered delaying the response by saying he'd need to consult with his father and the council, but the man knew he'd come to the outpost with their full authority.

The idea of strengthening the position of this Roman's empire did not sit well within, but it would ensure the safety of his tribe.

He nodded. "It will be done."

"And one more thing." Tacitus crossed his arms, his eyes narrowing. "You must rid your tribe of any druids."

Shock coursed through him, but he gritted his teeth and kept his face neutral. "Our druids?" he asked, stalling for time.

Domnall stepped forward, but Connall put a staying hand on his brother's chest. *Not now, brother.*

"Yes. Those who are your priests." Tacitus frowned at the interpreter, who nodded back. "That's the word."

Interesting request, this was. He'd heard the Romans allowed their client kingdoms to worship as they pleased, so why were they wishing to single out their druid priests?

Sending a quick prayer to his ancestors for the fine line he would attempt to walk, he replied, "Our priest is no longer with us." And he wasn't lying. Mungan wasn't in their party or at Dunadd. Connall also hedged by pretending that the Roman understood the term druid correctly. Well that it was so, otherwise they wouldn't have let him in the fort.

No way were they going to rid themselves of their intellectuals.

Later that afternoon, a fat dog with a bone clutched in its jaws darted between Connall and his wife then tore down the dusty, unpaved lanes of an open market outside the fort. To better protect her, he stepped closer to Ashley, his hand on the small of her back.

"I've never seen so many people in a market," Domnall shouted from behind as he and two other men formed a human shield. The rest of their party guarded their supplies. Beyond stretched sectioned-off fields for cultivation, though with the winter it lay fallow.

Ashley tugged on his kilt. "I'd like to stop by the herb seller."

He glanced down and smiled. "Eithne also has a list for me." He peered around a stick of a man who had a sheep draped over his shoulders. How the man carried an animal that appeared to weigh more than him, he couldn't fathom. "There's one there." He pointed past her, liking how the movement angled his body into hers.

Ever since the bath, he was more convinced than ever that she would soon be his. It had been so difficult to force himself to wait for her to initiate, but he'd done so.

He guided her through the milling crowd until they reached the herb seller's stall. Amphora filled with rare oils lined one side, along with a rack of wooden boxes. Rope threaded overhead, from which hung clumps of dried herbs.

"Do you have any Queen Anne's Lace?" Ashley asked the elderly woman within.

They'd found that unlike the soldiers manning the fort, the tradespeople were similar to his own, their mother tongue close.

He added Eithne's requests to hers. But when the merchant handed over more herbs than he felt justified his offering of cured hides, he threw in one more hide. The woman was frail—more bone than meat—with no husband visible to aid her. "Now we're even."

The woman startled, her eyes going round. "I thank ye," she whispered.

He draped an arm over Ashley's shoulder and steered her back into the thoroughfare. Domnall and the other men fell into step behind.

The shouts off to the side barely registered, for the noise wasn't close at all to the level he'd experienced while in Ashley's land, but as they drew parallel, he espied Machar and others of his party on the edge of a crowd, their voices lending to the noise.

Foreboding settled in his gut. Romans with their large spears headed toward the fray. They were still some distance away, but he needed to act quickly. If his men were only watching, he'd usher them away. If they weren't mere spectators...

"Domnall, you and the others remain with Ashley." He eyed the approaching soldiers. "Better yet, take her to the encampment, and I'll meet you there."

As he drew near to Machar, he yanked on his upper arm. "What's happening?"

Machar fought against him for a moment until he realized it was Connall who'd accosted him. Relief softened his features. "Teàrlach." He pointed into the clearing. "Some trader took offense to how the boy looked at him, is the best I can tell."

Sure enough, his youngest—and smallest—warrior was being pummeled by a hulk of a man whose tattoos were not unlike those of his own people. Connall's gut eased a little, for 'twas clear the man was no Roman. But a scoundrel he was to go after someone unable to defend himself. Teàrlach was quick and nimble, though, and was doing his best to dodge the man's swings.

Connall pushed in between the two fighting men and raised his left arm, blocking the next blow. At the same time, he planted a foot in the man's belly and shoved. "You have something against one of my men, you can deal with me."

The man had an inch on Connall, and his face twisted into an ugly sneer. "Your men need to show respect. That one called me a name."

"By my ancestors, I said not a word," Teàrlach piped up, his breath and words coming in gasps as his chest rose and fell. "He just came at me. Wanting a fight, I think."

Connall blocked another blow and stepped into the man's space, the rush of battle singing through his veins. Though he wished for nothing more than to let his blood lust have free rein, he kept it in check. "Respect isn't earned by fists." With a quick movement, he took the large warrior by surprise, twisting his arm up against his back.

Shouts of "kill him" rang out, though Connall was gratified to see none were his own men. When he'd held the man's arm up high against his back long enough to make his point, and for it to be painful, he shoved him away with a kick to his arse. "Go back to your people and fight with opponents your own size."

The man stumbled forward until he dropped to his knees. Then he looked back over his shoulder, his eyes filled with hate.

Connall strode toward his men and clasped young Teàrlach around the shoulders, turning him around to head back toward their encampment. He trusted his warriors to watch his back.

Then two of his party surged forward. Connall swung around and sidestepped the attacker's lunge. Using the man's lumbering momentum against him, Connall yanked on his arm and unbalanced him, then swept his legs out from under him. The larger warrior landed flat on his belly, the breath escaping his lungs and blowing dust into the air. Laughter sounded, which had not been Connall's aim.

"Let's be gone," Connall barked to Teàrlach and the others. "The Romans are approaching, and I do not relish being here when they arrive."

They slipped through the crowd. They'd have to circle back to their encampment, but 'twas the prudent move.

Connall spared a glance—the large warrior was still splayed flat on the ground, his face crimson. If these were the people the Romans wanted them to fight, he'd not find it difficult to meet the request.

• • •

Ashley rushed up to Connall, adrenaline spiking through her veins, a metallic tang in her throat. "Are you..." She pulled in several breaths. "Are you all right?"

She'd *never* seen a fight before. Not in real life. It was much shorter and much scarier than on TV or in a movie. The men crowding the circle seemed to feed off the energy, testosterone thick in the air.

Though her voice was breathy, it reached Connall. He whirled around and stared down at her, his eyes flaring with anger, surprise, and...heat.

Connall frowned at Domnall, his eyes now only holding anger. "You were supposed to watch over her, not accompany her to this spectacle." He peered over her shoulder. "We need to keep moving. Follow me, and do not stray." He directed the last to Ashley.

"But I—"

"You will obey me on this." With that, he resumed his long strides around the back of the market.

Since she was planning on it anyway, she followed. Domnall and the others formed a tight guard around her.

"She gave us the slip," Domnall said.

Connall shook his head and scrutinized her from over his shoulder.

"I was worried about you," she said.

"I'm fine. It would take a lot more than that man to hurt me."

At the reminder that he could be hurt, she winced.

Which then made everything within her go still—she didn't want to ever see him hurt. But he was a warrior; that was inevitable.

It was all too much to take in.

He protected his men, and her, for that matter. What would it be like to have the love of someone like that?

And on top of all of that, he was kind. Throwing the extra hide to the herb merchant earlier had melted her.

Super-honest.

Caring.

Fiercely loyal.

All traits lacking in her ex-husband.

His powerful legs ate up the dusty ground, the muscles along his broad shoulders rippling as he moved. Ashley pulled in a shuddering breath as desire—hot and sharp—tore right through her and out the other side, leaving her feeling hollow and aching.

Oh man, oh man, oh man.

This is not good.

Thirty-seven more days.

I have to resist him.

But as he slowed down to let her catch up, her resolve weakened.

Would it really be the end of the world if she hooked up with a hot Highlander before she headed home? She should get *something* good in return for this mess. Right?

She gripped the sack of Queen Anne's Lace she'd purchased from the herb lady, thankful she'd followed through on that precaution.

Can't have a baby daddy stuck in the second century.

Chapter Nine

Four days later, Ashley pushed open the door of their hut at Dunadd, the leather hinges emitting a tiny *squeak-creak*. Late morning sun spilled across the interior, highlighting the bed and a corner of the trestle table, and a surge of homecoming smacked her so hard honest-to-God friggin' tears welled in her eyes. She'd missed this place?

Connall's straw pallet drew her focus. Heat flushed her skin—she'd forced him to sleep there so she wouldn't be tempted to jump his bones. After they'd left Bearsden, it had been even harder not to jump said bones.

He strode up the incline, having hung back momentarily to greet some of the villagers. His thighs bunched and flexed as he hiked, the cloth of his kilt draping him oh-so-enticingly. Their eyes locked, and that heat swirling along her skin arrowed straight to her core.

Crap. I'm about to be all over that.

Whenever they'd stopped on their return trip, he'd brought her food and made sure she had the most comfortable spot when they bedded down for the night. All very charming at first, but as their journey wore on—frustrating.

As if each sweet gesture were a weapon he deployed, and her defenses were proving increasingly useless.

"I thought I was stronger than this," she whispered, turning back into the empty hut. The thump of Connall's boots sounded behind her.

"Is there aught amiss inside?" His words were a rumble right near her ear, his heat a tangible presence along her back, sending shivers down her spine.

Bracing herself, she stepped into the center of the room. He ducked inside, his large frame unfolding to its full height.

All the attraction simmering between them swelled, taking up the interior, pushing more insistently against her, and making her earlier attempts to resist him seem downright heroic and not at all something she could achieve now.

Though tempted to give in to experiencing a tumble with a hot Highlander, she'd forced herself to wait until they returned to Dunadd. Her fantasy did *not* include having sex in a temporary camp with a bunch of other men around to watch, thank you very much.

But we're alone now.

And the possibilities bloomed. Still, would the Queen Anne's Lace work? Should she risk it?

He stood mostly in shadow, but he languidly surveyed her body. She shivered—it was as if he'd lightly brushed across her skin with his calloused fingers.

This is it.

But he took a step back. And another. He raked his hand through his hair and made a fist at the crown of his head, making that bicep of his bulge.

She clenched. She for-real clenched.

He cleared his throat, keeping his eyes locked with hers. "I'm needing to report to my father. He'll not be happy until he's hearing the news from our journey." His voice held a clear note of regret.

She released her breath in a slow *whoosh,* and a strange mixture of relief and frustration fizzed through her veins, as if all the lusticles in her blood stream were running around saying *we can't handle him anyway* and *oh my God what now?* If the lusticles had fists, they'd be propped on their hips.

Needing to shut herself off from his mesmerizing and lustful gaze, she turned and *clunked* her traveling bundles onto the trestle table. With trembling hands, she fished out the smaller bag from the herb seller and held it up. "And I'll bring these to Eithne."

Take that. And, since the tension had been cut, it was the perfect time to have The Talk. Let's be real, they were going to boink at some point.

"Before you go, I need to ask. Do you use protection?"

His brows dipped. "Protection?"

"When you have sex with others."

He stepped closer. "I'm still not understanding, but why do you wish to know? That might help me answer."

"So that you don't get a sexually transmitted disease." But even as she said the words, most of them were in English so that didn't help. "Er, so that you don't get…" She waved at her crotch. How to put it? "So that you don't get wounds there from someone else."

His forehead smoothed. "I take your meaning. I was tutored in the art by a druid—it was her specialty. And she cleansed both of our bodies in herbs and oils, and the members of their order regularly check their bodies. Since then, the few times I have done so, I've used a barrier made from sheep's gut."

Oookay. I asked, didn't I?

"Thank you, I'll just…" She held up the herbs. "Take these to Eithne."

He nodded and stepped to the open doorway. "And do

the laundry afterward. Our clothes need cleansing."

She folded her arms. And glared. "Real men ask nicely."

He smiled. "Real men know how to give orders."

Infuriating man. "I told you it was a job, and I was right."

The heat of his gaze raked over her and lit her core. "Not all aspects of our marriage will be a chore, I'm thinking." Then he turned and left.

She slumped against the bench, as if the moment he'd turned away had cut some cord.

Holy hell. It had been hard enough to resist him while they'd been on the journey. Now? She'd be lucky to pass the night without getting a taste of that Highlander. And the fact that he was the obey-me type? Well, that would make it easier to leave him afterward.

It was late afternoon by the time Ashley trudged back up the incline to the first terrace and her hut. It had taken her longer than she'd thought to deliver the herbs to Eithne and help the women get through the chores left for the day. They'd been grateful for her return.

She stuck her hands under her armpits. Despite the exercise, her fingers had turned to blocks of ice.

Her muscles no longer strained as she made her way up the incline, and her breaths weren't puffing out like some asthmatic steam engine.

Satisfaction surged through her, followed by a splash of cold—that meant time had *passed*. And she was getting closer to the deadline.

Thirty-three days before she could leave. She tightened her arms around her chest and bent into the wind as she trudged up. God, that still seemed like a long way away.

Thirty-three days? Here?

In order to stomach it, she needed to have some measure of control over her life. And first on her agenda? Fixing the gender inequality. Listening to Eithne and Affraic complain today, overworked and underappreciated, she discovered that part of the problem lay in the fact that they had no voice on their council. It was all run by men.

She pushed inside the hut, shaking out her arms now that the wind had been cut off. A little thrill kicked up in her heart—Connall was already inside, his large frame bent over the hearth. He poked a fire into a welcome blaze of heat, the pop and sizzle of the peat the only sound.

Already she was associating the smoky, pungent, smell with *home*. It didn't help that when she'd taken a bite of her first baked bread since she'd returned, and her mouth filled and prickled with its yeasty flavor, the memory that had always hovered out of reach snapped into focus—Grammy P's bread. Those summer visits to her great-grandmother's old house in Wisconsin had been the only times growing up that she'd felt cared for, cherished, special. Already into her nineties then, she'd died when Ashley was only eleven.

"How did it go with your father?" she asked, desperate to fill the silence.

He glanced up, one of his braids falling forward to swing by his chin. "We accomplished what we'd set out to do— procure an alliance with the Romans." He pushed away from the hearth and faced her fully.

Her heart fluttering, she settled on the bench near the fire. Near *him*. He stilled as if on alert, like a predator amazed that his prey had come within range. Then the moment popped, and he shifted forward, turned, and folded his large body onto the bench beside her, adding to the heat warming her up. She stuck her hands out to the blazing fire. *Here's me, totally ignoring his closeness.*

Prickles of warmth shot down her frozen fingers, and she

gasped at the sharp pain.

He angled closer, and his large hands enveloped hers. Man, his hands had that rough-but-gentle thing down to a science. And warm, too. He was always so warm...

"Let me see them." His voice gruff, but the concern clear. "Och, they're like ice, they are."

His enticing scent, and the masculine heat of him, mixed with the scents of cold winter air.

He briskly rubbed back and forth. Slowly, life crept back into her fingers. "I need mittens," she said, her teeth chattering.

"Mittens?"

"Yeah. They're like a piece of clothing fit for your hand. Keeps them warm."

He looked down at her with interest, his face only inches away. "Can you make these?"

Wow. They didn't have mittens? Or gloves? Though now that she thought about it, she'd not seen anyone wearing any, despite the cold.

Could she? She didn't know how to knit, so that was out. But she'd sewn trinkets for her Etsy shop. "Yeah. I think I can." She pulled one hand out from between his and studied her fingers. "I'd just need some cloth. And fur. And a sewing needle and thread."

"Eithne should be able to help you with the material you'll need."

Today's conversation with Eithne had given her an idea. She put both her hands in her lap and turned to face him, straightening her back. "Can you ask the council if I can speak to them?"

His brow furrowed, his eyes searching her face. "I can speak on your behalf. What would you like me to ask of them?"

She shook her head. "I'd like to speak to them myself. I

found out that the council is all men."

He nodded.

"And I want to see if they'll allow some of the older women to join."

Sure, she didn't plan to stay, but after all she'd endured from her ex, it didn't sit right—she couldn't let other women be completely dependent on their men if she could help it. And if she could leave this place having accomplished something meaningful, she would.

He cocked his head to the side. "Why would they want to do that?"

"So they can be a voice for the women."

He folded his arms across his chest. "The men are perfectly capable of acting on their behalf."

She bit her lip. These were different times and she had to be careful. "But they can't. Not really. Women can bring a different perspective. They see and hear things that the men don't."

Connall stared at the fire. "I'll see about getting you an audience." He uncrossed his arms and placed his hands on his knees, leaning toward her. "But you must understand— life has become more dangerous. Ever since those Romans arrived, they've pushed people from the land. Raids and wars increased. We believed things were finally settling down to peace until..." He scowled at the fire.

"Until you were raided this winter."

"Aye." He stood abruptly and leaned a forearm against the wall, staring down into the hearth fire. "We don't know where they came from."

The fire's light flickered across his strong profile. Even doing something as simple as leaning against a friggin' wall, he was decidedly masculine. All powerful muscles, poised and capable for action.

"What procedures have you set in place to prevent

another raid?"

"There's not much we can do. Lookouts are stationed atop the keep at all times. But that only grants us the narrowest window to effect a proper defense."

An idea formed. During their trek along the Antonine Wall, she'd seen several spots where the wall jutted out, and on top was a pyramid of sticks. She assumed it was some sort of signal fire. "Would it help if you could have more time?"

• • •

Connall poked an iron into the fire, appreciating that his wife was discussing tribal matters with him. He'd take any such evidence as a good sign. Additionally, he knew her well enough to know he should hear her out. She was a smart one. "Aye, but eyes would need to be stationed up and down the coast. What time we gained would be mostly lost while they raced back with a warning."

She leaned forward. "What if you could know as soon as those eyes spotted the invaders?"

"Not even Mungan's magic could accomplish such." Glad he was to have something to occupy his hands, however, as he poked the fire to a fuller blaze. Being so close to her was testing his resolve. At first, he'd been focused on accomplishing his goal—find a wife and keep her. But every day with Ashley showed him that this need—while still valid—was simplistic. He didn't want *any* wife. He wanted Ashley—her fire and ingenuity.

Her presence calmed him.

"We could create a signal tower."

He turned sharply to her. "Explain."

"We'd need to keep it simple so that we can build them quickly, but remember those structures we saw at the Roman fort? The wooden hut on stilts?"

He nodded. "They guarded the entrances."

"What if we created some structures like that, placed on top of high hills overlooking the water?"

He shook his head. It wasn't that he was dismissing her—he simply wasn't following. "We'd have no guarantee that the raiders would pass close enough for the men inside to attack."

She smiled, squirming on the bench with what looked like delight. "But that wouldn't be their purpose here. Smoke can be seen from a distance. We could stack wood at the top of one of them, ready to be set on fire. When the lookouts spotted raiders, they light it up. The men watching from the keep would know that smoke coming from that direction signaled danger."

Connall gasped and straightened, fresh energy coursing through him at the possibility. "That could work." He glanced over her shoulder, assessing the steps. "First, we'd have to search from atop the keep for spots where we could still see smoke from a fire. And if we use birch wood for the fire and topped it with damp wool, it would create more smoke."

"And if we end up having time, we could make a string of them. One could signal the next, and the next, until the closest one to here was able to set their wood ablaze."

His body tensed from the overwhelming urge to wrap her up in a hug and kiss his clever wife.

If this worked...

Chapter Ten

Excitement thrummed through Connall. Anything that could help his people was welcome. He marched to the door and yanked it open. "The sun hasn't yet set." He cast a glance over his shoulder. She'd risen and come partway to him, which for some reason gave him hope. When it came to her, he grasped at every thread of hope he could find. "Let's go to the top of the keep and see if we can find our first locations."

Her eyes lit up, and she closed the distance. Feeling as if he'd made progress with her already, he held out his hand and his heart swelled when she readily placed hers in it with no hesitation. He'd worried that returning home would remind her of her situation and her determination to resist him.

His heart full, he tugged her through the door and broke into a run, laughing.

She laughed beside him. At the last stretch of steps, they had to split apart to climb, single-file, but she was right behind him, her breaths even and her steps strong and sure—another sign. How different from when she first arrived.

Inside the keep, he grabbed a torch and, ignoring his

father's stare and those of the council members sitting around the hearth fire, he led her to the keep's steps. "After you." He pointed up with the torch, and she dashed past him.

When they reached the next floor, she stopped. "I haven't been up here."

He stepped up behind her and held the torch high, letting its light illuminate the room. It was the same size as the room below.

She angled her face up to his. "What do you use this room for?"

"Storage, mostly. But in instances of danger, we herd everyone in the village into this room and barricade ourselves within."

He motioned to the steps spiraling upward. "One more set of stairs. The sun is setting, and I'm eager to see what could work."

She strode upward, and he kept a steady hand at her back, for these steps were narrower and steeper. Soon she halted, and he carefully maneuvered up behind her, sharing the narrow step. Having her so near, her body lightly brushing up against his, set him aflame. He resisted the urge to bend down and nestle his nose into her sweet-smelling hair. He'd made progress, aye, but he didn't dare ruin it.

He closed his eyes—*must* ignore that urge and the stronger one which wished for nothing more than to grip her around the waist and pull her hard up against his growing arousal. Cursing softly, he opened his eyes—his lust quelled—and pushed open the door above their heads.

The wood clattered against the walkway with a *bang,* and light streamed in. He tucked his torch into a receptacle in the stairwell, for they'd need it on their return, and followed Ashley outside.

As a child, he always loved coming up here. While one couldn't see all the way around in one spot—for the domed thatched roof formed a barrier—one could stroll about and see all. He led her along the perimeter until they reached the westward-facing section. The most likely raiders came from the open sea.

He nodded to the two sentries. "We'll keep watch until the sun sets. Go warm yourselves by the fire." They rushed out, eager for the warmth of fire and spirits.

He braced a hand along the bulwark and shielded his eyes from the setting sun's rays. The wind—strong this high off the ground—buffeted him, and he shook his head to clear his hair away from his eyes. At the brush of Ashley's arm on his, he tugged her in front of him so that she was shielded on both sides. Her body trembled against his, and he pulled her up against him. To keep her warm, was all. 'Twas a coincidence that it was precisely what he'd been wishing to do not a moment before.

She searched the horizon, as eager to implement this plan, as he. 'Twas a brilliant idea, truly.

To the southwest, a line of hills ranged southward, overlooking the open sea. He pointed and spoke directly into her ear to be heard over the wind. "There. We could place the first one on that farthest hill."

"What lies south of there? We could put a second one on another hill or a cliff, extending our reach."

"Machar would know."

They hurried around to the north end of the walkway and repeated the process, finding another likely spot for a signal tower.

When the sun set, they'd found three great locations—two to watch the approach from the open sea, and one to watch the river.

"I'll speak to my father. I don't see why we can't start right away." He tucked her against him, her shapely body molding to his. The sun's rays lent the air a pink glow, reflected in the still waters of the loch.

Something eased inside him to have her here, working together to help his tribe. *Their* tribe. For she was one of them now.

One of The Horse People.

He refused to worry over whether she'd choose to return to her time.

His couplings with women in the past had been a matter of satisfying lust on both sides. And while, aye, he lusted after this woman, he also relished these moments where they shared space together. Shared a quiet moment. With no expectations or demands.

Ashley's hair whipped in front of her, the braid coming loose. She brushed the strands back, but more joined the others to twist and jump in the wind. He hummed and placed his palms on her forehead. She stilled, and he slowly drew his hands back, smoothing and gathering her hair as he went. When he had the locks gathered at her nape, he made a fist and held it there for her.

She tilted her head, her gaze clashing with his. Blood roared through him, for desire danced in the depths of her eyes. He wound her hair tightly around his fist and slowly, so slowly, lowered his head.

His mouth inches from hers, her sweet breath brushing against his skin, he searched her eyes, vigilant for any sign of hesitation. Ancestors help him, he wanted to crash his mouth onto hers and take. Claim.

Be gentle.

If he spooked her now, there might not be enough time before the spring equinox to mend the error. And a kiss, freely given, could stop there, could it not?

Her eyes fluttered shut, and her face tilted closer. He nearly groaned. Unable to hold off any longer, he closed the distance and skimmed his lips against hers. A barely-there pass, but oh it was as if his body knew sensation for the first time, for the velvety pillow of her lips dragged against his and it felt like *everything*. Urgency pounded through his veins, but he held himself in check.

He cupped the back of her head and brushed his other hand up her jaw, cradling her face. Again, he trailed his lips against hers, this time giving the lower lip a gentle nibble. Her breath escaped her on a gasp, and her mouth parted.

Just one taste.

His skin sizzling with need—need to take her, need to taste her, need to claim her—he brushed his tongue briefly inside her mouth.

So sweet. Like the honey he'd once filched as a lad, but spicier.

He gently stroked, getting lost in her, and she matched his movements. A tiny groan from the depths of her throat inflamed him further. *Mo Chreach.* He held the most delicate and beautiful flower in his hands. Her nectar…intoxicating. The headiness of it all, of finally tasting her, holding her, swamped his senses.

He stepped closer, eager to feel her body against his. His need prodded her belly, and she gasped into his mouth, but instead of pulling away, she increased the urgency of their kiss, her hands digging under his mantle to grab his shoulders.

And then his heart raced even faster, for she moved her hips slightly. *Yes.* She wanted him. He pressed her harder against the wall, trying to still her movements, for he'd not take her for the first time on the keep's walkway. He angled his head and deepened the kiss, which grew headier, more frantic.

And then a *bang* doused him as cold as a bucket of water. He sprang away from her, heart in his throat, and spun around so that he stood between her and the source of the noise.

But then his heart slowed to its normal pace, for 'twas

only the watchmen returning for the rest of their shift.

The sun had set.

He reached for her to escort her below and caught a flash of regret. His chest tightened. And then he cursed himself— his plan had been for *her* to initiate. And he should have stretched matters until *she* kissed *him*.

While he'd accomplished his desire to find locations for her signal towers, he'd ruined his plans by giving in to his desire for *her*.

• • •

"It's coming together." Ashley slid off her horse and peered up at the men who'd been laboring for the last two days on the structure taking shape on top of the hill—their first signal tower. The wind was stronger up here, whipping some strands from her braid and stinging her cheeks.

She adjusted her new mittens, wiggling her fingers inside them. She'd used leather for the palm side, and tartan cloth for the other side, and then lined it with rabbit fur. To keep them around her wrist, she used leather string, but it meant Connall or someone else had to tie them on for her. In a pinch, she used her teeth. She'd craft a better solution, but for now, they worked.

Whenever he put them on her, she straightened, feeling a bit like a boxer having their gloves tied on. Arming herself for battle—a battle against her growing attraction for him and her tenuous hold on her life back in San Francisco.

And she needed whatever metaphorical strength she could grab—she'd been so, *so* ready to have a Highland fling with him, but after she'd finally kissed him?

Oooh boy.

Bad, bad idea.

Because that kiss wasn't just a *kiss*.

And so...*sex*?

Her heart tripped—it wouldn't just be sex. Her fling window had sailed right on past.

Connall stepped up beside her, his arm brushing hers. His horse came to a stop on the other side of him, its head arching down to nibble on the grass. He smiled down at her. "Aye, it is."

The morning after they'd discussed the idea, Connall had been holed up with the council, who immediately agreed and devised a plan. Since it couldn't be purely of wood, like the Roman watchtower, or it would burn to the ground the first time they signaled, they'd had to alter the design. For one thing, the support beams were stouter, because it had to hold up a stone-lined roof.

A line of men trudged up the hill with horses laden with river rocks. She and the elderly women had been scouring the loch and river bank for the last two days and creating piles of the flattest they could find for the men to collect. They still needed more.

However, she and Connall couldn't resist loading up their horses and bringing over the first load so they could see the progress. This was as far up as their horses could go; the rest was a steep climb to the summit. To make it easier to haul the rocks, a relay of men lined the approach, handing up wicker baskets of stone. The entire slope had been cleared of trees, shrub, and fern to make not only the construction easier, but to also provide an unobstructed view to the Sound of Jura. From her leather hide, she'd learned the village of Crinan would later occupy the base of this hill.

The stilts and crossbeams of the tower were already in place, and the workers on the ground fed lumber to those at the top, who were busy lashing them together to create the lookout station.

Connall grinned down at her, pride shining in his eyes,

one of his front braids blowing under his chin from the wind, as if highlighting his strong jaw. He lifted the bags of river rock slung over her horse's back, his muscles bunching under his kilt. "We should be done with this first one in another few days." Her horse sidestepped and seemed to do a wiggle now as if delighting to be free of his heavy burden.

Slinging and arranging the bags around his own shoulders, Connall brought the stones the last couple of yards to the base of the incline, where one of the men took it from him and passed it to the next. Connall conversed with some of the men on the line, who all stared up at the top and nodded, grins wide on all their faces.

It struck her that this was the first time she'd seen many of them smiling. Some were still in mourning from the raid, and this project was helping to lift their spirits, if even only temporarily. It felt *good* to be doing something constructive. Leave a little stamp before she returned to her own time.

She nuzzled her horse's neck, enjoying his earthy scent as well as his warmth against her face.

Connall returned. "They're not reporting any major problems, but I'll need to be returning to supervise with the clearing and cutting of the rest of the timber."

"And I need to get back to hunting suitable river stone." She grinned, and her heart gave an unsettling lurch when he returned her smile.

Since that evening up on the keep, he hadn't tried to make any more moves. While that should have made her new-found resolve easier to keep, it just worked her up even more.

The robotic tones of the Borg sounded in her mind— *Resistance is futile.*

God help her, she furtively eyed his muscles. Those *biceps.* And how he cared for and interacted with his tribe.

"Let's be off, then." He stepped into her space, giving her

a delicious gulp of his rugged scent—leather-spiked musk—
and gripped her waist with his strong hands, lifting her back
onto her horse. He swung onto his mount with a deftness that
still amazed her, and together they carefully picked their way
down the shallower slope of the hill until they were along the
flat ground running between the hills and the open sea. They
were able to move faster here, because the ground was solid.
To her left the narrow strip of ground dropped sharply to the
water below, and on her right rose craggy stretches of granite
walls pocked with weathered shrubs. It was hard to tell how
much time had passed on their way out here, but she guessed
they had about an hour or so ride ahead. As he did earlier on
their journey, he rode behind her to act as guard.

They were about halfway to Dunadd when the wind
picked up, whipping the folds of her tunic and skirts against
her and spraying her with drops of sea water. She glanced to
the western sea, jerking her head to clear away stray hairs—
storm clouds, bruised purple and blue, crowded the horizon.

Dayum. That came out of nowhere.

Connall pulled up alongside, his black hair whipping and
swirling toward her, his horse's ears twitching back and forth.
"There's a cave ahead." He raised his voice to be heard over
the wind. "Your horse will follow mine, but let it find its own
path for there are holes he'll know to avoid. If we hurry, we
can make it before the storm breaks."

With that, he hugged his horse's neck and shot forward,
his mount zigzagging along the ground, dark sand and grass
kicking up behind. She did the same, and her horse needed
no prompting before it broke into a canter. The wind rushed
over her face, the cold stinging her cheeks. Her eyes watered,
but she trusted her horse, relaxing her grip on the reins. Up
ahead, Connall reached a break in the cliff and leaped off his
mount. He disappeared into a crevice and then emerged. She
reined in alongside.

"All is clear inside." He lifted his arms, and she readily fell into them. She was kind of disappointed that he didn't do the whole let-her-body-slide-down-him move, but then again, they were in a hurry.

Before he let her go, he did give her hips a quick squeeze. He grabbed both reins and led their horses inside. She held her leather-lined palm to her forehead to keep the hair from her eyes—the rain was now only a half a mile away, almost to the shoreline. A solid curtain of gray suspended from black clouds, obscuring the horizon.

She hadn't known it rained so much in Scotland until she'd come here. Connall dashed back out. "Collect what wood and tinder you can find."

Gathering firewood was tough with the mittens, but she made a quick pile on the ground and then raked them all onto her skirt and, carefully standing, managed to keep most of it balanced in the folds.

Connall, who was inside the cave when she arrived, threw down his load and scooped up hers just as the first drops of chilled rain hit her back. She hunched over and followed him into the oblong space, shivering. The smell of wet stone and decayed leaves struck her, but it wasn't unpleasant.

He fished flint from his belt pouch. Soon he had a fire blazing and was pulling saddles off the horses. He removed the saddle blankets and arranged them by the fire, facing the entrance.

He held out a hand, and she readily placed her mittened-fingers with his, enjoying his solid strength. His eyes darkened, and he reached up and stroked his knuckles across her cheeks. The gentle touch—it made her tremble.

"You're cold." He snatched his hand away and tugged her to the ground. He unfurled the top half of his kilt and arranged her until she was sitting between his legs, snug up against him with her back to his chest, the kilt draped tight around her shoulders and his knees on either side of her.

"Draw your legs up," he murmured in her ear.

She pulled her knees up to her chest, and he wrapped his legs and arms around her, draping the cloth around them. She hadn't really been that cold, but hell if she was going to protest. The man was like a furnace, and she was never quite warm enough here.

She relaxed into his arms and sighed.

"Better?" he whispered.

She nodded against his chest, feeling treasured.

Outside, the rain beat down, but they were far enough inside that the wind didn't spray droplets onto them or the fire. It looked as if it would keep them trapped for some time. Enough time to…

She'd told him she couldn't be his wife, but damn, she wanted him. And she was tired of resisting the inevitable. She tilted her head, exposing her neck. She would've done more to signal her interest, but he had her wrapped up snug, her arms trapped by his encircling body.

As the fire crackled before them, his chest rose against her back on a deep inhale, and she'd swear she heard a slight rumble. His soft hair brushed her neck, and she held herself very still, careful to not stiffen or shiver, in case he misinterpreted their cause.

Sensual awareness sizzled in the air. Ages seemed to pass before his temple brushed hers. His warm breath fanned her skin, and she hummed her appreciation, since sound was about her only option left. Other than just shouting: "Take me now, dammit."

She held that option in reserve.

Against the small of her back, he stirred and grew hard, and heat flashed through her. He wanted her as much as she did him.

His head shifted, bringing his mouth to juuuust brush

against her cheek.

Then his voice, low and raspy, his breath tickling her ear, increasing the sizzle going all up and down her skin and flashing her blood hot. "Are ye still cold?"

"No," she whispered.

"Are ye scared, then?" She was still trembling, she realized.

"No. Not when I'm with you."

He groaned and tightened his hold. Then his soft lips dragged across the shell of her ear to the pulse along her neck. The kiss—when it came—was so light, she almost didn't feel it. She arched her neck to show him that yes, she wanted *him*.

He skimmed the tip of his tongue down her neck, and she groaned. Where his kilt covered her shoulder, he stopped. He clasped the edge with his teeth and dragged it an inch or so.

Her belly tightened and her breaths came in pants.

God, how could this feel erotic, him exposing just her shoulder like this?

She didn't dare move.

He nuzzled his nose along the exposed skin and inhaled slowly. With alternating licks and kisses, he trailed his mouth back up to her ear.

"I want you." His voice—gruff, gravelly, and oh-so-appealing—sent heat storming through her.

He nipped her earlobe. "I want you very much."

Her body shook. "I...I want you, too," she managed to say, her heart beating so fast she worried she'd die before they had sex.

His sharp inhale rang through the cave, blending with the pelting beats of the rain. He brushed his lips along her ear. "Say it again."

The growled words amped up her desire. No effin' way could she deny him. "God, yes, I want you."

Chapter Eleven

Honest to God, she thought her words would have him whipping her around and getting down to business, but no. He placed another kiss on her neck. Slowly, he stretched his legs out, and then his hands unwound from holding her tight to him until they gripped her waist.

Here we go.

How did guys in the 100s get it on? Even though doggy-style was not usually her favorite position, the idea of him just picking her up and entering her from behind had liquid heat shooting from her chest down to her sex. It fit with the whole alpha-warrior thing he had going on.

But his hands pressed up from her waist, slowly mapping her sides and back down.

No. No-no-no.

This was *bad*.

A quick fuck she could rationalize—she would just *somehow* force it into that little item on her checklist. Highland fling, done. In a *cave*. Bonus!

But this?

Each drag of his mouth across her exposed shoulder, the stubble from his cheek and jaw scraping lightly, deliciously, betrayed his intentions. Just like their kiss at the keep hadn't been *just* a kiss, this—despite their primitive surroundings— wouldn't just be sex. As his mouth traced tantalizing paths all over her neck and shoulders, she trembled—with need and with this new realization settling in.

Oh, she could stop him.

She was sure he would if she asked.

But what had her trembling was a different betrayal—her own effing body and her own effing desire.

She didn't *want* to stop him.

Maybe—she pulled in a sharp breath—maybe she could still come out unscathed.

He gripped her braid, and she gasped and let her legs drop open, stroking her hands down his thighs and earning a groan near her ear, though she couldn't feel anything with her dang mittens on. His mouth and hands roamed, sucked, and licked until she was panting, and every bit of her skin along her shoulder, neck, and breasts was aflame.

Under her skirts, she grew wet, begging for his touch. He stroked back up her waist, and this time when he feathered his fingers across her breasts, he brushed the peaked tips of her nipples. Even through the fabric of her tunic, it felt like a brand, and she jerked against him.

Holy shit. She'd never been this turned on by a man's touch. Her skin was like one big live wire—he could touch her anywhere and she would jump.

God, she wanted to touch him, too. Explore all of his muscles. See what made him shiver. What made him gasp. She pushed her hands up out of the cocoon of his kilt and held them up. "Can you untie me?"

Whoa. Without even doing it on purpose, her voice had come out smoky-low, like some sex-kitten.

Instead of stopping the gentle stroking of her breasts, he leaned forward. From the corner of her eye, his profile came into view, with his lust-laden eyes and aquiline nose.

His hair and braid fell forward on the far side. "Give them here," he grunted, pinching the aching tips of her breasts.

At his order, she brought both up to his face, and he captured one loose end of string with his teeth and pulled. Slowly, every pull and tug echoing the desire building within. All the while, he continued teasing her nipples.

Spellbound, she caught her breath as he did the same to the other mitten. Instead of using his teeth to loosen the final knot on them, he brought his hands up to hers. She closed her eyes in anticipation and clenched her fingers into a fist inside the warm mittens.

When the tugging stopped, giddiness suffused her—now her hands would be free. But he pulled her wrists upward, draping them over his head.

The position pushed her breasts outward. Wha—? She opened her eyes and pulled her arms, but they didn't budge.

OMG.

He'd tied her mittens together.

Her sex clenched and liquid heat shot through her. *Holy shit. Wicked, wicked man.*

Now, with her legs spread wide, her hands captured behind his head, and her chest pushed outward, she felt so vulnerable.

Despite still having all her clothes on.

He skimmed down her forearms to the undersides of her arms, and then those strong fingers came into view as they stroked down until he cupped her jutting breasts. Breasts which were pushing forward and back as her breathing increased pace.

God, just the sight of his strong, capable hands cupping her was enough to make her clench again, but the feel of him holding the heavy weight made her squirm and close her eyes, resting her head against his shoulder.

He molded his chest against her back, and again his arousal gave a big *hello*. She pressed her legs onto his thighs, opening herself wider, feeling deliciously exposed. After a quick tweak of her cloth-covered nipples, the natural fibers abrading her, he stroked down her waist and out to the hem of her skirts. Then he dragged the cloth upward, the rough tips of his fingers brushing the bare skin of her calves.

A soft string of Gaelic burst from him, too low for her to understand, but the cadence threaded into the spell he weaved, quickening her breaths.

Jesus, he was sexy as fuck.

She used his neck as leverage to lift her hips, and he moaned and yanked her skirts free from the tangle of their legs. Now her bare ass was sitting on the saddle blanket, her skirt's fabric pillowed around their legs. His hands disappeared underneath the hem, his fingers skimming down the insides of her thighs. Feeling, but not seeing those fingers brush along her sensitive skin heightened her desire.

Just before he reached where she ached for him most, he brushed back out to her knees. She bucked in frustration and moaned. His breath chuffed in her ear with a soft laugh.

He moved his kilt away from between them and cinched her tight against his bare skin. The heat of his cock practically branded against her backside.

And it was killing her not to touch. Or see.

But somehow it also *thrilled* her.

"Touch me," she pleaded.

His lips moved against her skin. "Who's giving orders?"

He skimmed up under the edge of her tunic top, and she quivered at the first contact of his warm, warrior-rough palms brushing against the soft skin of her stomach. He cupped the heavy weight of her breasts. Not where she'd meant, but would she complain?

Heck no.

He pinched and tweaked her nipples into tight buds, and she brought her legs together, seeking some kind of friction. Heaven help her, she was squirming against him. The longer he stayed away from touching her sex the more antsy she became.

Um, he could check off "foreplay" as done-done-done.

Then he scooped an arm under her knees, gathering her legs together. His other hand reached down and splayed against the backs of her thighs, and he lifted her up like she weighed nothing, her feet dangling in the air. Then his silken hot cock swept across the folds of her sex.

The intimate touch, the promise of pleasure it held, seized and locked her muscles. If she'd felt vulnerable before, it had been nothing on *this*—poised on the precipice of being taken and unable to move, cradled in his hold, his hard length rubbing against her folds.

Not enough pressure on her clit to make her come, but— gawd—it was making her wetter with each stroke. Then on the next pass, he oh so slowly brought her down onto the head, using his hand to guide himself inside. She clenched around the tip, a little *omg-hello-welcome-welcome* hug.

He lowered her an inch, but the position he held her in prevented him from filling her completely. He eased her up again, and back down, his thrusts slow and shallow. What kind of positi—Oh! Because then he shifted her slightly and on the next shallow thrust, the tip of his cock hit her G-Spot.

Holy-shit-she-thought-that-was-a-myth.

She jerked and gasped in his arms, her walls clutching him as sensation zipped all around her veins and along her skin, but concentrating the most where he massaged her G-spot.

She thrashed her head back as he rocked her shallowly

on him, all sensation coalescing in that one spot, tightening and tightening. The feeling of building pressure was different than she'd ever experienced. It was scary and frightening and exhilarating as he kept his relentless pace, and she was completely at his mercy.

Then heat flash-bombed her muscles, her body locked tight, and an orgasm barreled through her so hard she screamed.

Ohmygodohmygodohmygod.

Next thing she knew, she was falling forward, aftershocks sparking and twitching through her, completely spent, her mind going *whatthehellohmyfuckinggod*, her body reeling from the aftermath of her very first G-spot orgasm. She braced herself with her hands on the saddle blanket, still trapped in the mittens.

Her skirts swished over her back as he lifted them, and a hand gripped her hip, the weight of it solid, hot, and very much signaling he was in control. His other hand slipped under her tunic top, the rough skin of his fingers and palms tracing up the back of her spine and down. She trembled, and on the next stroke up his hand pressed against her, and she followed his lead, leaning her shoulders down.

So doggie style, then. Instead of feeling used in this position, a primal surge of lust blazed its way through her veins. So male. So take-charge. She had no idea that turned her on. But he'd made sure she'd come first, and she couldn't say that about her only other sexual partner before this.

She rested her cheek against her mittened hands. In the flickering firelight, her Highlander was on his knees behind her, his powerful chest lifting and falling in deep, controlled breaths.

He'd removed his shirt, and his kilt lay in haphazard spills around his waist. His whole body was tensed as if he were holding himself in check, which meant she could see every line of his muscles and his six-pack abs. Dark eyes veiled, his attention shifted between his hands stroking her back and her hip to her bare ass pointing right at him.

The erotic sight... Her stomach dipped, and gooseflesh spread across her arms and the back of her neck.

From this angle, his cock was hidden from view, but just the anticipation of him thrusting inside her had arousal surging through her. She'd swear she grew wetter the longer he drew this out, the cool air of the cave and the storm kissing her bared sex. Then his eyes flicked to hers, and she caught her breath; they flared with heat and longing and barely restrained power. As he held her gaze, he moved his hand by her hip down until his blunt fingers slipped through her short curls and slicked across her folds.

He brought his fingers to his mouth and sucked them clean. He closed his eyes and moaned.

She clenched again as understanding flooded her, just as swift and powerful as a fresh wave of desire.

That action...

The slow methodical way he was taking her...

He was *claiming* her.

Every step creating a path to making her fully and completely his—entering her that first time in shallow thrusts to make her come from a G-spot orgasm, to tasting her, to... whatever he was about to do next.

A flutter of panic at the idea that she was being tied to him more than she'd bargained for signaled from deep within, but it was too weak to overcome her overwhelming desire for this man.

Then, his attention fixed on her, those fingers popped from his mouth and disappeared behind her, and she knew by the rhythmic tightening of his forearm and biceps, he was slowly stroking himself. Then the hand on her back eased forward until it gripped her shoulder, his strong fingers just inches from her face but hidden by the cloth of her tunic.

Then. Oh then…he thrust. Thrust into her hard and sure, bucking her forward.

She dropped her forehead to a mitten and gasped. Oh holy altar to all penises, this man was large. And she was tight and it had been so long, he didn't fully enter despite how wet she was. Heat seared her insides as he stretched her.

He eased his hips back, his cock leaving her in a slow drag, the friction of which was *insane*. Then he tightened his grip on her shoulder and thrust back inside, plunging farther this time.

Deliberate. Purposeful.

The first full claiming of her as he worked his hard length deeper with each thrust until with a shout, he slammed back into her, fully seated.

Her breath tore from her, and she bit her lip, afraid she'd start babbling about how incredible he felt inside her, filling her fully for the first time. How *right* it felt. How that scared her senseless and could he go back to thrusting so she could pretend they were just fucking?

Instead, he was still. So still.

What was he—? She placed her chin on her upper arm to turn and look, but stopped. Because oh-my-God-did-she-know that just looking at him right now might pull her in deeper into his orbit.

Fuuuuck.

Open your eyes. He's just a man.

She relented. But, oh, what a man. His eyes were closed, his bottom lip between his teeth, his head dipping back slightly, highlighting the strong column of his neck. His Adam's apple bobbed on a swallow. Then, barely perceptible except she was watching him so closely, enthralled, his whole body trembled and then stilled.

That he seemed to also mark this moment, relish it,

melted a part of her into a holy-shit-you're-amazing goo. Then he lowered his head, his eyes dark with need. Never taking his eyes from hers, he eased out, his hand gripping and massaging her shoulder and the other kneading her butt cheek.

The moment stretched, then snapped as he rammed forward. Then their movements were frantic as each searing stroke awakened a deepening throb of pleasure where they were joined, until it became all she could see, all she could feel, all she could hear. But sweet relief remained poised, right at the brink, swelling her, threatening her, and she whimpered and quaked with need.

Then he licked his finger. The cool shock of the wet tip flicking her nub—that was all it took. Scorching pleasure cascaded through her, rushing through her veins, and now she *did* close her eyes because *holy shit*. She shook and shook and shook as convulsions wracked her.

His movements stuttered. "Ashley," he whispered, his voice bouncing off the cave's walls, wonder and need filling out the vowels. Never had her name sounded so...laden with awe.

Then he became frenzied, less controlled, and the solid weight of his chest covered her as he drove into her one more time. He bit her shoulder on a moan, and his length kicked and throbbed inside her walls, the heat of his orgasm a delicious searing.

His cock eased slightly out and back in, and he curled his hand around to her stomach and tugged her tighter against his hips as if he couldn't get close enough for a final thrust.

She gulped quick breaths, her heart beating so hard it pounded in her ears and throat. She collapsed onto the blanket, and he eased off to her side, groaning. He rolled onto his back, pulling her with him. She gladly curled into his side and fought to catch her breath, her arms tucked up against his chest, since they were still tied together.

The intensity of the moment clutched her senses, clutched her throat. To her horror, tears welled and her breathing hitched.

No.

She swallowed the hot tears, the hot panic. She inhaled slowly. Pushed her breath back out.

It was *not* phenomenal. Nope.

It was just exactly what she'd wanted, and now she could go back to her own time.

Yep. Go back a satisfied woman. Go back knowing what sex *should* feel like.

She repeated that lie to herself as she soaked in his warmth and masculine scent. And his sweetness as he snuggled her tighter against him and kissed the top of her head. Then he tugged on her wrist, and she brought them into view. A slight smile on his face, he gently worked his fingers on the knot until her mittens were unlaced.

Then she shook them off and did what she'd been dying to do ever since she'd first seen him back in San Francisco, and even more so today—she skimmed her palm up his abs and across the chiseled chest and cupped his powerful bicep. Her fingers barely reached halfway around.

See? This is just physical.

That was all the energy she had left, and her eyes drifted shut.

But would it be so bad to stay here, with him?

I'm so screwed.

· · ·

Ashley's grip around his bicep loosened, but not the grip the woman had around his heart.

As he lay there, said heart beating from the exertion, an

odd mixture of triumph and exhilaration poured through his veins.

Aye, he'd known their joining would be unlike anything he'd ever experienced. But one could still be overcome, and a bit in awe, by the *shape* an expected experience took.

He'd gained her affections—gained her as his wife for true—by exercising patience. When she'd uttered the words, "I want you," their sweet tones filling the cave, he never knew such joy. For such a woman as *her*, to desire *him*.

He wanted her to have no doubt as to their equal participation, even as he set about claiming her fully. As *his*. He'd yet to bring her request before the council, and now that she'd become his, there'd be no need—she *trusted* him now.

But as her breathing evened, and his own finally calmed, he felt a new truth. He was *hers*, irrevocably and completely.

And while that weakness should shock him, should *scare* him... It didn't.

Chapter Twelve

Two days later, Connall reined in his horse outside the stables on the lowest terrace, now completely rebuilt from the fire. Rònan forked fresh hay into piles around the outside run, but Connall barely greeted the man in his haste.

Ever since that feverish encounter with his wife in the cave, he was starved for her. Starved for running his hands along those sweet curves. Starved for seeing her face when she found her pleasure. Starved for, aye, the cuddling she loved to indulge in afterward.

Oh, he'd had her again. And again. Implanting his essence deep inside his wife. Implanting all the burgeoning feelings inside her that he dared not utter aloud. But it was never enough. That first night in the bed she finally let him share with her, they'd made love by the hearth fire, and the next day, without saying it was their plan, they'd brought a load of stones to the build site for their midday break. And stopped at the cave, though there was no storm.

This morning, after they'd parted to attend to their many chores, he'd sneaked out to their cave with the softest furs he possessed to make her more comfortable. He'd also searched for the clever pin she'd crafted for him, but as yet had not found it. He'd noticed it missing several days ago and it bothered him that he'd been so careless as to lose something she'd made.

His loins stirred in anticipation of finding her and beholding her beautiful face upon seeing his gift of soft hides in their cave.

He rubbed down his horse and put away the tackle, making sure there were fresh oats for the beast, and then, breath quickening in excitement, he worked his way around the incline, aiming for the kitchen where she'd most likely be.

But as he reached the main courtyard, he stopped. He'd been so keen on seeing his wife, it only struck him now—with every villager crowded into the courtyard—that the terraces had been devoid of their faces, their chatter. He strode up to the edge. "What is amiss?"

"Nothing that we know of," Sionn the blacksmith replied. "But there's a Roman inside."

A Roman? "Just the one?"

Sionn nodded.

Odd. He knew from his father that the earlier visitation had been a whole retinue of guards, along with a handful of emissaries and their attendants.

He glanced at the door to the kitchens, where Ashley was working, and grimaced. He blew out a frustrated breath—their pleasure would have to wait. After pushing inside the keep, he waited a moment for his eyes to adjust to the darker interior. At first he didn't see any Roman. With a jolt he realized his mistake, for there was a stranger in the grouping around the hearth, but he wasn't dressed like a Roman.

In fact, if Connall had been asked, he'd have guessed the visitor was another tribesman, except he lacked the telltale blue ink that marked a warrior come-of-age. His father waved him into their circle, and Connall slipped into a gap.

His father raised a hand, indicating the stranger. "This is Nonus Octavius Vibianus, who has only now arrived with his commander's tidings."

Connall nodded to the man. "A hundred thousand welcomes to Dunadd."

Easily as tall as himself, Vibianus, however, wasn't a warrior. Wiry but not unhealthy. And while the angles of his features and warmer tones of his skin marked him from another land, his clothes and the styling of his hair were like his own people.

"You aren't dressed like a Roman."

Vibianus shook his head, his temple braids swinging. "I'm an arcani."

He frowned at the unfamiliar word, even though the rest of the words were in his own tongue. Unlike all the other Romans he'd encountered, this man needed no interpreter.

"It means 'secret ones.' We're charged by the emperor to interact with the tribes between this wall and the one to the south. Sometimes we act as scouts. Or, in this instance, as a ready messenger."

His father turned to him, his face grave. "Our part of the alliance is to be paid sooner rather than later, it seems."

The arcani supplied the rest. "Your people will need to muster a force to send to Bearsden in five days' time for a fight against the Caledonians. We'd hoped to bribe them into peace, but they are recalcitrant. It's time we marched north."

Though he relished a fight, an unfamiliar emotion settled in his gut.

Regret.

He glanced in the direction of the kitchens again, as if he could see through several walls. Then he briefly dropped his head.

Regret that he'd have to leave his wife so soon.

And then he brought himself to his full height and faced this arcani and his fate. A lashing of anger tightened his shoulders. Anger that an emperor he never met could take him away from her.

He ground his teeth and willed his hands to unclench from the tight fists he'd formed, pushing the swirling emotions down. It was time to act as a warrior and protector for his people.

· · ·

Ashley snuggled up against Connall's chest, the sweat from their lovemaking cooling on her skin. The hearth fire sizzled and popped behind them and lent a pinkish glow to the hut's interior. Every day since their first encounter in the cave, they'd made love there on their return trips from the site, as well as every night in their bed.

She bit her lip and traced her finger around his nipple. He was an awesome mix of carnal and sweet. Unlike her assumption in the cave, doggy-style was *not* the extent of his knowledge. That night he'd taken her slowly, face-to-face, as he kissed and stroked her unrelentingly to a mind-blowing orgasm.

More and more she caught herself daydreaming about what it would be like to stay here. Then she'd shake herself for even thinking it, because it was dangerous, on *so* many levels, to stay. Even though her life had sucked in San Francisco, she had access to hot showers, toothpaste, and modern medicine. She didn't regret fleeing that shithole of a situation, but couldn't she have fled to a safer spot in her *own* time?

Thank God she'd been taking the pregnancy-prevention herbs. But that was one of the dangers, wasn't it? Besides the pregnancy itself, the herbs might not work. And then where would she be?

It had been easy enough to eat the seeds of the Queen Anne's Lace she'd bought in Bearsden with no one wiser, but the stash was dwindling. And it wasn't like she could go to Eithne and say, oh hey, I know the tribe wants babies, but do you have Queen Anne's Lace to spare?

And even if she could think of some way of asking Mungan, he'd already left this morning after only two short days at Dunadd. That meant one full moon had now passed, and the next would potentially see her tether weakened.

And a new danger emerged, driving the point home—Connall was leaving in the morning to fight in a friggin' *battle*.

Ever since the Roman had visited four days ago, Connall had been as thoughtful and diligent as ever, but a slight wall had arisen. She tried not to be hurt, because she got it—his mind was focused on the upcoming fight. Even now, he wasn't quite *here* with her, despite the amazing sex they'd just had.

Her throat swelled as tears threatened, and she swallowed hard.

Oh God, she cared for him.

And some barbarian could slice right into the skin she was touching. She stopped stroking his nipple and buried her face in his chest, hugging him tight.

His arm encircled her. "Shhh. All will be well." He kissed the top of her head.

"You can't *know* that." Dammit, that had come out high-pitched, though it was muffled because her face was pressed into his body.

Swallowing her fear for him, she straightened up on her elbows and pushed her hair out of her face.

"How long will you be gone? Will you be back before…" Wow, just even voicing the idea that she had a deadline looming was hard. A deadline where she had to decide whether to remain here—with him—or go back to her old life. A deadline that was twenty-four days away.

And when had her friggin' brain—or God, her heart—morphed it into a *decision*? When had she stopped seeing it as a given that she'd go back?

She shivered at the implication—and the fear for him blended into a fear for herself. Was this the magic at work? Was she accepting her life here? With him?

Pain flashed briefly in his eyes. "I will be back before the spring equinox. I swear it. Even if I have to leave before the battle is waged. The Romans will not miss one man." His eyes searched hers. "Have you made a decision, then?"

There was one part of her life here that wasn't quite ideal. While he was a complete marshmallow when they were alone, he tended to be all he-man-I'm-in-charge when they interacted with his people, which was annoying as hell.

"If I decide to stay and be your wife, you need to treat me as an equal."

His forehead creased, but he nodded.

She narrowed her eyes at him, because that had been too easy. He probably didn't really understand what that meant yet. But he would. His ass needed to be woke.

When he came back. Because that's all she'd allow herself to believe.

He stroked a finger across her cheek. "I will return. Do not fear for me."

She smiled but knew it was tremulous. She leaned forward and brushed her lips across his, needing to taste him again. Taste him so she could memorize him and this moment.

At first their kiss was languid, a bittersweet expression of parting. And that effin' wall was still there, keeping him separate from her.

Fuck that wall. She poured herself into the kiss, desperate to break through. Desperate to make him not forget her. Desperate for him to want her enough that he'd return alive.

And then their kiss grew heated as his hands cradled her

face and he took control. Even though they'd just made love, urgency built within her again.

Yes! One last chance to have him again. One last chance to break through to the man she'd been starting to fall for before he left for a friggin' *battle*.

He flipped her onto her back. "Do not move."

She smirked at him. "Real men ask nicely." It had become their thing whenever he gave an order. Though most of the time it was because he truly needed to learn.

He smiled. "Real men know how to give orders."

This time he made love to her with a new urgency. And as she cried out her release and he stilled inside her with his own, his eyes flicked to hers.

And *there* he was. The depths of his green eyes no longer eerily flat.

He was here in this moment with her.

But he'd be gone in the morning.

Several days later, Ashley caught herself. As happened so often lately, she'd been doing an activity and had just...stopped.

This time it was a shout that startled her into awareness, and she found she was in the middle of churning butter, her fingers gripping the plunger.

She dropped her hands. Eithne, who'd been stirring a pot of stew by the hearth fire, put down the ladle and stood, wiping her hands on her skirt apron. A frown creased her pillow-soft forehead. "I wonder what's amiss?"

"I don't know." Her tone was snappish, and she winced, as Eithne had been nothing but nice to her. But the truth was, she was pining. Pining for that dang Highlander. And eaten up with worry. Last night as she'd lain in their cold bed, brushing her hands across the space where he usually slept, she realized she was now spending more time thinking about him than of her old life in San Francisco.

She stood, ready to go out the door to find out what was going on, because the noise had only grown. However, one of the younger warriors tasked with building the signal towers rushed in, his chest heaving. He steadied himself against the doorframe.

"There's been an accident."

Her heart clenched. Connall!

But no...it would be too soon for his return. "What happened?"

"Teàrlach slipped while hauling rocks up the signal tower ladder. He fell, and the basket of stone fell, too, nearly crushing him."

She gripped the door frame, leaning into it—relief that Connall was unharmed whacked aside by guilt for feeling relief and then worry for Teàrlach making her a tad unsteady. "Where is he?"

He glanced over his shoulder, his brown braids swinging in an arc. "They're bringing him in on a litter." He brought his hand down over his face and then looked at her, his eyes pleading. "Do ye know how to heal? Our healer was taken in the raid, and Mungan is still absent."

"I thought you had more than one druid?"

"Yes, but druids have different specialties—the one who trained as a healer is gone."

Her stomach turned queasy as the responsibility he was hoping to place on her hit.

Her? A healer? She started to shake her head but stopped. "Not by training, but I can try divining. There's no guarantee I can find the answer, or even if I do, that I'll know how to apply the knowledge." Holy hell—she could hear her siblings laughing, and possibly her dad as well. *They expect you to do what now?* Her—the baby in the family everyone called spoiled.

Her—the coddled wife of an investment banker.

Her—the overworked coder slash Etsy shop crafter trying to pay off that scoundrel's legal debts and running from his illegal ones.

But the man stepped forward. "It's more hope than we have now, isn't it?" He sprang through the door, speaking over his shoulder. "Follow me. They're bringing him to the courtyard now."

Eithne shooed her out, and Ashley ran after the warrior. A trail of men worked their way up the incline. They'd be here in minutes. "I'll be right back. Let me get my divining leather."

She dashed down the slope to the hut she shared with Connall. What if the man was so severely injured nothing could help him? What if she couldn't think of the right search terms to come up with an answer? What if she *failed?*

Her hands trembled as she grabbed her divining equipment. It *had* to work, it *had* to. People looked up symptoms all the time on Google. Okay, sometimes that led down a rabbit hole of increasingly worse diagnoses, but she needed to keep her head.

She darted back up the slope. *So,* so *glad that's easier now.*

She arrived just as the men were lowering the wounded man onto an open grassy area near the north wall. One of the men was completely naked, because they'd used his kilt to carry Teàrlach.

Averting her eyes, she rushed up to the group and the men parted, making room for her. She knelt beside Teàrlach. Sweat plastered his dark-red hair to his skull and dirt streaked his too pale face. She quickly scanned his chest and limbs but couldn't see any obvious injury. "Where is he hurt?"

They pointed to his ankle, which was already beginning to swell.

Teàrlach spat. "It's only been turned."

"Then why did ye go fainting the moment you were putting weight on it?" Sionn asked.

Oh God, she had no clue how to tell if it was broken or sprained. She closed her eyes and thought of how she'd search for this on Google. As a question formed, she gathered a handful of dirt and threw it across the leather. It took several tries to narrow down and adjust her questions while she also had him move his foot. Her audience stole glances at her while they looked on their friend or neighbor with concern.

Please work.

"It's just a sprain," she concluded. "He'll need to stay off it for several days and keep it elevated."

"This means we'll have to stop working on the signal tower," one said.

"Why?" she asked.

"With half our warriors off fighting for the Romans, we didn't dare send too many to work on the project. It's why he was injured—too few to help."

She turned to the guy who'd alerted her. "So you've been without a healer since the raid?"

He nodded.

"Do we have any onions? We could make a poultice to help with the swelling."

"No. We're out and haven't scavenged for more."

"I wish the council would have granted my request to speak with them. This is exactly the kind of thing a woman would prioritize and bring up."

An older man she knew sat on the council cocked his head at her. "What do ye mean, lass?"

She shook her head in frustration. "I'm sure the men on the council are aware we're low on onions, but they might not realize they—"

"No. I mean what request?"

She sat back on her haunches, willing herself to remain

calm because it was probably just her Universal Translator not getting her meaning across. "Connall said he'd ask you and the other members of the council if I could address them."

Several people around her gasped, but the older man gave nothing away in his expression. "Interesting request. But Connall never asked this of us."

He *what*?

Disbelief, followed by a shot of anger, surged through her, and she plopped down onto her butt.

Ooh, if he wasn't off fighting in a damn battle, she'd hunt him down and give him a battle of her own.

He'd *promised*.

A frustrated grunt as Teàrlach tried to sit up and failed brought her focus back to him. She placed a hand on his shoulder and squeezed. Color was beginning to return to his face, which she assumed was a good sign.

"Does he live with anyone here?" she asked the concerned faces peering down at her.

An older woman stepped forward. "I'm his grandmother."

"All right. Make sure he gets plenty of rest and that you keep him off that foot for several days and keep it elevated. I'll check in with you every day, but you need to understand I'm not a healer."

"You look like one to me," she replied. "I'm grateful to you. He's my only family left." She blinked, and her lips rolled together.

The others murmured, but all she saw reflected back at her was awe, gratefulness, or respect.

Phew.

As she packed up her divining leather, though, she couldn't find pleasure in her small victory here. All she could think about was the fact that Connall had *not* talked to the council.

How could she live with a man who didn't respect her?

Chapter Thirteen

Ashley wiped her forehead with the back of her hand, careful to keep the flour off her face. Light from a rare sunny day poured into the kitchen from the slits in the walls. Man, kneading dough was tough work. Forget doing upper arm reps on a cable curl, this shit would get her Michelle Obama biceps in no time.

Ever since she'd found out Connall hadn't talked to the council, she'd been chatting with the women she worked with every day, getting a feel for their opinions. One of them had told her early this morning that the council would be meeting today, when the sun reached the zenith. Which was soon.

"Are you in?" she asked.

Eithne nodded—her normally gentle face firmed into battle-axe mode—and set aside the supplies someone had just brought in from the storage room. Ashley turned to Affraic, who also nodded, her narrow head matching her narrow shoulders and hips, though Ashley had learned she could be just as tough as Eithne. They circled down to the lower terraces and collected some of the other older women who'd also agreed to Ashley's plan—crash the council.

They climbed up the incline, six of them total, exhilaration and excitement powering her muscles. Exhilaration at the prospect of demanding they have a say and excitement at the possible changes this would effect for the tribe.

At the closed door, she turned to the others. Worry clouded their eyes, but also determination. "Ready?" she asked.

They nodded. She held out her fist, and they stared at it, foreheads crinkled. "Put your fists on top of mine."

One age-spotted hand followed another until they looked at her with "what now?" expressions.

"One for all," she said, pausing, waiting for them to finish, but of course they didn't know the rest. "And all for one, that's what you're supposed to say," she finished with a mutter. She was about to pull her fist away, but several piped up, though not at the same time, so the impact was a bit anticlimatic, "And all for one."

She smiled. "We'll work on that, all right?"

Girding her proverbial loins, she pulled open the door and stepped inside. Torches set into the walls cast a yellowish glow over a round table filled with older men. Conversation sputtered to a stop as the council members twisted in their seats to stare, their faces a mixture of surprise and puzzlement.

"Here goes nothing," she whispered.

Confident her compatriots were following, she strode inside until they were arrayed in front of the assembly.

Connall's father stood—Eachern, she'd learned his name was. "What is the meaning of this? We're in the middle of council."

She raised her chin. "That's why we're here. We'd like to address this body."

Shock registered across the chief's face, and the other men muttered. He glared.

Ha. Bring on the Intimidation Tactics, mister.

If he wanted them to leave, he'd have to bodily remove her. She wouldn't slink away.

His head bowed slightly. "Have your say."

Oh wow, okay. Heart beating like mad, she said, "I'd like to request the council to add several of the older women into their number."

Now the rest of the men stood, but Eachern motioned for them to sit back down. They obeyed, but their eyes trained on her, some narrowed, some wide with curiosity.

The chief clasped his hands behind his back and widened his stance, facing her fully. "And why do you wish this?"

"Because it's not right that women aren't represented on the council."

"The men represent them well enough. We see to the needs of everyone in the tribe. If some have concerns to be addressed, they can ask their menfolk."

"But they can't adequately represent them. It's not possible."

"Why not?"

"Because there are some issues that are unique to women. And does every woman in your tribe have a male family member? What about those who don't? We can also bring a unique perspective to whatever issues you face. We contribute to the welfare of the tribe just as much as the men do, and we should have a vote on the council." She took a deep breath at getting that all out. She'd memorized what she wanted to say, knowing she might only have one chance to lay it all out there.

Shouts erupted. Each seemed determined to make their opinion, and voice, the loudest, and so none of them were heard clearly.

"Gentlemen," she said, stepping forward. She waved her arms. "Can we get the discussion back on track?"

But none paid her any attention. She lowered her arms. It was pointless. They needed time.

She didn't have much to give them, but she'd made her point. The other women looked at her with wide eyes, and some with tremulous smiles.

No. *They'd* made their point. Together.

She turned her back on the men and silently marched to the door. Once outside, Eithne fell back against the closed door and exclaimed, her voice breathless, "Oh my, that was exciting. I almost peed myself."

"Eithne," Affraic chided.

"Well, I didn't. So no harm done."

They all laughed at that. When their laughter died down, they turned to her. "What next?" Eithne asked. It was a heady feeling having them—*anyone*—look to her for guidance.

Ashley contemplated the closed door, the men behind it no doubt still shouting at each other, completely unaware that they'd left. "I don't know what they'll decide, but I know *our* next step."

"What's that?" another asked.

She faced the other women. "Until they get their panties unwound, we should form our own council. The six of us. We can discuss what needs we have and work to resolve them however we can."

Eithne smiled. "I'm unsure of what these panties are, but the rest sounds like a grand idea."

A head bobbed into view from the terrace lower down, and when the newcomer fully appeared and caught sight of her, he made straight for her.

"Can you do a divination for me?"

"I can try." More and more of late, different members of the tribe approached her to divine something, and her reputation as an oracle grew.

It was thrilling to have such value, to be useful, but what

would happen if she left?

As she followed the man down the slope, with the vast landscape as her only handrails, an odd feeling stole over her, and goose bumps danced along her skin. This was so *exactly* opposite of her old life in San Francisco.

Sure, she felt useful—a bit—with her tech job, but mostly she was drowning, unable to work fast enough to rid herself of her ex-husband's debts.

But that life felt more and more like a dream. *This* felt more and more like her reality.

• • •

Connall nodded to a guard along the perimeter of the Roman encampment and worked his way through the maze of caltrops, an earthenware jar of precious oil in his palm. He glanced back over his shoulder. Not for the first time, he marveled at the Roman army's efficiency. All day, they'd marched, and when they stopped, they'd erected a village of goat-hide tents in neat rows along an east-facing slope and dug an encircling trench for protection. All before they'd bedded down for the night.

Work that would be for one night only, according to the commander, Silanus, for they would continue their march northward before the morning was over. Word from the Roman scouts relayed that the enemy would be met by midday.

Silanus had also gifted him with this expensive oil made from olives, whatever those were—a rare commodity, he was told, that had traveled from a land so distant their vegetation and climate were different.

When he received it, his first thought had been to give it to Ashley, and he wondered if she valued the oil from olives and whether she would be pleased with him for bringing it.

And that's when he knew it was the perfect sacrifice. Earlier, the Romans had gathered around a stone altar and poured wine over a hot brazier. As the wine sparked and hissed into the air, the soldiers lifted their hands to the sun, their heads covered, and prayed to some god named Mithras.

He would feel better if he did a proper sacrifice, however. Up ahead, the river rushed along, cutting through the rocky landscape, its waters jumping and frothing in its eagerness and fervor. Connall smiled. The goddess of these waters would be strong indeed. He picked his way upstream until he reached a particularly lively spot and knelt on a patch of grassy shore. He held the jar up in offering and bowed his head, sending a prayer to the river goddess that his men would fight brave and true and all would return safely to their hearths.

When he finished, he strode into the onrushing water, ignoring the chill hitting his calves, and lodged the sacrifice as best he could amongst the rocks. That accomplished, he sloshed back to the shore and sought Silanus to receive instructions for his men.

The Roman, who'd been leaving his tent, motioned forward. "Follow me. This is an opportunity for you to learn more of our ways." Thankfully, the leader of this army spoke his own tongue.

"Should I gather my men?"

"Not necessary. It will take but a moment. You can relay it back to them."

Some of their ways were intriguing, and he avidly observed those which would help his tribe. But some were altogether strange. At a clearing, another Roman squatted by an iron cage. Inside were several chickens.

Silanus spoke. "It's a portable auspice kit."

"Auspice?"

He nodded. "We never go into battle without divining the outcome."

Ah. This Connall understood, though the methods were different. How were the chickens to divine anything?

The diviner placed pieces of cake along the ground and stepped back, his expression grave. Frowning, Connall studied the cage, but the chickens only poked their wee necks through the bars and partook of the meal.

The diviner raised his chin, a satisfied cast to his features, and said something in their tongue.

Silanus slapped him on the back. "Victory. Let us break camp and meet the enemy." Conversation started up as the Romans departed, their expressions ranging from happy to smug.

Connall stared at the cage. "How could you divine that from what we just saw?"

Silanus folded his arms, pride evident in his thrust-back shoulders and widened stance. "The sacred chickens ate the cake and allowed bits of grain to fall from their beaks."

"And that is good?"

"Very."

The diviner carefully draped a cloth over the cage and lifted it from the ground with extreme care. Connall had his doubts of the Roman method, but Silanus and the Romans seemed well pleased. He'd have to take their confidence as his own.

As efficiently as they'd encamped, the Romans broke it down. Knowing they'd fight this day, Connall and his men circled around their campfire and brewed wild thyme for vigor and courage. When the call to march sounded, Connall and his men joined the middle ranks. Excitement hummed through his veins at the prospect of battle and a sure victory, for they had both his sacrifice to his own goddess and the divination of the Romans on their side, if their method of divination were valid.

Soon, he would fight.

Soon, he'd return home to Dunadd. To Ashley.

Ashley.

A pang cracked through his battle-focus. He'd found it increasingly difficult to suppress thoughts of Ashley back at Dunadd alone, without him by her side. Perhaps he'd been wrong to deny himself—if he allowed thoughts of her to have free rein, its power could dwindle. So, he indulged on the rest of their march by contemplating what she might be doing at this moment. Did she think of him during his absence?

Would she choose to remain?

Had he made the right decision in denying her request to address the council? At the time, he'd justified his decision by recalling what happened the last time he'd advocated on behalf of a woman. But as the days passed, he began to think that was flimsy indeed. For that had been when he was but a child.

No. He'd been right to deny it. In time, she'd learn to trust that he had her best interests at heart.

He touched the spot on his kilt where her pin would normally be, still absent, for he'd not been able to locate it before his departure. And he tried not to let the Romans' superstitions rub off on him that the only tangible piece of her he possessed was no longer in his keeping.

The acrid tang of spilled blood infused Connall's nostrils as he swung his body around and blocked the blow from a charging Caledonian. His left arm holding his targe vibrated, the attacker's sword glancing off with a dull scrape. Steam rose from the ground, the result of warm blood hitting cool air. He adjusted his stance. It would not do to slip in the mud and gore.

His men, all naked as was their custom, were in tight

formation around him as they cleaved their way—along with the Romans—through the enemy. Like his own people, the enemy battled naked, but they also smeared their bodies in woad-dyed paste, streaking them in grisly blue swirls.

Quickly dispatching his attacker, Connall pushed forward. Their main task was accomplished, however. The Romans had wanted his men to counter the first wave who attacked on chariots, for the defense against such an attack was more familiar to them than to the Romans.

The whole time he fought, the words of Ashley's first foretelling echoed through his bones—*ware the Painted People at the cragged rock*—for such a formation loomed over the battlefield from a nearby hill.

Another blue-streaked warrior charged, sword raised, his face twisted with a hate that seemed more personal than mere blood lust. Puzzled, Connall blocked the man's powerful swing with his targe, and then kicked the man's knee. His opponent stumbled but cocked his arm back for another swing. It was then that Connall recognized the man—the Caledonian who picked on warriors smaller than him. The one he'd taught a lesson to back at Bearsden.

Renewed strength and energy suffused his muscles as he met and countered each move of the warrior. Though evenly matched, the Caledonian tended to favor his right side. As soon as an opening appeared, Connall took it—a feint to his right, a blow to the man's head with his targe, and then a quick slice across the warrior's throat.

He took no pleasure in ending the man's life. It was part of their tribe's survival. The Romans were their new allies, and these were enemies of the Romans. It was as simple as that.

A persistent sting registered, and he glanced down. Red trickled down his chest. His own. The sight renewed his determination. Taking advantage of a rare lull in the battle, he quickly stabbed his sword in the ground and daubed his fingers into the blood. Then he drew a sacred circle on his forehead and a jagged line across his chest.

Half of battle was intimidation.

He yanked his sword from the ground and swung around at the sound of another enemy yelling his approach.

Letting the full fury of his blood lust power his voice, Connall lifted his face and shouted, "We are The Horse People. Be ware!"

He blocked his attacker's swing and worked quickly—more quickly than usual—for blood loss would eventually weaken him, and he'd be of no use to anyone.

Parry, thrust, block, he and his blood-spattered warriors relentlessly cut forward, but his breathing grew labored. His men, still all standing, gathered tighter and switched to defense. His mind grew dizzy.

Ashley will not be glad for this turn of events.

Chapter Fourteen

The long, low wail of a horn pushed its deep notes into Ashley's consciousness, startling her awake. What the hell? It paused and sounded again, urgent and dire. She threw the blankets off and lurched out of bed, stumbling in the early dawn light barely illuminating her hut.

The cold air slapped her bare legs and arms. Shivering, she yanked on her tunic top, skirts, and warm mantle, stuffing her feet into the fur-lined leather contraptions they called shoes.

Skipping the tedious process of donning her mittens, she tucked her hands into the relative warmth of her arm pits and pushed her door open with a shoulder.

The horn's urgent tones blared louder now that she was outside. "What's happening?" she asked her neighbor Fionnuala—an elderly woman who kept to herself and had also stepped outside.

Fionnuala motioned downslope. "It's the men. They're returning from battle."

Ashley's heart lurched. Connall!

She hustled into the trickle of people heading down, the nervous energy rushing through her making her movements jerky. She pushed and twined her way through until she reached where the bulk of their people were lining up on either side of the path leading to the loch. A string of battle-weary men plodded up the incline, so Ashley scooted to the side, nudging her way between two other villagers.

As the warriors approached, she eagerly scanned their faces for the one she wanted to see most, but he wasn't in the front where he should be. Worry and fear became a sharp taste on her tongue.

Most were on foot, having just disembarked down at the docks, but near the back, a figure sat hunched forward on a horse. Black hair fluttered behind him, the familiar, sharp cheekbones and proud nose set in a face paler than usual. Dread slithered through her heart.

"Connall!"

At her screech, all heads turned to her, and she dashed down the slope. He raised his head, his face creased in pain. When recognition dawned, he straightened and his features smoothed.

She rushed to his side, hopping sideways to keep up with the horse's gait. "Connall, are you all right?"

The stubborn man nodded, but his hand came away from his side and clenched into a fist on his thigh. Revealing a makeshift bandage, bloody and caked with grime, wrapped around his torso, just visible behind the folds of his kilt.

Knowing he wouldn't want her to fuss over him in front of everyone, she restricted herself to reaching up and squeezing his thigh. "You're home now," she whispered so only he could hear.

Gratefulness flared in his eyes so briefly, she wondered if she'd imagined it.

Man, she wanted to drag him off that damn horse and

simultaneously kiss him, shake him, and swaddle him up in cotton balls. Instead she wrapped her arm around his calf and walked proudly beside him. Tension hummed through her, and it seemed to take forever to make their way up the incline as the villagers welcomed him and the warriors back home.

At their hut, Connall stiffly reined in his horse and slid to the ground, his movements slow as if moving through molasses. He stood erect in front of her, his face unreadable.

It unnerved her. Why didn't he move? She nearly vibrated with the need to hug him, but she was constrained by his strange stance. He was home, though. And alive. She should be happy about that.

Domnall, who'd been walking on Connall's other side, came around. "I'll help him to your hearth."

Help him?

And it was only then she noticed the light sheen of sweat coating his skin. His unfocused gaze.

Connall swayed slightly, and Domnall caught him up and draped an arm over his shoulder. Together they hobbled over to their hut.

Her knees momentarily dipped as a bolt of fear spiked her heart beats. *It's worse than I thought.*

Willing her jelly legs to cooperate, she rushed ahead and yanked open the door. Domnall nodded his thanks and brought Connall inside, who was now clearly drained. As if all his remaining strength had been expended on making a dignified return home. *Oh God, oh God, oh God.*

She hurried to the bed and threw back the blankets. "Lay him here, and I'll get the fire going. Tell me, please, what happened? Will he be all right?"

"I'll be fine," Connall grunted. He sat heavily on the bed, his large body bouncing slightly, and his face contorted in pain. But the stubborn man didn't lie down.

At the same time his brother straightened and said, "Taken a fever, he has. We sealed the wound, but the gods must not be happy with him." Domnall glanced down at his brother, his lips thinning, and his forehead creased.

The words *it's not a punishment from the gods* choked her throat and she pulled in a deep breath and swallowed. "The wound's infected."

Matching frowns greeted her, though Connall's head turned much more slowly toward her.

She rounded on Domnall. "Get Eithne for me. I have work to do."

"Work?" Connall croaked. "I'd think..." He dragged in a slow breath and wet his lips. "I'd think you can take a rest and talk sweetly to me now that I'm returned home." His upper body swayed.

"I was referring to you. You're part of my job description, remember?"

His eyes flew open and it took a moment for his gaze to find hers and focus. "I told ye, that was not my intention."

She pushed a confused Domnall out the door and smiled back at Connall, though she couldn't help biting her lip. *He looks so weak.* "I was only teasing." She crossed to where he still sat on the bed's edge.

Men.

The same in every time period, it seemed. She pushed on his shoulders until he fell back onto their heather-filled mattress. "Lie down and let me fuss over you, all right?"

When he didn't protest this time, she frowned.

Oh God. Please, let him be all right.

Okay. First things first. Boiled water.

She rushed over to the iron kettle on the hook and retrieved water from outside. A week ago, tired of going down to the river every day to bathe, she'd set up a large waterproof barrel to collect rainwater and used it for daily sponge baths, saving the full river bath for once a week. She coaxed the fire to life and set the pot on the iron rod suspended over the flames to bring it to a boil.

Next. Bandages.

She tugged one of her skirts from a shelf and ripped it into strips, the tearing sound filling the small confines. She tossed them all into the now-boiling water.

By then a scratch sounded on her door, and Eithne peeked inside.

Ashley straightened from the fire and wiped her hands on her skirts. "Come in. I'll need your help."

The older woman entered and quietly shut the door. "I heard Connall was wounded," she said in a low voice.

"Yes. And infection has set in."

Eithne cocked her head, because "infection" had come out in English.

"He has a fever. I need to cure it."

"What do you need me to do?"

Ashley grabbed her divining kit, spread it out on a bare spot on the floor, and formulated her question. *What herbs are available in Iron Age Scotland that will combat infection?*

She threw the dirt, but no answer appeared. Panic fired along her veins. That was a simple enough question. Lately, she'd noticed the answers were more sluggish in coming to her, but she'd never had it not answer completely if it was something Google would know.

Shit. Not now, of all times.

She pulled in a deep breath and closed her eyes. Connall's harsh breathing filled the hut, making it difficult to push out all thoughts, all worries. Again, panic clawed up her throat, but she breathed through her nose.

C'mon, Zen.

Finally, as calm as she could hope to be under the circumstances, she tossed the dirt. She could feel the answer coming, but it was like trying to remember a word that was just out of reach. She breathed in through her nose on a count of three, and out again. *One. Two. Three.*

The answer finally came, and she turned to Eithne. "Can you bring me any Herb Robert or heather you might have?"

Eithne nodded. "There's a bit left in the storage room used by the old healer, I think. And there's plenty of heather hereabouts."

"Thank you."

"This will help him?"

Connall's skin appeared even paler.

"I sure hope so," she whispered.

When Eithne left to retrieve the herbs, Ashley fished out the sterilized strips of cloth from the boiling kettle and hung them over the clothesline she'd strung up on one side of the hut. All the while, she darted glances at Connall's prone form. Since the clothesline was near the fire, she prayed it wouldn't take too long for them to dry.

She crouched down beside the bed and pushed aside the folds of his kilt, exposing the bandage. Where was the knot? She frantically felt around. Unable to roll his large body to the side, she hurried over to the shelf where they kept their tools. Luckily, a funny kind of scissors had been invented. They worked like tongs, but with sharp blades.

Back at his side, she eased the blade under the fabric and cut away the filthy bandage until only the cloth caked to his wound remained. She sat back. How to get it off without hurting him or removing a chunk of skin?

She'd have to *undry* the blood.

She hopped up and tested a large strip drying on the line with her finger tips. Cool enough to handle and, more to her purpose, still warm and wet. She pulled it down and spread it against the caked bandage, but it wasn't nearly enough moisture. She tore off another strip and dipped it into her outside bucket of water and carefully wrung it out over the wound.

She needed to get that bandage off.

Finally, after careful application of water and working the moisture into the fibers and the dried blood, she was able to peel the cloth away without disturbing the wound, though some of the dried mess around it peeled away with it.

She gagged at the sight. And closed her eyes, her heart beating like a drunk thing.

Shit, shit, shit.

This was bad.

She'd missed him while he was gone, and while that had scared her, as well as the abstract fear for him, seeing him wounded like this cut her deep. Deep enough that she had to acknowledge a simple truth—it would be so easy to lose him in this time period. And losing him?

That was the deepest cut of all.

Someone kept nudging Ashley's shoulder, and she swatted the annoying creature away.

"Ashley, wake up," a familiar feminine voice said near her ear.

Her shoulder was nudged again, and Ashley blinked eyes caked with sleep.

Where was she? What was going on?

Darkness cloaked the hut, with only the barest pink glow emanating from the fire. Eithne crouched into view, her face barely visible in the gloom.

"Ashley, you fell asleep," she whispered.

So? Sleep was good. She straightened, and her neck pinched.

Ouch.

Then she blinked and looked down. She was sitting cross-legged on the floor and had fallen asleep with her head propped on the edge of the bed. Okay, yeah, sleeping that way wasn't good. Why was she—?

Connall!

She jerked around, her arms stretching forward, seeking him. He was asleep, his features still scrunched from feverish dreams. His head wrenched to the side, and a low moan emerged.

Hands caught her under her arms, and she was being guided upward. Eithne murmured in her ear, "Let's get you properly to bed. You'll be of no use to him if you're tired and take sick yourself."

Ashley's body ached, and her mind raced, trying to piece together the haze of the last day. She'd finally scoured all the gunk from his wound, having found out it was sealed shortly after battle with the tip of a hot iron. She'd almost thrown up just picturing how painful that must have been, and she wished she'd been there to hold his hand through it, though he probably wouldn't have let her.

She'd flushed the wound, cleaned it with an herbal disinfectant she'd made, and wrapped it up tight with the clean linen she'd boiled. At one point she'd forced him to wake up and swallow some kind of nasty concoction to help reduce fever, judging by the grimace he made.

Speaking of… "Help me get him to swallow some more of that stuff."

Eithne's upper body was stronger than hers, so she directed her to get him semi-upright.

His eyes, glassy with fever, blinked open.

"Connall, swallow this," she urged, bringing the hard leather cup to his lips.

Luckily, he was too out of it to do more than twist his mouth, but she forced it open and got him to swallow down several gulps.

Once he was horizontal again, she straightened. "Thank you, Eithne."

"You need to move him again, you get me or Domnall to help you." She gripped Ashley's shoulder. "Now you get some sleep, dearie. I'll see you at dawn."

"I will," she said, touched by the woman's concern. "And thank you for checking in on me in the middle of the night."

"Of course."

Ashley carefully picked her way over Connall's large frame on her hands and knees, unwilling to disturb him. Reaching the far side of the bed, she crawled under the covers and snuggled up to him on his good side. His skin was still too warm, and he still thrashed, but was it her imagination that it seemed to lessen with her stretched along his side?

. . .

Through a fuzzy haze, Connall became aware of muted *thunks* and a softly whispered curse. The curse, he was gratified to hear, was in his wife's voice.

I am home.

Contentment seeped through him until he remembered the battle. He startled awake.

How had he gotten here?

As he blinked the room into focus, which was awash in a late afternoon sun, snatches of memory surfaced. The battle. Domnall grimly touching the hot brand of an iron to close his wound, the uncomfortable journey back on their boat as he shivered with fever and was flushed with sweat despite the chilly air.

And then being too weak to walk for their homecoming and being propped up onto a waiting horse.

How humiliating.

And that was how his wife had seen him return. How everyone had seen him.

Another curse sounded behind him, and then a feminine gasp. His wife's lovely face swung into view, her forehead marred with creases of concern.

"You're awake." She collapsed onto the edge of the bed by his hip and placed her head in her hands. Her hair, not done up in a braid as usual, cascaded forward, hiding her face.

Her shoulders convulsed, and a choking sound emerged from behind her hair.

He frowned. Not quite the homecoming he'd expected.

"Are you...are you crying?"

Her head whipped up, revealing a splotchy-pink face with tears trickling down her cheeks. Her eyes flared. "Yes, I'm crying," she said with angry heat.

"You're crying because...I awakened?"

She swatted his side, and he winced. She then immediately patted the area. "Oh my God, what's wrong with me? I'm so sorry." Her eyes locked with his. "And yes. Because I didn't think you ever would, you bastard. Do you know how long you've been lying on that bed, completely insensible?"

He shook his head.

"Four days. *Four* days and four nights you were burning up with a fever, and I was at my wits end trying to figure out how to heal you in this damn time period, and my divining power is lessening, and I'm smelly and you're smelly and I'm hungry and you're probably starving and everyone's worried about you and they keep coming in and asking if they can help and I have to tell them I don't know what the hell I'm doing and I keep dropping things and I... I..." Her eyes grew round, and her mouth closed.

"I missed you, too," he rumbled.

But she didn't smile, her eyes only going rounder. "Don't

you smile at me. Do you know how close you came to dying, mister? And I almost couldn't save you?"

"Would that have upset you?"

She smacked her thighs with her fists, and he winced in sympathy for her abused thighs. "Of course it would have upset me."

Wishing to comfort her, for she was obviously distressed, he tried to gather her close, but his heavy arms fell back against the bed. By the ancestors, he was in a weakened state. "Come here."

"I smell," she said.

"Well, apparently so do I, so we're no worse for each other. Come here."

She flew so fast against his chest he gasped. And though it took great effort, he managed to bring his arms up to cradle her against his side. She was so upset, she didn't realize she was lying right across his wound, but he didn't care—an immediate sense of relief, of peace, of rightness swamped him when he held her against him again.

He swallowed hard, his throat parched as if someone had set up a bonfire inside and dried him out.

But one thought overrode everything—she cared.

And while that should have made his heart soar in triumph, instead he felt his chest tighten. By the ancestors, he'd caused her much anguish. For the first time, an insidious thought struck him—was it fair to put someone through this kind of life? His world *was* more dangerous than hers.

Chapter Fifteen

Several days later, Connall pushed open the keep's door and strode into the courtyard. Earlier that morning had been the first time he'd been able to leave his hearth and the exercise was welcome. He'd grown weak from his bout with fever, and he needed to return to fighting form. His tribe depended on him. For the first task, he'd trekked down to Achnabreck and gathered some dirt from the sacred site. He'd then mixed it in with Ashley's dirt, hoping it would aid her divining, for she'd been anxious that her gift was disappearing.

Now, he'd finished having an audience with his father and the council. Irritation stiffened his gait—Ashley had demanded an audience of them during his absence. While the council hadn't decided on whether to grant their request, he was shocked to discover the older members of the council were arguing in its favor.

As her husband, *he* decided whether an issue of hers should be aired with the council. He stomped across the well-worn path. As soon as he could find her, he'd have a talk with her. But first, he wished to visit the progress on the new signal tower.

Before his steps could bring him fully across the sandy courtyard, his wife emerged from the kitchen, her arms holding an empty barrel.

When her eyes clashed with his, she set her burden down and marched right over to him.

He opened his mouth to chastise her for going to the council when she said, "What are you doing out of the hut? You should still be in bed. And I heard you're planning to ride out to the signal tower?"

Several villagers and some of his men who'd been strolling by stopped. The weight of their stares settled on him.

"I'm well enough," he ground out.

She placed a hand to her hip and pointed to their hearth downslope. "You need to return to bed and finish healing. Do you want to get reinfected? Or open your wound? You're not out of the woods yet."

Her speech was peppered with unfamiliar words in her tongue, but he understood her tone well enough. While he'd been pleased at her fussing over him ever since his fever had broken, this was rather embarrassing to do so publicly. Grins sprouted on the faces of some of the villagers and warriors. He took a deep breath. *Be calm—it only means she cares.* And that pleased him.

"And it's definitely too soon for you to venture to the signal tower."

This was quite enough. And coupled with what he'd just learned, it was clear she needed a reminder of who was in charge. He'd found her strength of mind invigorating before, but that was in the privacy of their hearth. He could not afford to have her undermining his authority with his tribe.

To lead them well, he needed their respect.

He had to put a stop to this.

"I know full well what I'm capable of doing. You're not

to question me."

Her eyes flared, and she opened her mouth. Then she looked around at their growing audience, and he was gratified to see she closed her mouth again. But if the set of her shoulders and the fire in her eyes told him anything, he'd hear about this later around their hearth fire.

• • •

When Connall entered their hut that night, Ashley set down the new batch of healing paste, trying not to let the crockery bang. He shook out his mantle and hung it on a hook by the door, then glanced over his shoulder. By the set of his jaw he knew she was about to let loose on him.

Which made her even angrier.

"You said you'd treat me as an equal," she stated as calmly as she could.

He cocked his head, his forehead wrinkled by a frown. He stepped farther into the room.

"Before you left to fight for the Romans, I told you that I can't be your wife if you don't treat me as an equal."

"I do treat you as an equal. More than equal, in fact."

She gestured toward the door. "What you did out in the courtyard was not treating me as an equal."

"How did that have anything to do with it?"

He honestly seemed puzzled. She rounded the trestle table and sat down on the bench, crossing her legs and arms. "What does being equal mean to you? When I asked that of you, what did you take it to mean?"

"Treat you the same as I treat others. However, I treat you as more than their equal. You are my wife."

She closed her eyes and blew out a breath. "I meant, equal to *you*."

He crossed his own arms. "But you're not. I'm the chief's

son."

Okay, a different approach, then, because obviously this was a foreign concept. "Why did you reprimand me in front of everyone?"

He took a step forward. "You questioned my judgment in front of the others. I cannot abide that."

"Why not?"

He looked up at the ceiling as if trying not to lose his temper with *her*. He lowered his chin. "I'll allow that your people have different ways of doing things, so I'll explain."

So. Mansplaining was a thing here, too. *Great.*

"By all means. Go ahead."

He didn't recognize her sarcasm. "I'm most likely going to be their future chief."

"Most likely? Aren't you the oldest son?"

"That doesn't signify. It does place me in a better position to be given the responsibility."

"How are chiefs chosen, then?"

"They're elected by the council and approved by the druids."

"So why does it matter that I appeared to question your judgment in front of others?"

"I need to be able to lead them effectively, and I can't do so if I don't have their respect."

She made her hands into fists and clamped her folded arms tighter against her chest. "Giving an opinion doesn't mean it's taking away your respect."

He shook his head. "That's not how they'll see it. With the raid taking a good portion of our women, the tribe is too vulnerable in these dangerous times. We need a strong, capable leader to replace my father when the time comes. Which, I hope, is not soon."

"But we can be stronger if we work together as a team."

"That's not how it works here, Ashley. I'm needing their

respect, and I'll not be having it if my wife is undermining me. It's as simple as that."

God, and here she'd been toying with the idea of staying. Maybe this place was just not right for a modern woman.

Square peg, meet round hole.

Her throat swelled as fresh emotion swamped her— pain joining her anger and frustration. Shit, she'd somehow allowed herself to fall for this man.

He must have misinterpreted her silence, because he said, "I'm glad you understand. This is also why you shouldn't have gone behind my back and addressed the council."

"What? You didn't keep your word when you said you'd take care of it."

He shook his head. "No. I considered it and decided that everything is working fine as it is."

"Why didn't you tell me?"

"I didn't think it was necessary."

She put her elbow on her knee and dropped her forehead into her palm. She massaged it and let out a frustrated growl. "I can't do this." Resigned, she looked back up at him. As he continued to stare at her in puzzlement, she took a deep breath. "Listen. I can't be in a relationship with someone who doesn't let me have a voice. I did that once and have been paying for it ever since."

"Once?"

"Yes. Once."

He strode over and sat beside her on the bench, his body turned slightly toward her. "What happened?"

"My ex-husband."

His brows raised at that. "Oh yes, I remember you mentioning that. We have precedence for that here as well. What happened?"

"I let him control everything."

He nodded. "So you understand, then. Your times are

not different from mine."

She tossed her hands in the air. "Actually, they are. *Some* men are still like that." *Dinosaurs.* "But I was an idiot. I married a guy I trusted because he had a high-paying, high-powered job and he, well, seemed like a grown-up. I was head over heels in love with him and wanted to prove to my family I was an adult.

"All I proved was that I *hadn't* actually grown up. I was the youngest of my friends to marry. We had a huge fairy-tale wedding, which meant we also had a lot of excess gifts from the registry. All the formal stuff. So we cashed all that in and combined it with some money we also received and formed a nest egg. We hadn't decided *what* we were going to use it for yet—either our dream home or for our future kids' tuition."

Man, she'd been so stupid. Her ex was ambitious, and she saw it as a virtue for being a good provider, believed the best of him. Excused his distance as him being overworked.

"I don't understand what most of that means, I confess. What in there is wrong in your eyes?"

She stood up and faced him. "I'm just getting warmed up. He insisted on being the one to manage our finances, and I didn't have a head for it. He was an investment banker. Anyway, turns out he was a crook. I woke up one day to find out he was a scam artist, he owed some scary people money, and had taken our nest egg to make some shady investments."

And because she'd let him control all the finances, she didn't realize until it was too late.

"Ashley. You're using words and concepts I have no idea of their meaning."

She stepped in front of him and crossed her arms. "Here it is, plain and simple. I trusted him to do what was right for me—for *us*, as a couple and family. And he betrayed that trust. It placed me in a very vulnerable position, and I vowed to never let a man control my life like that again."

She closed her eyes and opened them. *Be strong.* "Which brings me to *you*. You disrespected me by deciding things were fine without even a discussion first. You can't just *do* that. If I'm to be your wife, you can*not* assume you know what's best for me. If you do, I'll be leaving, one way or another."

Connall stood, a flash of fear and anger in his gaze, quickly masked. "You don't trust me?"

"Not with you knowing what I need. But it's not an insult for me to want to control my own life. If we're to be together, you need to understand that." Why oh why did she seem to fall for guys who didn't? Maybe all men were controlling d-bags.

He stared at her a moment longer, then calmly scooped up a fresh shirt and went behind their "bathroom" screen to clean. But as she looked at his retreating back, she couldn't help a flare of hope that he'd be different. Somehow. That with time, he'd get it.

Late the next afternoon, Ashley worked with Eithne and the others to unpack the food they'd hauled up to the first signal tower with their horses. It was a feast, because the whole tribe was ready to celebrate. She lugged a basket filled with bread and set it down next to the other baskets. She straightened and flexed her fingers, looking up at the signal tower. Though she *wanted* to feel excited, she just felt...flat.

Just pack her up and send her off on the big-fucking-deal train.

A sour taste from last night still coated her tongue, and she and Connall had gone to bed in separate places—her on the bed, and him on the old pallet on the floor. And she'd barely slept. Now, the whole tribe was gathered at the base because, with Connall on the mend, they'd decided to head here and pitch in as a unit.

And now it was done.

Several folks were already sitting on rocks nearby, their fingers picking a lively tune on some very strange-looking instruments. Some of the older women began dancing, their faces splitting into huge grins.

Everyone was happy. Happy to have finished their first of many signal towers, which would go a long way to protecting the tribe. And it had been Ashley's idea. And it had felt good to do that for them. Made her feel a part of them—part of The Horse People.

But all through the day, as they put the last touches on the signal tower, Connall behaved as if their argument had settled matters. The whole situation underscored how different their worlds were, and whenever she'd asserted her will today, he'd given her a glare. As if she'd forgotten and he was reminding her.

And as he strolled alongside one of his brothers, nodding gravely to something he was telling him, she realized he would *never* understand. And she couldn't live with someone like that.

Later that evening, as they all sat around a bonfire, Connall approached. She held herself stiffly, unwilling to show him any weakness.

He crossed his arms and widened his stance. "Ashley, we need to talk."

She looked up at him. "All right. What is it you'd like to say?"

"I don't think I was clear enough last night, and for that I apologize. In public, you will need to acquiesce to me."

She arched a brow and brought up her chin. How dare he. "Oh. You were clear. And no, I won't."

With that, whatever little hope she'd held that they'd understand each other sputtered and died.

Chapter Sixteen

Horns tooted a festive tune the next day as everyone in Dunadd lined the path to see off the first party of warriors to man the new signal tower. Some looked pale from imbibing too much last night.

Connall folded his arms and ground his teeth. Relations with his wife had not returned to normal. But he could not afford to relent on this—she must understand that it was for the good of the tribe. Too much was at stake.

Especially when that Roman arcani visited them again, this time to warn that the Damnonii, a tribe to the south, were raiding for slaves. He was grateful that their new alliance with the Romans was already fruitful; the tower had been finished just in time.

Beside him, Ashley stood stiff and unrelenting, and Connall sighed.

She'd learn soon enough.

As soon as the warriors reached the level ground and galloped off to their new assignment, he cupped his hands to his mouth. "Meet at the courtyard, for we have news everyone is needing to hear."

Glances both curious and cautious fell upon him, and he made sure all were before him as they headed up the incline.

Once they reached the top, he nodded to his father, who stood waiting for them on the speaking stone.

His father studied the assembled crowd, his face grave. "The Roman visitor this morning brought news of fresh raids. Everyone must be extra vigilant now, and no one is to leave Dunadd unattended."

Grumbling sounded, but his father held up a hand. "We have no guarantee they will come from the direction of the signal tower. While we will, of course, watch for the alarm from that quarter, we need to be aware that the raid could come from any direction."

. . .

As everyone shuffled away after the chief's announcement, Ashley caught Eithne's eye and gave her the prearranged hand signal. Eithne nodded and slipped into the crowd. Since the council still hadn't granted the women a voice yet, the six of them had continued to meet in secret, and the hand signal was how they alerted the others to an emergency session.

As casually as she could, she strolled toward their meeting place—the kitchen. No one questioned Eithne's, Affraic's, and Ashley's presence there, and, so far, the presence of the others hadn't drawn any attention, either. They were invisible.

She washed some bowls, eager to have something to do while she waited for Eithne and the other women. One by one they arrived, their faces flushed, and took a seat around the main work table. They looked to her for direction, and she felt the full weight of that responsibility.

She wiped her hands and joined them. "All right. Any concerns about preparations for a possible raid that the council hasn't addressed?"

Eithne leaned forward and looked up and down the table and back to her. "We should ensure that a proper supply of food and water is stored on the second floor of the keep."

Ashley nodded. "What do you need to get that done?"

After they hashed that out, and they gave an update on their efforts to stock up on onions and other foodstuffs that also had healing properties, she asked, "Anything else? How about any elderly who might not be able to make it up to the keep in time? My neighbor lives alone, and I worry about her. There could be others."

They divvied up who would help whom at the time of the alarm. One of the other women said, "It's not just the elderly. What about Murdina? She's due to have her babe at any moment. She lives on the lowest terrace. She was one of the few who survived the last raid, and she lost her husband then."

"Oh God. That's awful." Ashley's heart went out to the poor woman—to lose a husband was bad enough, but when she was pregnant, too?

They all began talking at once. Ashley raised a hand. "We need to wrap this up. Eithne, you and I will be in charge of seeing she's brought up safely." Ashley stood. "If no one has anything else, I think that's settled, then."

She held her fist out over the table. Chairs scraped the floor as the others stood. Grinning widely, they placed their fists over hers. Ever since their first shadow council, this was how they ended their meetings. "One for all," Ashley said.

And then smiled when the other ladies said, without hesitation and all at the same time, "And all for one."

So later that night, when Connall imperiously informed her that if the raid happened he expected her to head straight for the keep, she nodded without replying. She'd head to the keep, all right. But only after she ensured that Murdina was brought up safely with her.

Several days passed in a tense state of watchful awareness. Ashley was reduced to giving only polite nods to Connall whenever their paths crossed in public. At night, when he returned to their hut, she didn't even give him that much consideration. It was killing her to be so distant, but she needed to take care of herself first.

She and Eithne were just emerging from the storage room when a horn blared from the top of the keep. Three short blasts followed by a long one—the agreed upon alert that smoke from the signal tower had been spotted and to prepare for an incoming raid.

Without saying anything, she and Eithne set their burdens down and ran for the first terrace.

Connall burst out of the keep at a full run and caught up to her. He had a shield and sword, and his hair was tied back in a queue.

"In the keep. Now." Without waiting for an answer, he continued his downward dash. She, of course, ignored him. The women were depending on her to hold up her end of the duties—so few women and children were left. Feeling like a fish swimming against the current, she worked her way down the incline to the lowest terrace with Eithne.

By the time she pushed her way into Murdina's hut, Ashley was out of breath. The pregnant woman was squatting on some kind of wooden stool with their midwife holding her arm.

The midwife glanced up. "Her water just broke. She's not going to be able to walk on her own up that incline."

Shit.

"We need to make a stretcher."

She glanced quickly around the room. Three stout spears leaned against one wall. Ashley grabbed two and looked to Eithne. "We need rope."

"Bran should have some."

"Is he on this terrace?"

"Aye, for he's in charge of the docks, and he fishes for the tribe."

"Perfect. Just take the rope. We'll return it later."

Eithne hustled out, and Ashley laid the spears parallel on the ground. Next, she stripped the bed of the heaviest blankets. She stared at the spears, working out in her head the quickest way to make a web of rope on which to lay the blankets and Murdina. It wouldn't be the most comfortable stretcher, but it would do the job.

All the while, the mother-to-be made no sound other than an occasional sharp intake of breath.

"Is she all right?" Ashley asked the midwife.

The older woman nodded. "She's in a great deal of pain, but the contractions are far apart. It's her first babe."

Eithne burst into the hut, trailing a long line of rope.

Ashley jumped up and helped her get it all inside. "Here's what we're going to do." Ashley knelt by a spear, taking the end of the rope. "I'm going to tie a knot here and pass it to you. You wrap it twice around and knot it and hand it back to me."

Working quickly, they created a crude web between the two spears. As Eithne tied the last knot, Ashley grabbed one of the blankets and tied a corner on each end of the pole, just to make it a little more secure.

She was about to lay another blanket on top when the hut's door banged open and a wild-eyed woman barged in, her blond braid nearly undone, with bits of hair sticking to her tear-streaked face. "Aiden," she screamed.

Everyone froze.

Eithne was the first to recover. She darted up to the woman, who was just looking at each of them and back outside, repeating "Aiden" over and over.

"What's going on, Alana? Where's Aiden?"

"He's missing. My baby is missing. I need to find him. Help me!"

Ashley stood. "Calm down. Tell us exactly what happened? Where did you last see him?"

But the woman bolted for the door. Ashley leaped forward to grab her arm but missed. Dammit. They needed to work *together*. She dashed after her just in time to see the mother slip past villagers. In the wrong direction.

Shit. Shit. Shit.

She charged back into the hut, grabbing the doorjamb and swinging inside. "Can you manage the stretcher on your own?"

Eithne nodded. "We'll get her up the slope."

Satisfied, Ashley darted after the frantic mother of the missing child. She needed to get her up into the safety of the keep. But as she neared the bottom, all was chaos. Warriors fought warriors amidst shouts and screams. Ashley stumbled to a stop, chest heaving in and out. *Shit.* She couldn't make it through that wall of fighters.

Where is Alana?

It ate her up inside to turn around and run back up, but in this, Connall was correct. They needed everyone heading *up* to the safety of the keep. There was nothing she could do for the mother now or her child. She dashed back up the incline, her legs burning now from all the running, and rounded up the last stragglers on the first terrace.

"Leave your things," she shouted to one older woman. "Your life is more valuable. Go." She pointed up the hill. "Go now. The raiders are just below."

That got the woman moving. Ashley checked the rest

of the huts on this level and then followed the others up the incline. At the second terrace, Eithne and the midwife struggled with the cumbersome stretcher, but Ashley needed to make sure everyone on this level had also vacated. She ran to each hut and, finding them empty, she hastened to Eithne.

"Here, I'll take this end. You go up and take one side from the midwife."

Ashley adjusted her grip on the ends, but a pair of men appeared. "We have her in hand. We were tasked with bringing her to safety but were delayed."

They were?

Why hadn't she or the others been told?

A bang sounded next to her, almost making her drop one of the poles. Una, one of the other women on their secret council, was helping Ashley's neighbor from the hut.

Ashley frowned. "You two should already be inside the keep."

Una motioned to her neighbor. "Tell that to her. She refused to leave."

"They want to burn my hearth, they can burn me with it. I'm too old for this."

"Then who will teach the wee ones-to-come the tribe's sacred songs? You know the oldest, some of which hold great power." Una propped her fists on her hips and glared.

"Hush with your blathering; I'm coming aren't I?" And the older lady pushed past.

One of the men took Ashley's end of the stretcher.

"Alana?" Eithne asked, coming up to her.

She shook her head. "She disappeared."

"Where did you last see her?"

Ashley explained and Eithne's eyes unfocused. "The south ravine." She gripped her arm. "If that's open…"

Her heart lurched. "What do you mean?"

But Eithne was booking it back down the incline, her

white hair billowing behind like an avenging angel's wings. She caught up to her.

"Eithne, where are you going?"

"The men's council blocked off the south ravine because with our reduced numbers, it was too much to guard. But it had been a favorite run for the children, and with the recent rains…"

"It might have washed away, and Aiden…"

"As one of the few children left, has taken advantage of it to play."

Sure enough, as they reached the approach to the south ravine, the bottom of it had washed out, leaving a slim tunnel beneath a giant boulder wedged in the gap.

She skidded down the incline. "Quick, go get help. We need to block this again." As Eithne ran back up, Ashley gathered up the largest rock she could lift and perched herself on a low edge of the boulder. From below, the main mass would keep her hidden.

Palms sweaty she forced herself to breathe calmly.

As the minutes ticked by and only distant shouts reached her, she began to relax but tightened her grip at the sound of scuffling. An arm appeared below her, pulling its owner up.

She'd planned to wait until the person's head appeared to make sure it wasn't Aiden or Alana, but the muscular forearm stained with blood was no child's or woman's.

Heart screaming *holy shit,* she raised her arm and as soon as a head appeared, she whacked him. He grunted and slid downward, his body twisting and blocking the gap.

His heavy breaths filled the air, and chills raced down her spine. She didn't think she could *kill* a man.

Thankfully she was saved from having to decide as several warriors, led by Eithne, appeared at the top rolling another large boulder before them.

"Stay where you are," one shouted.

Eithne stepped to the side and the warriors pushed the boulder down the ravine. It landed against her much larger one with a solid *thunk*.

At a sharp cry and a scuffling sound, she climbed up the boulder and peered over—the attacker had slid partway down the ravine.

Wasting no more time, she jumped back down and accepted the help of the warriors to climb back up to the main thoroughfare.

By the time they made it to the door of the keep—still open wide, thank God—Ashley's muscles were shaking from spent adrenaline.

As they made their way inside, the doors slammed shut behind her with a *thud*. The scraping of wood against wood followed as the older council members barricaded the door.

Outside, shouts were growing closer when they finally reached the second floor. The elder council members followed up behind them and barred the door leading down.

Now they had to wait.

Ashley slumped against the wall and slid to the ground, her legs giving out. Her whole body shook.

She worked to catch her breath and glanced at all the assembled villagers, worry clear on their faces. And now that the hectic activity of getting everyone safely up into the keep was accomplished, she had nothing more to do but think about Connall and the others out there fighting off the raiders.

Despite all her anger and frustration at him, still she worried. *Please be okay.*

Chapter Seventeen

Out in the courtyard, Ashley worked alongside Eithne tending the wounded. The sun was already on a fast slide into the western ocean. For most of the day they'd been holed up in the keep, restless and scared and startling at any loud noise or scream. Finally, a warrior knocked the all-clear signal on their barricaded door, breaking their tense wait.

Thankfully none from their own tribe numbered among the dead, and the wounds were all minor. Prior to the raid, she'd made up a large batch of the antiseptic ointment, and she worked on flushing the wounds and getting them wrapped up.

But a pall hung over the villagers, none yet willing to venture down the slope to their homes, even though Connall and the others had declared it safe. Only a short while ago, warriors had found Aiden's mother, cut and muddy but alive.

Somehow, via the south ravine, she'd made it past the raiders in search of her son, and when she couldn't find him, and the raiders were passing back through, she'd hidden in a slight crevice covered by a patch of gorse.

Ashley couldn't fight a sick feeling in her stomach whenever she thought about Aiden, how scared the little boy must be.

"I'm not cut out for this kind of life, Eithne," she choked out, wiping her nose. They worked their way over to the next warrior deemed most in danger of infection.

"You're as capable as any of us," the older woman admonished.

Shouts from the door of the keep brought her head up. Connall strode out, followed by a contingent of warriors. He didn't spare her a look as they marched down the incline.

"Where are they going?" she asked.

"To look for Aiden before the sun sets fully. There's a chance the raiders didn't take him. That he hid like his mother."

Ashley bit her lip and looked down, her heart breaking. God, she hoped they found him.

• • •

Rain slid down Connall's exposed skin and had long ago drenched the fabric of his kilt and mantle. The folds stuck to his thighs as he and his men trudged up the last incline to the courtyard. Not a soul appeared to greet them on their way up, and his steps were heavy—from scouring the nearby land through the night, to lack of food, but most of all because they'd not found the boy.

As he'd surmised, the tribe was still encamped on the upper courtyard. His gaze immediately tracked to where Ashley crouched, spreading ointment on the arm of one of his wounded men.

His jaw worked. She'd disobeyed him. For he'd seen her back out on the lower terrace *after* he'd ordered her to the keep.

Aiden's mother dashed up to him, her face streaked by tears. "My Aiden?"

Connall could only shake his head. The mother stumbled into the keep, keening, and the sight—while it tore at his insides—also firmed his resolve.

He clasped his hands behind his back and straightened his shoulders, addressing the assembled villagers. "It is with a heavy heart that I'm reporting our search for Aiden unsuccessful. We were able to fight off the raiders before they could do any damage, or abduct any others, but we're going to assume he was taken. While our warning system helped us fight off the attack, the boy would not have been taken if everyone had obeyed orders and retreated to the keep as soon as the alarm was given."

Ashley stood, her forehead creased. She opened her mouth, probably to give some excuse as to why she'd disobeyed but glanced around at their audience and closed it.

Without another word, he strode for their hearth home, knowing she'd follow.

When she whirled in behind him, he held up a hand. "Truce."

She stopped and folded her arms across her chest.

"I realize you were only trying to help the tribe, but we need to come to some kind of compromise."

She pulled in a deep breath and nodded. "I'm listening."

"I promise that in the future, I will always listen to you and try to implement your good ideas, for you are truly a valuable member of the tribe. If not for the signal tower, more than Aiden could have been lost. However, in return, you need to drop the council request. And when there are situations that are a matter of life and death, you will follow my directives."

"But there are things the men's council doesn't even notice. You *need* those women on the council."

"Can you act as their advocate with me? I promise that whatever concerns you learn of from them, I will listen to."

Since she still appeared to hesitate, he said, "I saw you on the lowest terrace during the fighting and the sight..." He cleared his throat and stepped closer to her. He tugged on her braid. "The sight sliced fear through me, as sharp as any sword. Having you amongst the chaos of battle and not safe in the keep placed you and the others in danger. If you'd been hurt, I'd never forgive myself."

Her shoulders slumped. "All right. I agree."

And while he was grateful to have secured her agreement, he took no pleasure from it. He could only hope it was a necessary compromise to ensure not only better relations with her, but also strengthened the tribe.

Waves rocked their ship as Connall and his war party cut through the waters of the Sound of Jura. Because of the Romans, they knew who'd raided them, which aided them greatly, for nothing about the raiders they fought yesterday distinguished them in any way from others living in these parts.

The Damnonii were a vicious tribe located south, and the chief and council had given permission for them to follow and attempt to retrieve Aiden.

Connall yanked on the line running to the aft sail, adjusting it slightly.

By the ancestors, he hated what he'd had to do to Ashley. And he kept telling himself it was for the best for the rest of that evening.

But ever since she'd agreed to the compromise, she'd been listless. And last night, yet again, she would not let him into her bed.

He rubbed the back of his neck and looked out over the choppy silver water.

She'd come around. She would.

He just had to exercise the same patience he'd used with her before. But first, he needed to make sure their war party returned before the spring equinox only four nights away.

"Our ancestors and the local gods are smiling down on us today," Connall whispered to his brother Domnall. He jutted his chin toward the misty shore where the indistinct shapes of five boats shimmered gray and blue, their white sails tied fast to their masts. Most were empty save the one in the center, which contained two hulking shapes, as well as one other shape. A shape much smaller, and one Connall hoped and prayed was that of the small boy they searched for—Aiden.

As the second night of their quest bled into daylight with no signs of the raiders, his anxiety had grown. Anxiety not only for the sake of the boy, but also because he knew he needed to return to the stronghold in two nights.

But now, if all went well, they would return in triumph. And though eager, he'd not make the mistake of turning that feeling into haste and risk ruining this.

The Damnonii boats were moored in a crescent-shaped inlet, and he and his men had carefully kept their boat close to the shoreline when they'd approached this lip of land.

He addressed his men. "We must act quickly, but with stealth, for we know not when the raiding parties will return to the boats and lend aid." He pointed to the small island guarding the inlet. "We will sail along the sea side of that isle, but myself, Domnall, and Machar will keep our heads down in case these Damnonii can count."

"Why does that matter?" asked one of his men.

"Because we're going to slip out once the isle is between us and them and make for its shores. The rest of you will sail on to the next lip of land as if you're just passing by."

They all nodded, waiting for him to continue.

"Moor there—out of sight, mind you. But post a lookout. We will make our way to the inlet side of that isle, slip into the water, and approach them from behind. We three can hold our breaths the longest. And those fools are spending most of their time aiming their noses inland, wishing they were part of the raid and not babysitting Aiden. Once you see us begin to subdue those two, make for us with all speed. Hopefully, the surprise of our approach will end it before you arrive, but in case not, you can lend aid. But most importantly, you will carry us—and Aiden—back to the safety of our stronghold."

He looked to his brother and Machar. "Domnall, you take the sentry on the left, Machar, the right. I'll be in the middle and will pull Aiden to me. All clear?"

When all gave a nod, they unfurled their sail and tacked across the inlet. He crouched in the hull, slipping his shirt and tartan from his frame. When Fearghus softly whispered, "Now," he slipped over the side, his knife strapped to his ankle the only thing he wore, and swam with powerful strokes to the nearby shore.

Hearing his brother and Machar beside him as his feet touched shore, he didn't bother directing them—they knew what to do. All three slipped into the dark recesses of the tree-crowded isle. Once on the far side, they crouched and used shade and boulders to hide their quick dash to the inlet's waters. Though Connall was confident this was the party they sought, he risked a quick glance. They were close enough now he fancied he could see the fleas crawling along the men's tartans, though in truth they were still a hundred feet away.

The small boy, hunched and shivering, was the only one

looking in their direction, and Connall allowed himself to feel a moment's relief—the boy was Aiden. When his eyes caught Connall's, they rounded in surprise and relief, but the lad was quick-witted enough to not give them away by either movement or sound. Connall raised a finger to his lips, checked the knife to ensure it was still strapped in place, and slipped into the water. Before sinking under the calm waters, he filled his lungs with air.

Chapter Eighteen

Connall's chest burned from holding his breath, but he calmly counted the moments since he'd first slipped into water—he would make it. He knew how far he could count underwater. The water was crystal clear and the mist in the air above was already burning away by the time they neared the boats.

He looked to either side. Domnall and then Machar caught up to him, mere feet from the boats. Just as Domnall nodded, Connall caught movement above and heard a shout, muffled by the water. One of the men was half turned toward them, his face frozen in surprise.

As quick as an otter, Domnall shot out of the water and grappled the second warrior before he could react to the alarm given. Changing the angle of his thrust, Connall sprang up alongside Machar, now that he'd be dealing with someone not unawares.

The glint of a spear whipping around had him lifting his arm to block, giving Machar time to grab the warrior by his braids, exposing his throat for a quick slice of his knife. But the brunt of the weapon hitting his forearm was not as forceful as he'd expected, and Connall glanced down in surprise.

Aiden had kicked at the man's belly, surprising him enough to make his aim falter.

This little heroic stunt unbalanced Aiden and he fell back into the water, his hands still tied in front of him. He sank quickly, the shore angling deep at this point in the inlet.

Mo Chreach! Connall dived back into the water and scooped him up, then kicked off from the bottom and shot to the surface. The boy sputtered and gasped, and Connall thrust his hand through his own hair, clearing his vision and taking a deep breath.

Up ahead, his men were rowing hard for them, and after checking behind him to ensure that Domnall and Machar had dispatched both—they had—he arranged Aiden against his side, his head above water, and swam hard for the boat.

As soon as he was within inches of it, hands descended and dragged a sputtering and coughing Aiden into its safety. Connall gripped the rail and levered himself up. A dip and two thumps indicated Domnall and Machar were safely onboard, and without losing a beat in their rowing, his men aimed for home.

They weren't yet out of danger, though. Connall took up an oar and heaved back on the next pull, the loch's waters already starting to dry on his naked body from the late morning sun. They kept their rhythm-chant low—except for whatever shout that one warrior had given, all the rest of the interaction had been in near silence, save splashes, coughs, and grunts. If their ancestors kept smiling down on them this day, they'd make it to the bend and be out of sight before any of the raiding party returned.

As the raider's crafts disappeared from view, Connall pulled in a deep breath and disengaged his oar.

He assessed Aiden, whose gaze was still locked on Connall, as if he'd never looked away since they'd reached the safety of the boat. And maybe he hadn't. No doubt the boy was flooded with conflicting emotions—the latent fear from his capture and relief to be rescued—though he hid it well. Only his eyes spoke of it.

And Connall went still—he felt as if he were looking into a younger version of himself. Surely his own eyes had looked much like this if anyone had seen him as he'd stumbled from his hiding place and finally caught sight of his tribe's stronghold.

He grabbed his clothing and dressed, settling next to the lad, who had his knees drawn up to his nose with only his big eyes showing above. His hands were still curled into his body.

Connall drew his knife from his ankle-strap and nodded toward the boy's stomach. "Will ye let me cut those for ye?" he whispered.

The boy nodded and extended his wrists out from the shelter of his body, though not by much. He carefully angled his knife into the small space the boy gave him and worked the bonds loose. When the leather fell, Aiden launched himself upward and latched his arms around Connall's neck. He had just enough time to get his knife out of the way.

He held the trembling boy, but just as quickly as he'd launched himself at Connall, he sprang away and sat abruptly against the boat's side. He drew himself straight, striving to appear unaffected.

How could he comfort him without him drawing up defenses? What would he have wanted to hear when he'd been in the same frightened position as this lad?

"What you did back there was brave, Aiden. Thank you for your part in the fight."

That earned him a glimmer of a smile, but it still looked as if the boy struggled against tears. He hiccupped once. "I shouldn't have been caught in the first place. Mam told me not to play in the reeds, but…"

But a child will ignore the advice of an adult for the sake of play.

His chin went up. "I tried to fight them off, but...but...I..." His lips compressed, and his eyes widened.

"You?" Connall prompted, knowing the boy needed the respect of hearing him out, even if it was something he thought shameful.

"I failed. I wasn't strong enough," he finished, his voice smaller. He turned his face away.

Connall gripped the boy's chin and brought his face back around. "You tried, though. Do you agree?"

Aye, he'd felt earlier that he'd been looking upon a younger version of himself, seeing his fear and relief, but now he felt as if he were talking to that younger version as well.

The boy nodded in Connall's light grip.

A tight knot of emotion lodged in his throat, and he pushed past it, his words rendered a wee rougher in the passing. "Then that makes you very brave indeed, to pit your size against theirs. Do you think anyone here could expect you to overpower someone as big as myself?"

"Not many warriors your size can best you," Aiden whispered.

"That's right, but you fought regardless."

"Yes," he whispered. And then again, his voice stronger, "Yes, I did."

His chest filled with pride as a strange sense of relief and...forgiveness flooded him. "You are only a child, there's no shame in not having the strength to best a grown man." Connall moved his palm from the child's cheek to the top of his head. "You might be a child, but within, you have the ferocity of a warrior. Don't forget that."

Connall was rewarded with a tentative smile, and he took his place again to row for home. At first, Aiden huddled against the sides, but then his natural curiosity rose to the surface as the novelty of having an audience of warriors completely to himself made itself apparent. The rest of their journey, they fielded one question after another, ranging from how to sail and row to how to fight. It was only as their boat reached the loch abutting their stronghold that the boy finally nodded off.

This time, as Connall trudged up the incline to Dunadd with his men, his spirits were somewhat lighter, though he was just as weary.

The villagers, alerted to their arrival by the horn his men had sounded at the dock, were arrayed on either side to welcome them home.

Alana was the first one to rush down to meet them, and Connall swung the tired boy from his shoulders and handed him off to the loving embrace of his mother.

"Thank you so much. I'm so grateful to you for rescuing him. He's my life." She snatched the boy up onto her hip and hugged him tight, sobs of relief coming out in gasps as she held her boy's face and stared at him in wonder.

Aiden's eyes drifted shut, and his mother tucked him to her bosom and dashed back up the incline.

And while the villagers greeted his warriors on their successful mission, he'd expected a much more joyful reception. The atmosphere had the same heavy weight to it as the last time they were raided on the winter solstice.

Connall searched the faces on their way up, but the one face he most wanted to see was not among them. For a moment, an icy fear gripped his heart—had she returned to San Francisco?

But that couldn't be, as he'd made sure they returned before the spring equinox tomorrow.

When he finally found her in the kitchen with Eithne, she merely gave him a dispirited smile, her eyes flat. They only sparked briefly when she asked after Aiden and learned he'd been rescued, but then they returned to a listless state.

Mo Chreach. He'd broken her spirit.

He backed out of the kitchens, further confused when Eithne shook her head at him in disappointment. He strode up to the keep and located his father and the council members, telling them the news.

When he turned to leave, his father stopped him. "What are ye going to do about your wife, son?"

He swung back around. "What do ye mean?"

"The whole of your absence she took to staring out over the terrace."

Hope sparked in his chest. "Toward where we sailed? Perhaps she missed me and merely looked for our return." He tried to inject levity he didn't feel into his words, despite the hope the words gave him. Even he knew he was speaking foolishly.

"No, son. She was not. She was staring toward Achnabreck. And this morning she asked if Mungan would be returning in time for the spring equinox tomorrow."

Connall's chest tightened. "I see. Thank you for telling me."

He headed straight for the door.

Aye, he'd done what he'd needed to do for the safety of his tribe. But by the ancestors he hated to see her unhappy. And to know he was the cause. He hadn't meant to break her spirit.

There was only one solution, then.

No matter that everything in him screamed *No*, he couldn't bear to keep her in a place and time where she could not be happy. Where she could not be her true self.

He needed to let her go.

Chapter Nineteen

Ashley lay stretched out on the bed in their hut, staring at the ceiling. When Connall had suggested the compromise, she'd relented because she really wanted to make things work between them. But the kicker had been his revelation about how she'd placed herself and others in danger.

Perhaps she *had* tried to take on too much here. And her eagerness to help—to be *useful*—had led to putting people in danger. Putting *Connall* in danger.

And so she'd worked hard to subdue herself.

Even when the door creaked open and Connall's familiar steps sounded, she couldn't be bothered to turn her head and look at him.

Oh, she still felt drawn to the sexy bastard. That just made this whole situation that much more annoying. *Traitorous body.*

"I've spoken to Mungan." His voice came out low, from the vicinity of the hearth fire behind her head.

That got her attention. She swung her legs to the floor and sat up. He'd planted himself on the bench by the fire.

"And?" The word came out on a half croak.

When her eyes caught his, they flicked away. "He's prepared to send you back to San Francisco tomorrow. All is ready."

Pain lanced her heart so hard she leaned forward and covered her middle. "You want me to go?"

His jaw worked, and he stared at his tight fists where they rested on his knees. "I think it's for the best."

Oh… Oh, wow. She didn't think it would hurt this much. She'd tried to fit in with his tribe, to be a contributing member of The Horse People, but obviously her modern outlook didn't mesh with them. She wasn't right for this place and time.

She took in the strong planes of his face, the determined set of his jaw. His flat, withdrawn gaze.

She swallowed a hot lump of emotion. Okay, then.

She was going back.

Without a word, she tugged the leather satchel out from under her bed to pack her meager belongings. Perhaps if she packed it exactly like before, the satchel would transform back into her messenger bag and laptop.

He cleared his throat. "You'll need to leave before sunset tomorrow, Mungan said, so he can use the first rays from the half moon to send you back."

It's what she'd wanted from the start. She wouldn't be a good wife for him.

Then why did it feel so wrong to leave?

Her throat closing tight, she kept her head down so that her hair blocked her face. If he saw the tears that were starting to threaten, that would be beyond humiliating. Her throat swelled and grew hot, and she swallowed hard. She would *not* cry.

• • •

Aye, he was a coward. All day today, he'd kept his distance from Ashley, but he could never stray too far. No, like the coward he was, he hovered just out of sight, watching her move, memorizing her gestures, her sway, her voice.

Even now, he was tucked in between the wall and their hearth home. His attention, however, wasn't on the vast emptiness of the moors and glens to the north, but on the emptiness in his heart and the sounds he could catch of her, like a starving man focused on the only meal that would ever satisfy him. What he could hear wasn't much—the occasional curse, or a clunk as she moved around inside, making her preparations to leave. The truth was, if he saw her depart, he'd lose his resolve.

Last night when he'd located Mungan and inquired about sending her back, Connall was shocked to learn the true cost of the spell Mungan had cast—it took a year off Mungan's life. He had made him swear, however, not to tell anyone else this fact.

"It's what I want," the spellcaster had said. "My way of giving back to a tribe that took me in as a foundling."

Since he was only a few years older than himself, Connall had no memory of a time when Mungan wasn't with the tribe, but he'd heard the story like everyone else had—Mungan had been found as a six-year-old wandering the moors and speaking a strange language and wearing even stranger garb.

When the door quietly shut nearby, Connall dropped his chin and blew out a breath. This was it.

He glanced over his shoulder and drank in the last sight of her as she trudged the short path from their home. Too soon, she was swallowed up by Eithne, the other older women, and half the village who surrounded her and followed her down the slope. From what he'd heard, most were accompanying her to Achnabreck.

Everything in him wanted to leap into that crowd and

pull her back inside their hearth. To say, *no, she's mine, she's staying,* but then he remembered her listless state upon his return. *He'd* done that to her.

The fire he'd admired about her was gone.

How could he be happy with himself, if his needs for the tribe left her unhappy?

He couldn't.

Mungan's spell to find the woman meant for him had not been specific enough. He'd found the woman meant for him, aye, but not the one meant for his tribe as well. Though it negated the whole point of bringing her to his land, he had to do this. Had to sacrifice his personal need for her for the good of the tribe. Had to sacrifice his happiness for the sake of hers.

Better for her to be in her land where she'd be happy, he told himself.

A little while later, unable to watch the progression to Achnabreck any longer, Connall pushed away from the keep's bulwark—the best vantage point to watch her and the accompanying party become specks in the distance.

At one point, he could swear that the figure he knew to be her had turned her head and looked back upon reaching the opposite shore, but he couldn't be certain. He'd raised a hand in farewell but knew he was too far away for her to see it.

He strode to the trap door that would lead him into the keep and knelt, gripping the iron handle. A glint from an unclouded, lowering sun—a rarity—striking a small object along the wall made him pause. Frowning, he straightened and walked over to the side facing the loch and crouched.

Nothing.

But he'd swear he'd seen something metallic.

He shuffled back a step and pushed his hands through the few leaves which had somehow worked their way up here from the wind. A sharp pain pricked his middle finger.

Cursing, he shoved the leaves away and found it—the kilt pin Ashley had crafted for him.

Carefully, he picked it up and stood, cradling it in his palm. How did—?

He glanced around, and his heart squeezed. This was where they'd first shared a kiss. Their *first* kiss. When they'd come up here to locate the ideal spots for her signal towers.

Memories of all the times they'd been together assailed him. Helplessness and despair gripped him. How could someone be so right for him, but so wrong for the tribe?

That fierceness of spirit he admired so much and which kept him on his toes—he'd thought he could keep it stoked in private but subdued in public. He'd failed to see in time, that by indulging himself, he'd weakened the tribe. If the only way he could lead them meant she had to be unhappy? Broken?

He gripped the pin, strode to the wall, and leaned his elbows against it, his head bowed. Could he have been wrong?

No.

It would be selfish of him to put his own needs and wishes above that of the tribe. Above her. And he couldn't forget, she'd wanted to return the whole time she'd been here.

Tightening his jaw, he pushed away from the wall and opened the trap door. He worked his way down the steps and out into the courtyard, his steps hastening as if being chased by the memory of their time together up on top of the keep.

Would those memories fade in time?

He was doing the right thing. Wasn't he?

As he approached the door to their hearth home, their neighbor opened the door and called his name. He turned and made his way to her, the summons unusual for the reclusive woman.

"How can I help you, Fionnuala?"

"You're a fool."

With that pronouncement, she shook her head, the loose skin under her chin wagging, and turned back for the door to her hearth home.

"Wait." He reached out and gently touched her shoulder. "I'll grant you that this is most likely true, but what do you mean?"

"If I have to tell you, it proves my point."

"Are you... Are you referring to my wife leaving?"

She rolled her eyes. "Let me tell you something, young man. If it hadn't been for her, Murdina wouldn't have been carted up to safety while she was in labor. It was Ashley and her council who made sure all of us older women who lived alone had someone assigned to us to bring us to the keep. And she made a stretcher—a *stretcher*—out of thin air to help that woman with child up there." She pointed a shaking finger at the keep. "And she resealed the south ravine pass."

Connall stood with his mouth open, for not only was that more than he'd ever heard the woman say at any given time, but because this was the first time he'd heard any of this. A surge of pride swelled in his chest, followed immediately by remorse. Of course, she'd do her utmost to protect these people. Then the rest of her words registered.

"Her council?"

But she was done enlightening him, apparently, for she yanked her shoulder away from his touch and shut herself back into her hearth home.

Growling in frustration but unwilling to push his luck with the woman, Connall marched into his own home. He slung his fur mantle onto its hook, and his gaze unerringly tracked to where she'd normally be sitting if she were here.

But she wasn't, of course. Because he'd sent her away.

He opened his fingers and looked at her pin, remembering when she'd first gifted it to him.

The old woman's words came to him again—her council?

So, she'd formed her own council of all women. He smiled—that was something she would do.

Then his smile faded. If the men's council had given the women a voice, the women wouldn't have felt the need to do things separately.

If they'd given the women a voice they'd have been united in purpose and Aiden's abduction might not have happened.

He glanced over to the wall as if he could see the old woman in her hearth home.

He closed his fingers over the pin. Yes, he'd been a fool.

He thought that being united meant the women listened to the men and obeyed, but it just meant the tribe wasn't working in concert. And before that, he'd believed he only needed to exercise patience to win her.

It wasn't patience he needed. It was a willingness to actually *listen*.

Oh, he'd made a mess of things, all right. He grabbed his mantle and pushed out the door. The sun hadn't yet set. He might still have time. Time to fix everything.

The tribe needed her. He needed her. The tribe was stronger with her.

And so was he.

• • •

Ashley shivered as the last rays of the sun illuminated the carved lines and indentations in the otherwise smooth shelf of rock. Next to her, Eithne and the other women on the council fidgeted, their feet occasionally stomping the ground to warm them up.

Behind them the half moon rode the tip of a distant mountain, in an already darkened eastern sky. As the sun's power diminished and the moon cast its soft rays on her, the air thickened with potential. With energy.

Perhaps it was from finally seeing the druid at work. Mungan had been fussing around the site ever since they'd arrived, setting everything up along the rocks. *This* felt very druid-y, seeing him mumble and pinch herbs into indentations in the rocks and place staffs in different spots. He kept squinting toward the setting sun and then to the moon over her shoulder and then back at the site where he was arranging everything just so.

Her attention invariably strayed to the wooden walkway below at any perceived movement, and each time, she tamped down the disappointment that tried to work its way into her resolve.

He's not coming.

Mungan strode up to her and waved toward the circle. "If you'll stand over here and face the moon. When I motion, walk sunwise around the circle of staffs."

"Sunwise?"

He pointed to her left. Oh—counter-clockwise. Ashley stumbled toward where he indicated. The druid placed his hands on her shoulders and adjusted her placement, a scent like ionized air mixed with the pleasant warmth of herbs wafting from his robes.

"There ye are." He stepped back, his piercing gaze latching onto hers, and began to mumble more words.

Oh shit, it was happening. It was starting. *That* jolted her, lifting some kind of cloud from her mind. The cloud that had made her feel so listless and ineffective. And the more he mumbled his spell, the more Ashley was convinced—this was *wrong*.

Eithne and the rest of the villagers who'd come to see her off shifted. Eithne shook her head, her eyes pleading. Earlier, each one had come up to her to tell her to stay. That they wanted her here.

"Ashley," Eithne admonished. "You're making a grave

mistake." This was met with another round of requests for her to stay.

The village needed her.

She was *important* here.

She was Epidii, one of The Horse People.

Never in her life had she ever felt as if she belonged. Until she came here.

She wanted to *stay*, dammit.

If Connall didn't want her, well tough.

The idea was a heady one, fizzing through her like the first sip of Coca-Cola. She *should* stay. She should *stay*.

The druid *can't* send her back. Connall would just have to deal with her because they *were* married.

As the thoughts circled round and round, pulling her more toward their truth, the druid stopped his mumbling and gave the signal for her to walk. She opened her mouth to tell him to call off the ceremony and announce her decision to him and the villagers, but a shout from behind startled her.

She glanced over her shoulder. Connall pushed through the fern, his black hair streaming behind him, his face set in determined lines, his chest heaving in exertion.

Her heart did a holy-shit lurch in her chest. *He came.* But…why?

Chapter Twenty

"Stop!" Heart in his throat, Connall bounded up the last stretch of the incline. Everyone in the village stared as he passed, but his attention was fixed solely on Ashley's lovely face.

By the ancestors, when he'd seen her already standing at the apex of the circle, he'd feared he was too late.

She hadn't started walking yet, so Connall forged ahead, hiking the few steep steps up onto the rock carving. He shouted, "I'll make ye an equal!"

Gasps sounded behind him. Her eyes grew round. But still she said nothing.

She didn't take a step to start her part of the magic, either.

He stumbled to a stop before her, his chest heaving. "A true equal." Anything. Anything as long as they were together. He pulled in another breath, winded from fear, not from the short dash here.

Because working together, everyone was safer, and everyone was definitely happier.

Most of all him.

And, he hoped, her as well.

Murmurs pummeled against his turned back, and he whipped around. He glared at all of them, stepping so that he was between Ashley and the others. "If the rest of you see how I treat my woman as a weakness, then you don't deserve either one of us. I'll go back to her land with her."

Eithne yelled, "You're the only one with a hard head, not us."

Laughter burbled up at this pronouncement, and he stood a moment, taking that meaning in. None of the faces watching him held censure or looked at him with any less respect.

He stared around Achnabreck, the site of where he'd lost his older brother. The site where he'd brought the woman he loved home.

And as the ramifications of what she said registered, and the villagers' reactions, he felt lighter. Lighter than he'd felt since...since the day his brother had been taken at this very location and Connall had cowered in fear.

As he moved his shoulders in a slight shrug, as if sloughing off the last vestiges of that weight he'd carried since he was young, he realized a new truth—he'd been holding onto the shame of what happened. And it had clouded his ability to lead effectively. Aye, he'd forgiven himself when he'd rescued Aiden, but he hadn't truly understood how it had affected his life. His decisions. Until now.

He whirled back around, for there was only one person whose opinion mattered. Was he too late for *her* forgiveness? Too late to mend her broken spirit? "Stay."

Her eyes narrowed at his commanding tone. "Real men ask nicely," she said, her voice strong but low so only he could hear.

His knees buckled as a wash of relief swept through him. Instead of locking them tight, he allowed himself to lower to his knees in front of her. She gasped, her eyes getting rounder.

"Ashley. Will ye have me? Your strength melds with mine and makes us both stronger. I cannot..." He swallowed and cleared his throat. "I cannot imagine living the rest of my days without your fiery spirit by my side. I love you."

Ashley caught her lower lip between her teeth, and her eyes filled with moisture. "I love you, too," she whispered. "I'd decided to stay whether you wanted me or not."

His heart swelled with pride and love. "Because you're as stubborn as me."

"And because *someone* needed to take this job of being your wife."

He laughed, his heart feeling full to bursting. He scooped her up and swung her around, the cheers of his tribe as accompaniment.

The druid, however, cleared his throat. "You need to know, that since her season is up, her powers are gone. She'll no longer have access to the skills the magic imparted to her."

Connall looked at him over Ashley's head, and then down at her. "That's not what made her special."

· · ·

After Connall's declaration and her life-altering decision, they stared at each other for what seemed the longest time. They only became aware of their audience when conversational chatter and the accompanying shouts and rustling of a group departing finally penetrated. Mungan placed a hand on both of their shoulders. "We are leaving before the night becomes too long."

She still found it weird that he was not only a young druid, but a hot one for those who were into his kind of impish looks.

Connall enfolded her into his chest, looking over at the spellcaster. "We will follow soon," he said, the words rumbling from his chest pressed to her ear.

His heart beat steady and strong.

Ashley trembled as he held her tight and all the adrenaline of the past few moments worked its way through her. Together they turned and watched the last of the tribe walk down the incline back to Dunadd. The last in line, Mungan smiled at them over his shoulder before he followed the rest.

Connall's strong fingers brushed her cheek and angled her chin up. Love and acceptance shown from his eyes.

I'm so lucky. So lucky to have this moment with him.

"Ashley," he whispered and lowered his face to hers.

It was a gentle meeting of lips brushing lips as if he reveled in the ability to taste her again, and she closed her eyes.

This. This man.

When it came down to it, he was just a big marshmallow inside. His warm breath, his taste stirred a rush of feeling that welled, stronger and stronger as their mouths luxuriated in tasting each other.

Tasting the promises so fresh from these lips.

But soon the kiss grew in urgency, and Connall stepped into her, placing a leg between her thighs, a hand splaying against her lower back and tugging her closer to him. His other hand cradled her face, his tongue stroking inside her now. A hot flash of need rushed through her veins, and she sucked in a breath.

"I missed you," she whispered against his mouth.

He groaned and gripped her hip, his mouth crashing into hers, and she undulated against his thigh, seeking pressure where she felt so empty for him. She broke the kiss and gasped, staring up at him. Then she placed her hands on his shoulders and pushed him back a step. "Did you mean all of that? What you said before?"

"Every word." His hand left her hip, and he smoothed both palms along her jaw, his gaze piercing. "I love you, and

I promise that every day I will show you that I do. You shall not regret making your life here, with me."

· · ·

Connall had intended to only have a moment away from the tribe to kiss his wife, unable to wait any longer to taste her again. To seal their promise.

That she chose to stay here, with him, humbled him.

But when she'd pushed him backward, his back had grown...warmer. He'd stepped inside the magic circle. While he wanted to make love to her with every fiber of his being, he'd been conscious of the cold for he knew she was more sensitive to it than himself. The magical heat inside the circle sizzled up his spine, speaking to him, telling him that here was the moment. Here was the time. Here they'd be safe. Safe to seal their bond.

He wouldn't be surprised to learn that the spell Mungan had started was not to send her back, but to create this circle of warmth and safety for them.

He stroked his thumbs across her cheekbones, and she shivered. But he knew it was from his touch and not the cold. He took a step back, and she followed, and the moment she stepped into the circle, any lingering tension from their exposed position or from the cold seemed to ease from her muscles.

Joy flared in her eyes.

Then she gave him a coy smile that heated his insides, and she unhooked the silver brooch clasping his mantle closed at his neck, her knuckles brushing his skin. She pushed on his shoulders and the cloth dropped in a pool at his feet. He shivered at the love he witnessed in her gaze and from the touch of her hands.

This was his wife.

He smoothed his fingers down the pale column of her neck, the moon lending its light to make her skin glow. He stroked a fingertip along her pulse point, which now beat faster.

She pulled in a sharp breath. "Connall," she whispered, her voice full of wonder.

He leaned down until his mouth brushed the shell of her ear. "Let me make love to you," he murmured. Her body trembled at the touch of his breath and his words against her ear.

She turned until her own mouth was at his ear. "Yes." And then she gently bit the soft flesh.

He groaned, his knees nearly buckling as heat and urgency fired through him. Drawing on all his strength, he suppressed the need to hike up her skirts and push between her luscious thighs. Instead he unwound his kilt, watching her track every move of his hands revealing himself to her.

He toed off his sandals and stood before her completely naked, completely vulnerable. The magic from the circle warmed the air, and the tattoos along his skin felt as if they moved and tingled.

She brought her hands up and slowly drew her tunic over her head and stepped out of her skirts. She also removed her shoes, and when she straightened and faced him, Connall swayed at the beauty of her—the dip of her waist, the full curves of her breasts—highlighted by the moonlight.

A shudder seemed to go through her, from her toes, up her legs and to her fingers, as she gazed on him in wonder.

Everything felt *right*.

He spread his fur-lined mantle across the stone. Then he straightened and held out a hand, palm up, and her lips curved into a smile. She eagerly slid her palm across his and interlaced their fingers.

He sank down to his knees on the mantle, and she copied

his movements, almost mirroring his motion and position. Her fingers traced the blue tattoos across his shoulder and down his biceps, and he closed his eyes, reveling in the feel of her soft, exploring touch.

Then those fingers nudged his shoulders, and he followed their gentle urging and laid onto his back. She straddled his lap and stroked her hands over his chest, and Connall gritted his teeth at the strength required to hold back. Never had he wanted a woman as much as he wanted her. And while everything inside screamed to grip her hips and impale her on his rigid length, he restricted himself to roaming his hands across her shoulders, watching in fascination as goose bumps of desire followed in the wake of his palms.

Then she inched backward onto his shins, bringing her out of reach. His hands fell useless to his sides. "Ashley?"

Then she smiled and leaned forward. And *licked* him. All up the length of his aching cock.

His hips bucked at the shock of desire that coursed through him. Then she brought her mouth fully onto him, and he groaned at the new sensation—of her hot, wet mouth, the pull and suck.

His hips bucked again, but she had his legs pinned, restricting his movement. Pressure built at the base of his spine as he jerked and gasped.

"Enough," he growled. "If ye continue, I'll spill my seed. And that's not where I'd like to be spilling it."

Her eyes flared with heat, and she released him. "God, what you just said...Wow, that was hot." She licked her lips and crouched over him on all fours, her breasts gently swinging. He took himself in hand, stroking up once to feel the evidence of her mouth on his member. And then he very nearly did spill his seed. He ground his teeth and captured her gaze with his own. "Come to me now, will ye. I wish to be sparing your back."

And honestly, he liked the idea of ceding control to her. If they were to be equals, it needed to be in every aspect.

She slowly lowered herself. He nearly closed his eyes at the exquisite sensation but forced them to remain on hers. The effort, and the love and awe reflected in her eyes, nearly undid him as she brought him, inch by inch, into her body, accepting him, welcoming him.

When she was fully seated, her lips parted and her chest rose and fell on a slight breath. And then her body shuddered for a brief moment as she adjusted to his girth and to their joining.

Heat—from the magic in the air, from the urgency—rushed across his skin, and she began to move in small undulating movements, her eyes never leaving his.

He traced his hands up her slim waist and cupped the sweet, heavy curves of her breasts. She moaned and bent closer, and he skimmed a hand along her spine down to her buttocks and squeezed, pressing her tighter to him.

And as he held her in his arms and she made shallow strokes against him, a feeling of joy and wonder flowed through him, riding the pleasure that grew and grew until it was a tight ball of heat.

"Ashley," he gasped.

"I know," she replied.

For this was more than satisfying a need. Each small stroke felt as if they were entwining themselves closer and closer into each other. Their breaths matched, their heartbeats became one, and the beauty of the joining, the sharing, felt so monumental he couldn't fathom it. He only knew that this woman was his everything.

Then her mouth dropped open as her whole body stilled and then shuddered, her sex milking his length in exquisite, tight pulls.

Knowing he'd be following her in but a moment, he

gripped her hips, raised her slightly, and pushed into her one final time. His lower back tensed, his balls tightened, and all the emotion building between them seared down his spine, and he exploded inside her.

As he pumped his pleasure into her—pumped *life* into her—and her body still shuddered from her own fulfillment, he held her face, held her gaze.

"I love you," he whispered, his cock still kicking.

"I love you, too," she breathed.

Then he wrapped his arms around her and held her as tight as he could, her skin to his, feeling himself soften inside her.

And as they lay wrapped in each other's arms and fought for breath, he glanced up at the half moon now farther along in its journey across the sky.

Magic had brought them together. But it was their own magic which kept them together. Made them strong together. And he could never be more thankful.

Later, after they'd made love a second time with a fierce passion—as if giving in to the need and urgency they'd both wanted to express the first time but held back—they slowly dressed and stepped outside of the circle, the night's cool air brushing his skin once again.

He clasped her hand, and they turned and looked upon the stone and then to the moonlit wooden walkway below, leading to Dunadd, leading to their hearth home.

From his belt pouch, he fished out the pin she'd crafted. "Will ye pin this on me?"

She smiled up at him. "You found it."

"Aye. Today."

And grateful he was, for it had not set well with him that he'd no longer possessed this. And finding it again had started to bring his hard head around.

...

With fingers trembling from excitement, Ashley pinned the metal sword to the cloth covering his chest. So much had happened since she first gave this to him. Even since he'd lost it.

He squeezed her shoulders. "Ready to go home?"

Home. Warmth spread in her chest at that word and what it meant for them. She looked up into his eyes. "Yes."

He led her down the incline to the horses hobbled nearby and helped her mount.

Oh man, she was sore down there and this was not going to be an easy ride. He swung onto his horse and brought it alongside hers. He looked past her to Achnabreck, a slight frown crossing his features.

"What is it?"

"It's strange, but ever since I came here to stop you and accepted that I had nothing to be ashamed of regarding my behavior when the raiders came—"

"The ones who took your brother?"

He nodded. "Ever since, as if shedding that shame opened up space within, I've felt a memory tickling at me, but it refuses to come."

"What kind of memory?"

"Something that I overheard and which I'd not remembered before now." He tightened his fist against his thigh and his horse sidestepped. "But I can't bring it fully formed. It eludes me."

She reached over and covered his fist. He visibly relaxed and glanced down at her.

"Don't tug at it," she whispered. "Let it come on its own and it will."

"But what if it's something that will help us find who took my brother?"

"Even more reason to not struggle with bringing it forward, or it may never surface."

He cupped her face. "Of a certainty, I found the right woman for the job of being my wife."

She laid a light punch against his side and laughed. "Indeed, you did. But…" She searched his eyes and frowned. "But you know you don't need to find him to redeem yourself."

"I know," he whispered. "But I'd like to find him for his sake. And because he's my brother and I miss him."

"Then we will."

Chapter Twenty-One

Two months later

Ashley leaned back in a carved chair in the keep and glanced around the council table to where Eithne sat. The older woman met her gaze and smiled. After Ashley had returned for good to Dunadd, some major changes had been made to the workings of the tribe. The biggest change? The council was evenly made up of women and men.

Today they were discussing the merits of Domnall also using the druid's magic and finding a wife from another time, because one thing had not changed—the tribe was still woefully short of women of child-bearing age.

The chief nodded to everyone. "It's decided, then. Domnall, you will step through at the Summer Equinox."

Domnall, who wasn't a member of the council but had been invited to the meeting to discuss this, drew his shoulders back and nodded. "I will not fail you."

"And I can coach you before you leave," she said.

Mungan stepped from the shadows, and Ashley startled,

even though she knew he was there. "We don't know that he'll end up in your time period. The magic will bring him to the right place and time."

"I know. But I can still help prepare him. Give him advice about what to do and what not to do."

Connall leaned forward. "As can I. Their method of eating is odd. There are people in buildings who stand behind a long table and ladle food already prepared onto your plate."

Domnall frowned. "What do I need to provide in exchange?"

"Nothing. No barter required."

Wait. "What?" She pulled on his arm. "Are you telling me you ate at a soup kitchen the whole time you were there?"

"It's where my friend Norton brought me, aye." He turned back to his brother, and she shook her head, laughing softly. "And another thing, one method of greeting is to tap your chest thusly"—he rapped the spot over his heart—"and say, 'Beam Me Up, Scotty.'"

She slapped a hand over her mouth to stifle her laugh, and Connall looked at her sharply, eyebrow raised. "Is that not correct? I may have the words wrong as they were in your language, but I believe that's how you greeted me in the café."

She nodded, her eyes watering from suppressed laughter. All she could do was wave a *please continue* hand.

Connall eyed her and smiled, then turned to his brother. "Ye need to ask the prospective lady if she enjoys washing men's underwear if you want them to not be stiff in anger."

Now she snorted and elbowed him. "I'll show you stiff underwear later."

He grinned at her. "Promises, promises." He draped an arm around her shoulder and pulled her closer to him, and she reveled in being in the shelter of his strong arms, reveled at the easy affection he showed her in front of everyone.

Mungan nodded to the chief. "If you have no need of

me until then, I will be visiting some distant lands. But I will return in time for the Summer Equinox."

"Very well," Eacharn replied. "Take what supplies you need."

When the chief adjourned the council, they all stood and placed their fists into the center of the table. Connall nodded to her.

"One for all," she said.

"And all for one," everyone replied at once, their male and female voices echoing in the close confines of the keep.

Some left straight away, while others resumed giving Domnall advice on his impending departure. Connall and Ashley sat back down and, while all eyes were trained elsewhere, Connall's free hand crossed over to her and rested gently on her belly. His fingers spread in a protective gesture, and happiness and affection and love welled within her on a sudden tide. She blinked to dash away some moisture from her eyes.

She placed her own hand over his and smiled up at him. He brushed his nose along her cheek. "I love you," he rumbled low.

Below their linked hands, a new life grew. She'd told him only that morning, when she'd woken him with a kiss and then said, bringing his hand to her belly, "Looks like we're increasing your herd after all."

And though they made love every chance they found—for they couldn't get enough of each other—she was convinced that the baby had been conceived that night in the magic of the spring equinox.

So much for Queen Anne's Lace.

Or had it been the druid's magic, after all?

Author's Note

You will not find this Highland tale peppered with words and expressions such as *dinnae fash* and *bairn* and *ken* and the like, for those are words from the Scots language (a distinct language separate from English and Scottish Gaelic), whereas the Highlanders would have been speaking mostly Scottish Gaelic. And since writing Connall's point of view in Scottish Gaelic wouldn't have been smart or possible, I used English and tried to use the syntax and grammar of Gaelic to give a flavor for the era, and used English words for concepts he would be familiar with.

Dunadd, meaning "fort on the River Add" in Scottish Gaelic, is a real Iron Age site in Argyll, Scotland. Several hundred years after the events in this book, it became the seat of the kingdom of Dál Riata. Unfortunately, not much historical record for this site exists for the time period of this book, so I took liberties in imagining the layout of the site, as well as events, using what little I found in my research to go from. We do know slave raids happened at this time, and that the Romans did occupy the Antonine Wall at this time and engaged in skirmishes with the Caledonians and other tribes in the area. The arcani were like modern-day secret agents who were tasked with keeping an eye on the natives between Hadrian's Wall and the Antonine Wall. Sometimes, they blended in so well with the local tribes they "turned."

As far as Connall's people, the Epidii, they were a tribe recorded by Ptolemy in that region, though the name is a Latinized version of what neighboring tribes called them since it's P-Celtic (from a Briton or Pict informant). If the Romans had asked Connall's people instead, the Latinized version would have been something like Echidii to adhere more to the Q-Celtic form of The Horse People. I've chosen to stick with the name as recorded by Ptolemy, since that's the common name.

Whether or not Connall's people fought naked is still fiercely debated, so I opted for the more visual version. And there is also ample evidence that the Celts had a system of wooden roads long before the Romans came along, so I felt justified inserting them in this context. And if anyone's visited Dunadd, they might be puzzled by the water I have lapping against their fort, but evidence shows that there was indeed water there at the time this story takes place.

There are several theories as to the origin of the Scottish Gaelic-speaking peoples of Scotland, with some saying the Irish immigrated to that region later to form the kingdom of Dál Riata and then spread to push out the Picts. More recently, Dr. Ewan Campbell and other scholars have argued that the people living there were indigenous, and due to their remoteness from the other tribes in that region, their language didn't develop into P-Celtic like those east and south of them. I've sided with this more recent scholarship for this story and made the culture and language that of the early Scottish Gaels, even though there is other recent scholarship that disputes it.

And Connall's father's name is a liberty I'm taking with the origins of Clan MacEacharn, which is typically associated with the region south of Dunadd, though still in the area said to be occupied by the Epidii. And since Eacharn means Horse Lord, well, it just fit too perfectly for me not to use it.

This brings me to the final historical character – Emperor Norton. He was a real man who lived in the late 1800s in San Francisco. Look him up on Wikipedia—you won't be sorry! Of course, he'd have been long dead by Ashley's time, but I've taken the liberty of making him and his supposed two dogs—Bummer and Lazarus—seem immortal, joining a long line of other authors to immortalize and honor them in this way.

Acknowledgments

First of all I'd like to thank Liz Pelletier at Entangled because without her, this story wouldn't exist! She hit me with an idea one day—hey, what about writing a story set in ancient Scotland where the woman are all gone for some reason and a druid sends the hero forward in time to find a wife, and he uses Craigslist. I was like, LOL, I'm On It! How could I resist? It spoke to my love for ancient history and the early Celts as well as sounding like a lot of fun.

As always, I'm hugely indebted to a number of people who helped me out with the historical aspects of the plot, description, and characters. I'd like to specifically thank the following for helping me; any mistakes or inaccuracies, however, are my own.

Jody Allen of Rings True Research who read my outline for historical advice and inaccuracies. And to *the* Dr. Ewan Campbell, the archaeologist who originated the theory that the Gaelic speakers of Dunadd did not come from Ireland— he was gracious enough to answer a question I had via email.

And, ohmygod, to Shaila Patel and Jami Gold, who read

my chapters as I was writing them so that I could adjust and revise as I went in order to make my deadline. I'd never done that before—usually I wait until I've finished a whole draft and had a chance to go through a thorough self-edit, but I didn't have time for that. They always have my back and give me helpful, and sometimes painful, feedback, but it's always worth it to make a story stronger.

Special thanks goes to Jami, Buffy Armstrong, and Shaila for always being available via Facebook chat when I needed encouragement or yanking back from some fruitless rabbit hole of research detail or for helping me brainstorm some tricky plot problem.

To my editors Liz Pelletier and Lydia Sharp, who helped me get this into final shape! You knew exactly how and where to get me to dig deeper.

I also want to thank the following who helped me during my research trip to Scotland in 2018: the lady working the counter at the Kilmartin Museum for giving me a good primer on the area and loading me up with history books of the region; Donald, the captain of the boat *The Morag*, who accommodated my last minute request to join his tour from Tighnabruaich up around the waters above the Isle of Bute and back. He was a natural storyteller and kept us entertained while also serving tea. He also kindly answered all my boat/water-related questions and tipped me off to using ferries to get in some of the views my characters would have seen while on water. Storms come from the west, he also told me, which wouldn't have been something I'd glean from book research. Though I didn't follow his advice to have my characters sail up around the top of the Isle of Bute as the incredible, craggy inlets at the south tip served my story purposes better. Sorry, Donald! If they had followed Donald's advice they would have been much safer from that storm. And to Heather and the staff at Ben Arthur's Bothy in Arrochar where I was staying, who kept me supplied with steak pie and Irn-Bru and other Scottish fare almost every night. It was nice to feel like I had a "home base."

And to the docent at the Auld Kirk Museum in Kirkintilloch who, when I asked if there were other places I should see related to the Antonine Wall, told me of an historical reenactment happening during my stay. She told me to look for her husband Martin, dressed as a centurion. This proved to be a mother-load of great information—nothing beats seeing and talking to people who steep themselves in an era. So thank you to Martin and the other members of The Antonine Guard who answered various questions I had about the Romans and their gear and culture, who let me take innumerable pictures and recordings as well as reenacting a prayer to Mithras for me.

To my employees at the bookstore who put up with my grumpy-groggy self when I'm on deadline, and especially Alex McLeod who's always willing to be a sounding board when I have a thorny plot problem or, in this case, coming up with the line about "increasing the herd." Thanks, Alex!

To the members of my facebook fan group—Angela's Time-Traveling Steampunk Regency Assassins—for their help and support! And to my readers, whose encouragement and support are invaluable.

To my facebook and twitter friends who are always willing to answer questions I pose, whether it's about writing, or character ideas, or an opinion sought.

To Bree Archer at Entangled for the gorgeous cover—I couldn't be happier! Love the silhouette of the castle in the skyline!

And finally to my family, who have always believed in me and make it possible for me to pursue writing.

About the Author

An avid reader herself, Angela Quarles writes books she'd like to read—laugh-out-loud, smart romances that suck you into her worlds and won't let you go until you reach The End. She is a RWA RITA® award-winning and *USA Today* bestselling author of contemporary, time travel, and steampunk romance. *Library Journal* named her steampunk, *Steam Me Up, Rawley*, Best Self-Published Romance of 2015. Her time travel romance *Must Love Chainmail* won the Romance Writer's of America's RITA® in 2016, becoming the first self-published author to win in the paranormal category. Her debut novel, *Must Love Breeches*, made the *USA Today* bestseller list in 2015. Angela loves history, folklore, and family history and combined it with her active imagination to write stories of romance and adventure. She also owns and operates her own independent new & used bookstore in Mobile, Alabama, connecting readers to books every day!

She has a B.A. in Anthropology and International Studies with a minor in German from Emory University, and a Masters in Heritage Preservation from Georgia State University. She was an exchange student to Finland in high school and studied abroad in Vienna one summer in college.

Find Angela Quarles Online:
www.angelaquarles.com
@angelaquarles
Facebook.com/authorangelaquarles
Mailing list: www.angelaquarles.com/join-my-mailing-list

Discover more Amara titles...

AWK-WEIRD
an *Ice Knights* novel by Avery Flynn

There's more to me than just being awk-weird. I own my own flower shop, have some great friends, and I have my eye on adopting the most adorable kitten. But when a Thor-lookalike who happens to be a professional hockey player hits on me at my bestie's wedding rehearsal party... You better believe I climbed that tree like a cat. There's zero chance I'll end up ever seeing him again...right? Until the pregnancy test comes up positive. What happens next? Oh my God, I wish I knew...

THE AUSSIE NEXT DOOR
a *Patterson's Bluff* novel by Stefanie London

It only took American Angie Donovan two days to fall in love with Australia. With her visa clock ticking, surely she can fall in love with an Australian—and get hitched—in two months. Especially if he's as hot and funny as her next-door neighbor... Jace Walters has never wanted much—except solitude, and now he's finally living alone. Sure, his American neighbor is distractingly sexy and annoyingly nosy, but she'll be gone in a few months... Except now she's determined to find her perfect match by checking out every eligible male in the town, and her choices are even more distracting. So why does it suddenly feel like he—and his obnoxious tight-knit family, and even these two wayward dogs—could be exactly what she needs?

THE HONEYMOON TRAP
a novel by Christina Hovland

Lucy Campbell never expected to see William Covington again. And she certainly never expected him to be her new boss at the TV station. How the heck is she supposed to work for him with all these butterflies in her stomach? But when she has to take a new assignment, she's in for a world of hurt...because now she has to pretend to be his wife. On their honeymoon.

THE WEDDING DEAL
a *Heart in the Game* novel by Cindi Madsen

Former quarterback Lance Quaid just inherited the most losing team in the NFL. He's got only a few weeks until draft day to turn things around, and he can't do it alone. Thankfully, his HR manager is more than capable, if only she'd stop looking so sexy while she's yelling at him. When Lance begs her to join him on a trip down the coast for his brother's wedding so they can finalize details—on a strictly business basis—she agrees...after they fill out the necessary forms, of course. Sparks start flying as the team starts coming together, but both of them know anything more than the weekend would be a colossally bad idea—after all, the extra paperwork would be a nightmare.

Made in the USA
San Bernardino, CA
05 December 2019